The Dare

Ian Tew

New Book   Author web site iantew.co.uk
Memoir of A Seafarer
Available on Amazon

Table of Contents

CHAPTER 1

He was young to be in command, even if it was only for sea trials of a harbour tug, but it was still a command and that was what he wanted. He was thrilled at the prospect but tried his best not to show it.

'Take the new tug, *Jurong*, out and thoroughly put her through her paces,' said the manager, leaning back in his black office chair, his brown eyes holding Tom's as though looking inside him to see what was there.

'Here's the sea trial programme,' he continued, handing Tom a small, printed pamphlet entitled *Jurong Sea Trials*. 'Make sure everything is completed and don't run aground.'

He stood up and shook Tom's hand.

'Welcome to Cosel and I hope you enjoy working with us,' he said, again looking Tom in the eye.

Tom left the manager's office and its curtained windows. On the one hand, he felt elated, yet on the other, he couldn't help thinking he was being tested. That searching look from those very brown eyes was unnerving and he hoped his own return was steady and confident, masking the turmoil he felt inside. It was all so new and exciting and so utterly different from his previous life.

The burning bright sunshine and harsh light shook him out of his reverie, the heat already making him sweat. Pull yourself together and act as though you know what you are doing, he berated himself. He walked through the yard past a barge on the slip, the noise from the air-driven chipping hammers pulsating through his brain, and reached the waterfront. There alongside the quay was his first command, her new paintwork gleaming in the tropical sunlight, smooth and unbroken, as befitted a new ship. The smell of the shipyard, grease from the slip, mingled with that of dead barnacles, while an indefinable brine smell from the dirty water, paint and wood shavings belied the newness of his first command.

There was no gangway so he climbed on board and entered the small wheelhouse. Looking forward he saw the bow was closer than he had imagined, realising she was not much bigger than a decent-sized motor yacht, although rather a different shape. He flicked away the twinge of disappointment that she was not larger and set about familiarising himself with her layout and bridge controls. It did not take very long, as he had been around yachts and ships all his life, so he knew his way around knew what to look for. The engine room was very neat and compact, the bilges still completely clean and the paintwork unmarked. Various workers were still on board finishing off, but they took no notice of him. There did not appear to be any crew, no doubt all would be revealed on the morrow.

Back on the bridge he took stock, planning how he would manoeuvre her off the berth with her single screw and no bow thruster. He saw there was no chart and made a note to obtain one. He was unfamiliar with this part of Singapore, knowing only the main port and anchorages, and not Jurong, on the western side of the island.

As he climbed ashore, his shirt wet with sweat, he was confronted by a European, dressed in a white shirt and blue tie, looking cool in the heat, his dark slacks well-pressed, who greeted him cheerfully.

'So you are the new boy,' he said. 'Going to do the trials, are we, for the latest addition to our fleet?'

He laughed.

'Well, yes,' replied Tom, slightly flustered.

'Welcome to Singapore and welcome to Cosel, the mad house which is our company,' he laughed. 'I'm Steve. I manage the yard.'

Tom shook hands, a nice firm grip, noting the man had said 'our' company not 'the' company, a good sign, which boded well for the future. He was cheered by the welcome he received so far since arriving in Singapore. Was it only yesterday, he thought?

'Come up to my office, you look as though you could use a cold drink,' suggested Steve.

Tom followed him into the large, faded, green-painted, corrugated iron shed alongside the slipway, the barge and the chipping hammers still making their infernal racket. It was a hive of activity on what appeared to be a number of fabrication jobs, and it was slightly cooler out of the sun. It seemed to Tom that the framework for another tug or large work boat was also under construction. It was good to see everyone was busy, a far cry from the UK.

Tom and Steve climbed a wooden stairway to a platform half-way up the river side of the shed. Glass surrounded the office on three sides, enabling the manager to keep an eye on the work below. The wall formed the fourth side, with a large window allowing a view of the wharf and the vessels alongside it. Steve ushered Tom in and walked over to the large fridge on the outside wall, while Tom shook the wet shirt off his skin, feeling the cool air from the air conditioning.

'What will you have?' offered Steve, the open door showing an array of soft drinks, Tiger and Anchor beers.

'A bit early for me,' Steve continued, pointing to the red Anchor beer tin, 'but don't let it stop you.'

'Sprite will do me fine, thanks,' replied Tom, slightly surprised at being offered a beer when it was only half-way through the morning.

Steve sat down in front of his desk facing the activity below while Tom sat opposite him with a view of the river and the yard opposite.

'Your first visit to Singapore?'

'No, I first came here as a cadet on a British India ship some ten years ago and have been coming on and off ever since. I was with Indo China on their Bay of Bengal Japan service, Calcutta to Yokohama and all ports in between. So

I know Singapore quite well, or rather the port and its environs, but I have never been to Jurong before or in fact this side of the island.'

'Back yard of Singapore,' Steve laughed, his piercing blue eyes twinkling. 'Singapore is a very different place to live in, rather than just visiting. I expect you know haunts I have never dreamed of, never knew existed,' he laughed again.

Tom felt himself relaxing in front of the cheerful yard manager who was obviously secure in himself and what he did. He looked fit and healthy, his face well-tanned, his fair hair parted in the middle. Tom reckoned he must be in his mid-forties.

'I've run the yard for the last five years from when the old man took over,' said Steve. 'We're building these small harbour tugs, renewing the Cosel fleet. Apart from port work, they mainly tow barges to Indonesia and Malaysia. I am hoping to land a contract to build a coaster for Indonesian clients, which could lead to greater things and make the old man happy.'

Tom raised his eyebrows, which Steve picked up.

'The old man, commonly known as Mr R, Rosenberg being his name, sixties, chequered career: Shanghai, Bangkok and finally here, Singapore. Fortunes made and lost and now onto his latest fortune. He knows nothing about ships, tugs or salvage but is a businessman and a very successful one at that. He's a good man to work for. The company is still small enough for him to know what is going on and he does not miss a trick.'

'I see. And the manager?' queried Tom.

'Ah! DB, Mr Dan Brown, been with the company since the beginning, what, 10 years ago? And stayed when Mr R took over some five years ago, when he brought me in to run the yard. D B runs the tugs, barges and salvage, as you know we have a largish salvage tug stationed in Singapore. I say we, the businesses are run separately but we all feel we are part of Cosel. The old man is very ambitious and keen to expand on all fronts, which suits me just fine.' Steve sipped from his can of Coca Cola, the pattern on the tin blurred with the condensation.

'Well, thank you for that. And the trials tomorrow?'

'I will be on board because I like being afloat. There will be a classifications surveyor to approve whatever he approves, it's all in the pamphlet you have. The yard chief engineer, a couple of foreman, a couple of hands will be onboard as well. DB seems a bit disinterested so I expect you will end up signing for the tug on behalf of Cosel Salvage so I can get my money.'

Steve laughed, the sound infectious, and Tom smiled.

First command, sea trials, signing for the tug as well felt as though he was being thrown in at the deep end and he had to pinch himself to make sure he was still in the real world, not some fantasy land, and that he would awaken to cold, dreary England.

'I expect you know we are waiting for the arrival of the new tug from Japan. I say new, she is second-hand and I expect the old man picked her up cheap and I will have to make her work. She is big in size, anyway, for us and we are preparing for her. She's expected to arrive in the next few days. The *Pansy*. The old man will have to change her name sharpish,' he laughed. 'Rumour has it, old Jan Smit almost refused to sail unless the name was changed. Jan is a big, burly Dutchman with a wife and three kids, been with the company as long as DB.'

'I am supposed to be sailing as chief officer to learn the ropes,' said Tom.

'I am sure you will get along fine with Jan, he is very knowledgeable and been in tugs and salvage most of his life.'

'Well, thanks for that, all very helpful.'

Tom stood up to leave, not wanting to overstay his welcome.

'You must come to supper and meet my wife, one day next week. I'll let you know after consulting with her.'

'That is very kind of you, I would love to. I'm staying at the Orchid Inn.'

'OK, until tomorrow. Oh, by the way, the yard supplies the refreshments.' Steve laughed, his blue eyes sparkling as he showed Tom out of his office.

Once outside, Tom wondered what he should do. He had familiarised himself with his tug for the next day, it was now mid-morning and he could hardly go back to the hotel, although a swim in the pool would be most welcome, but it would be rather like sloping off, going absent without leave.

He decided to go back into the main office and see what happened. He went in through the door from the yard that faced the slip with the barge on it; the chipping hammers were silent.

In the cool and apparent semi-darkness inside the office, the windows were all curtained like the manager's office. Tom stood, getting his bearings and allowing his eyes to adjust to the gloom. He saw a sign saying 'ops room' and thought this would be a good place to start. He opened the door and walked in.

A handsome Malay face looked up from the desk at which he was sitting, with a large log book in front of him, pen in hand.

'You must be Captain Matravers,' said the Malay as he stood, holding out his hand. 'Welcome to Singapore and Cosel Salvage.'

Tom shook the proffered hand.

'My name is Ishmael, I'm in charge of the operations room.'

'Yes, thank you, I am trying to orientate myself,' said Tom, pleased to be have been entitled Captain, though not sure he had earned it yet.

'I would be grateful if you would brief me.'

'Certainly,' replied Ishmael with a smile, his black hair shining in the artificial light. Tom noticed that there were no windows and the walls were painted an off-white colour.

'It's quite simple, there is one operator on duty 24 hours a day, manning the telephone, company radio, and VHF Channel 16, and he also writes the log. He has one assistant. There is a radio room on the other side of the road in the new yard on a barge, also manned 24 hours a day, for sending messages to the tugs away from Singapore and monitoring the distress channels.'

He pointed to the red telephone on the wall, within easy reach of the desk.

'That's the one dedicated to the radio room. This is our library, Lloyds intelligence information, etc., and that is the telex machine with the fax next to it.'

The telex machine started chattering with its distinctive noise, the keys rattling on the paper issuing out of it. Ishmael moved over to look at the message and said, 'From Lloyds intelligence.' He paused. 'No good for us, fishing boat in trouble in the Pacific, we don't operate there.' He paused again, and then added, 'Yet.' He smiled and said, 'All very simple and only Mr Brown, the manager, Mr Hibbets, the technical manager, you will recognise by the array of radios and gadgets he wears, the old man, Mr R, and the salvage master are allowed in here, anyone else by invitation only. The ops room is for operations only, not a meeting or chat room.'

The telephone rang and the operator, another Malay, answered it.

'During the day, the main switchboard is with reception and at night with us. It is important that as a salvage company we are contactable 24 hours a day and our senior staff are in communication at all times. You will be given a pager. That,' he pointed to a grey box on the wall close to the desk with a microphone, 'is the company radio with its own dedicated frequency. All the tugs are fitted with one, Mr Brown's car, Mr Hibbets' Landrover, the company vans and we have a few new Motorola portable radios, which are very effective, the range is about 30 miles. The codes are, Mr Brown, Mike 1; Mr Hibbets, Mike 2; Superintendent, Mike 3; Salvage Master, Mike 4. All very simple but works very well.'

Tom was impressed. The beating heart of Cosel Salvage, communications.

He left the ops room, returning to the main office, where a European in the first glass fronted office waved him in.

'Welcome to Singapore,' said a very English voice, standing and holding out his hand as Tom entered the office. He was dressed in a white shirt and dark tie.

'Welcome to Cosel,' he continued, shaking Tom's hand firmly.

'You must be Matravers, I'm Tony House, the marketing manager, for the tugs, barges and heavy lift crane. I'm not involved in the salvage. Have a pew,' and he patted the seat next to him on the sofa that he had moved to. Tom sat down, observing the same local chart of South East Asia hanging on the wall behind the desk as that in the ops room and covered in coloured pins, mainly in Indonesia.

A very pretty Chinese lady brought in a tray with tea, milk and porcelain cups.

'Milk, no sugar, please,' said Tom in answer to her silent query.

'Heard about you,' said Tony. 'You are doing the sea trials tomorrow with our newest and latest, the *Jurong*, I understand. Thank you, Mary,' he said as the Chinese lady left the office.

'Yes, and everyone seems to have heard of me,' said Tom.

'That is one of the things that happens with a small company like this, we're not unlike a family. I will be joining you; one, to get out of the office; two, I like being afloat; three, I like to have been on board all the vessels I market especially under way. I usually attend the on and off hire surveys of the barges as well,' he smiled.

'I noticed the sign over your door says Captain,' observed Tom.

'I served my time with BI and left as second mate because there was no promotion. I wouldn't have reached command until I was fifty. I came out here, joined Straits Steam, got my command, married a Chinese lady and been here ever since. I joined Cosel when Mr R took over, having known him from his days in Bangkok. If he goes on expanding I will be here until I retire,' he laughed. 'And you?'

'I served my time with BI too and left for the same reason, promotion was no quicker. Joined Ellermans for a couple of years but left, again for the same reason, and joined Indochina in Hong Kong. I found a job ashore in London with a firm of admiralty solicitors who occasionally acted for Cosel, met Mr Brown and here I am.'

Tom sipped his freshly brewed cup of tea, Earl Grey, the one tea he disliked, but obviously could not show it.

'Do you know anyone in Singapore?'

'Not really.'

'My wife is away at the moment so if you like you can borrow her car. It is the best way to find your way around the place. Could be very useful.'

'That is very kind of you,' replied Tom, almost overwhelmed.

'Come round to my house at 1800 and you can drive it away. Your UK license is valid here,' Tony handed Tom his card.

'See you on board the *Jurong* at nine tomorrow morning,' said Tony, rising from the sofa.

Tom returned to the main office, full of people working. A Chinese wearing shirt and tie waved him over to his desk.

'I am Daniel Bang, in charge of personnel.' He shook hands with Tom. 'Here is your contract, Mr Brown says you had better sign it before you take out the *Jurong* tomorrow or we won't be insured.' He smiled, handing Tom a folder. 'You can leave it on my desk if I am not here. Welcome to Singapore and Cosel Salvage and good luck.'

Tom decided he would have a look at the radio room and clutching the folder, left the office via reception and the main entrance, noticing the car park outside was full.

He walked across the road, his eyes still adjusting to the bright sunlight, into what was obviously the new yard. On one side there was a wooden office block, with a workshop underneath, diving kit spread out all over the floor and men working on it. There were various pieces of equipment lying around the yard and at the far end, alongside the bank, a barge. A single plank acted as the gangway onto the barge, which had two Portacabins and was festooned with radio aerials from a single mast at one end. Tom, sweating again in the hot morning sun, mounted the single plank, thinking it might not be so easy at night. The first Portacabin was locked. He entered the second one after knocking and found himself in a well-equipped radio room, various radios crackling and humming away, along with the air conditioner mounted on one wall. There were no windows.

A dark Indian looked up and gestured with his hand for Tom to be quiet. He was listening intently with one headphone pressed to his ear. The VHF on channel 16 was loud and clear, someone calling port control, a faint voice on one of the SSB's, saying something Tom could not quite hear. The Indian was writing in his log. He put down the headphone.

'You must be Captain Matravers,' he said, 'welcome to Singapore and Cosel Salvage.'

He held out his hand and Tom shook it. 'My name is John Gomes, radio officer. With two others, I man the radio twenty-four hours a day. I was just picking up the *Pansy*, giving her ETA.'

'Yes,' said Tom.

'1800 in three days' time, that's Monday,' said Gomes.

'Thanks, I am familiarising myself with Cosel, I'm due to join the *Pansy* as chief officer.'

'We heard,' said Gomes, smiling and continuing.

'Captain Smit is a very good captain, I sailed with him for a couple of years on the *Singapore*, Cosel's salvage tug. He is very knowledgeable, I am sure you will get on fine with him,' echoing Steve's words.

'So how do we operate here?' asked Tom.

'SSB's, single side band radios, for communicating with the tugs, one dedicated for the distress channels, VHF for port operations, company radio for dealing with the tugs when in range, and of course, the chart.'

'No salvage?'

'Nothing at the moment, but you never know when it is going to happen. Those yellow pins on the chart are the tugs and smaller brown ones are the barges, the big red one is the *Singapore*, presently on salvage stand-by in Eastern Anchorage. The black pins are ships in trouble and if there is a salvage, a big green.'

'Thanks for that,' said Tom. 'Do you mind if I use your desk for a minute, to read this?' he continued holding up the folder he was carrying.

'You are welcome,' replied Gomes, picking up a handset and speaking into the microphone. 'Base here, go ahead, *Java.*'

Tom opened the folder and started to read the employment contract. It was not quite what he had been told at the interview in the pub, but it was good enough. The salary was a little higher in pound terms but depended on the rate of exchange with the Singapore dollar. He noted he was to be employed by Cosel Hong Kong and made a mental note to ask why. Overall, he was happy enough and signed.

He left the radio room, waving at Gomes who was still busy taking the noon positions of the tugs calling in. He walked back to the main office and left the folder on Daniel Bang's desk. It was very hot outside. Feeling a bit spare, he poked his head into Ops and asked Ishmael how he could get back to the hotel.

'There is a van going into town and it can take you. Tomorrow morning it will pick you up at seven-thirty, so plenty of time to prepare for your sea trials.'

'Thanks, Ishmael, if I may call you that?'

'Be my guest and good luck for tomorrow.'

Tom went to bed early that night, not noticing the sterility of his hotel room. The air conditioning was on and turned high. He reflected on his day before sleeping. He felt he was on the verge of something important and life-changing; he felt alive, as if he was going to be part of something that was thrusting ahead, looking forward not back, expanding and looking to the future, not contracting and looking into the past; looking outwards, not inwards, unlike the UK; involved with itself, almost withdrawing from the rest of the world. It was like a re-birth, a new chance, a new beginning, and he was going to grab this opportunity with both hands, give it his all and make it a success. Something like this only came once in a lifetime.

CHAPTER 2

The next morning, Tom called ops to cancel the van, and dressed in a white shirt, dark tie and grey flannels. He drove himself to the office in the borrowed mini. The evening spent with Tony was enlightening and interesting, giving him more of an insight into Cosel and Mr R. He felt he had made a good friend and they both seemed to work on the same wavelength. He called in at Ops and found Ishmael sitting at his desk, the same as yesterday, and presumed he had been home the previous night. No-one had told him to call in at Ops, but it seemed the sensible thing to do.

'Good morning, driving in Singapore traffic okay?' greeted Ishmael, and Tom nodded his head, smiling. 'All ready for the trials? I see you have the trial schedule.'

'Yes, thank you, Ishmael, I have studied it and made my plans. I forgot yesterday I need a chart.'

'Of course, all ready for you here, together with a temporary log,' and he handed Tom the large-scale chart of Jurong and Singapore Western Anchorage.

'We are on good terms with the port authority and in general obey their rules,' he smiled. 'No vessel is allowed to move in Singapore waters without calling the port authority and obtaining their permission. If you try it and they find out, it is a one-way trip to Changi jail. So call them up, tell them you are going for sea trials and they will give permission. I have already told them on the phone. When you have returned and made fast, don't forget to call and tell them on the VHF and base on the company radio.'

'Okay, thanks, Ishmael.'

'Good luck!'

Tom left the office and walked down to the *Jurong*. Although it was only just after eight o'clock, the yard was a hive of activity and they were chipping on the barge. It was already hot. He climbed on board and entered the wheel house, confident of himself and his abilities, still feeling he was on the cusp of something important.

The sun had already heated the almost still air and the light was bright at nine when the trials started, although Tom did not really notice, he was too busy with his command. The tug seemed full of people and he was quite sure there were more people on board than her safety equipment allowed; still, no matter, he was certain all would be well. He was introduced to the superintendent who seemed pleasant enough, but did not catch his name.

Quite a crowd were gathered on the quay to watch the departure of the new tug, including DB, who was talking with a much older, shorter man whom Tom thought might be Mr R. Tony, dressed in a colourful shirt as though out for a picnic, was on the tow-deck, talking with Steve. The yard engineer was below in the engine room and his assistant was in the wheelhouse with Tom and the surveyor. The three of them filled the small space. Tom had planned his

24

manoeuvre carefully and it went off smoothly. The *Jurong* steamed out of the yard at slow speed, and into the main channel, turning to starboard, heading for Western Anchorage slowly increasing speed.

Tom felt elated in the afternoon after putting the *Jurong* neatly alongside her berth. The trials were a success, everything worked well, the tug manoeuvred satisfactorily. She achieved slightly over the design speed on the measured mile, the surveyor approved all the classification requirements and the certificates would be delivered the next day. All was ready for the tug to be handed over to Cosel Salvage.

'In my office,' said Steve. 'You coming, Tony?'

'Well, of course,' replied Tony who seemed in ebullient mood after his day out on the tug.

Steve's desk was covered with a white tablecloth. Small eats and bottles of champagne covered it instead of the usual papers.

On a separate small table under the river window lay the handing-over papers and two chairs. Steve's secretary was hovering near the chairs and Steve gestured to Tom, who sat down. There were a few yard foremen and those who had built the tug watching as Steve signed the papers, passing them to Tom sitting next to him, who checked that all was in order and then signed them on behalf of Cosel Salvage. Everyone clapped and Tony gave the toast simply saying, 'To the *Jurong*. Success to her and all who sail on her.'

It was a jolly gathering and Daniel Bang, whom Tom had not noticed in the general excitement, approached him.

'Well done. Mr R wants to see you in his office at 1800 sharp.'

'Okay, thank you,' Tom's effervescence taking a hit, automatically assuming he had done something wrong, something like being summoned to the headmaster. Better lay off the champagne, he thought.

'Successful day, well done,' said Tony as he left the party, still wearing his picnic shirt. It was now about 1700 and people were beginning to go home. Tom stayed on as it seemed as good a place as any to wait for his 1800 interview, but the party evaporated quite quickly. Rather than be the last person to leave, he walked over to the main office and waited in reception where there was a comfortable settee. He made his number with the receptionist. At 1800 he knocked on the chairman's door. The secretary had gone home, and Tom heard a voice command:

'Enter.'

Full of apprehension, Tom took a deep breath and opened the door. It was a big office with a large desk at the back wall, behind which the chairman sat, facing the door. To the left was a settee with a small table on which was an ice bucket and in this, an opened bottle of champagne. Two empty glasses were close by. The windows were curtained and there the floor was carpeted.

'Welcome to Singapore and Cosel Salvage,' said Mr R, waving Tom to the settee.

'Sit and pour the champagne, you don't think I'm going to allow my yard manager to drink at my expense and I not participate!' He chuckled, brushing his almost non-existent hair from his eyes, a gesture Tom would soon learn meant he was in a good mood and relaxed.

Tom poured the champagne and Mr R joined him on the settee, a much smaller man than he had imagined, but full of energy despite his advancing years.

'I invited you to meet me and I wanted to get to know you a little better. I know a lot about you.' There was a trace of some sort of mid-European accent. Tom looked surprised but said nothing.

'I watched you depart and return with the *Jurong* and if all our Captains could handle their tugs as well as you, our maintenance costs would be a lot less.'

Tom felt quite embarrassed and unused to such praise. He still said nothing.

'Yes, you were obviously in charge of the vessel rather than the other way round and I'm not a seafaring person. Congratulations on the successful sea trials! Tell me, did you read the handover document before you signed it?'

'Yes, of course,' replied Tom, surprised.

'And what did it say?'

'Basically, the tug had completed the sea trials satisfactorily and complied with all classification requirements and was built in accordance with the building contract.'

'And did you read the building contract?'

'No, I was not asked to because the yard manager's signature covered that.'

'Very good, not many other masters would have even read the documents. Those lawyers in London must have taught you something.'

'Thank you, sir,' said Tom formally.

'Call me Mr R, everyone else does.'

'Yes, sir.'

'Right, now to business. Cosel Salvage is going to expand and we are going to be the pre-eminent Salvor in Southeast Asia within a few years. To do that I need not just good, but top-notch people, who will act independently without supervision, and they are difficult to find. I think you are one such person. The only problem is that you know nothing about salvage except what your lawyers taught you, which, however, may prove very useful. To be any use to me, you have to learn the trade, and the faster you learn the better. There is an element of luck because you never know when the next salvage is going to occur. I am a businessman, but I find the business of salvage fascinating. My biggest worry is where the next dollar is coming from. There's no secure cash flow, it appears to be either feast or famine.'

He paused and drank his champagne, rather absent-mindedly refilling his glass. Tom took a cautious sip.

'Our first big tug is arriving on Monday.'

Tom glanced at the chart on the wall behind the desk and saw a red pin in the South China Sea. The chart was the same as he had seen in Ops and the radio rooms.

'So, together with the *Singapore* we'll form the basis of our expanding salvage fleet. We have the heavy lift barge, the salvage and mooring vessel, the harbour tugs and barges together with various equipment ashore. We have enough small tugs and barges, now to create the cash flow I need to support our salvage fleet when the tugs are on standby and not working. That's my plan and I need the people to make it work. Captain Smit is an excellent tug master but that is all he will ever be. You, however, I expect to be much more and I will be watching your progress with much interest. The reason I am telling you this at the beginning of your career is so you know if you perform well you will rise as the company expands. Don't forget, I'm on the last lap of life, you are at the beginning. I am giving you a potential opportunity.'

'I don't know what to say except, thank you, and I hope to fulfil the promise you see in me. I must say, in the last two days I almost feel reborn, it is so utterly different from UK, where it's all "them and us", but here, it seems it is us together for the future,' said Tom, overcoming his embarrassment at talking about himself.

'Just what I like to hear. I hear Tony House has lent you his car.'

'His wife's car actually, very good of him,' replied Tom, surprised the chairman would know such an unimportant detail.

'Well, explore Singapore while you can, the car will make it easy. You will be busy with Captain Smit refitting the new, well new second-hand tug. She'll be called *Sunda*. The big tugs are all going to be named after Straits: Singapore Straits, Malacca Straits, Messina Straits and so on. Drink up, I must be on my way,' said Mr R.

Tom left the office in a slight daze and sat for a while in the Mini, before driving back to the Orchid Inn, and taking a refreshing swim. He was being given the opportunity of a lifetime, he thought, as he swam vigorously up and down the pool, the only swimmer in the dark.

It was all up to him and somehow he felt sure he had it in him to accept the challenge. Who knows, he thought, drifting into fantasyland, take over when the old man retired.

He went to bed, happy that coming to Singapore was going to be the right decision.

CHAPTER 3

The arrival of the *Pansy* was an event in the history of Co-sel Salvage and everyone seemed to know, from the cleaning ladies to the chairman. No one went home early that Monday evening, all stayed to watch and be part of what seemed a turning point. Cosel Salvage was entering the world stage and the *Pansy* was the beginning.

There was a considerable crowd on the quay, watching as the *Pansy* was towed by the *Jurong* and another small harbour tug in the fast-gathering darkness. She was big, one of the biggest tugs Tom had ever seen, more like a medium-size coaster. The accommodation was amidships and there was a derrick forward of the bridge. As she came around the corner into full view, there was a collective gasp from the crowd. Big though she was, the white accommodation paint was scarred and streaked with rust; the hull, once black, was almost devoid of paint and she was high out of the water, the waterline covered with barnacles. The coming darkness hid the worst of it from sight.

Tom's heart sank; a floating wreck. Steve's words came to mind, 'Some junk the old man picked up on the cheap,' but he reckoned the machinery must work or she would not have been able to steam the thousands of miles from Japan. Then again, the prevailing weather was the north-east monsoon, which would have been behind her. As the huge tug slowly approached, Tom saw a large figure appear on the bridge wing, walkie-talkie to his mouth, obviously controlling the two tugs. He berthed her very neatly. The watching crowd applauded when she touched the wharf and shipyard workers made fast her mooring lines. The crowd quite quickly dispersed home, DB and the old man having left earlier.

Tom climbed on board and introduced himself to Jan, who vigorously shook his hand, exclaiming, 'Welcome! Heap of scrap, come below for a beer.'

Tom noticed a few empty beer cans on the table under the centre bridge windows.

The cabin needed painting and there was no carpet but the air-conditioning seemed to be working. The settee was plastic-covered, a rather nasty brown colour, and there was a single chair. The fridge looked new and Jan handed Tom a beer before he flicked open his can of beer and drank deeply, his large hand almost hiding the tin, his luxuriant moustache moving as he swallowed.

'Ah, welcome to Singapore and the madhouse that is Cosel Salvage,' boomed Jan. 'Still, can't complain. It's given me a good life and the old man is okay, but watch out for DB. What do you know about salvage?' he asked.

'Nothing about practical salvage,' Tom answered honestly, 'although I have learned a lot with my year in London with the marine lawyers. I have been around small boats all my life.'

'Good, I teach you good,' he guffawed, a big man in every way.

'Well, thanks, Captain,' replied Tom, slightly taken aback.

'Call me Jan. Now, to work. You are my chief officer and we have a lot of work to do to get this heap of scrap into a full salvage tug. I have been busy on the trip south,' and he opened a drawer and pulled out a pile of papers.

'This is my work list,' he said, pushing the bundle across the table. Tom saw it was all handwritten in an untidy scrawl.

'Find a typewriter and type it out, you will learn a lot from it,' Jan ordered. 'I had a message from Ops, there is a big meeting in the old man's office at 1000 tomorrow to discuss the refit, you will be with me. You will know what I want from typing that list out.'

Tom's heart sank, then berating himself, realised it was a golden opportunity to learn quickly what a salvage tug was all about. They went through the list together, adding and subtracting pages of it. Tom quickly came to respect Jan's knowledge, not just of equipment he wanted, but also of all he knew about ship construction and how he wanted to alter and improve the tug.

'Ops will help you get this typed,' suggested Jan. 'I'm going home. See you in the old man's office at 1000 when I will sign the work list,' and with that, he got up, his large frame filling the doorway as he left, a real character.

It was now well after 2100 and Tom was hungry, but he had hours of work to complete, typing out the work list. In Ops, the duty officer sat him down at a desk with a type-writer and he set to work. He finally finished some hours later, and gave his typed list to the assistant to make photocopies. He learnt an incredible amount and felt he would be able to justify most of what Jan wanted to do. He drove back to the hotel and had a light snack in his room before falling exhausted into bed. Mental effort could be as exhausting as physical labour.

The following morning, the old man's office was so full, extra chairs were brought in. Steve was there, and a contingent from the yard, DB, Daniel Bang, the superintendent - whose name Tom discovered was Barry Todd - Ishmael, the diving manager, technical manager and a few others Tom had not seen before. John Gomes was there, looking rather out of place amongst the core people of Cosel. The old man called the meeting to order and waved Jan's work list in the air.

'I may not be a mariner, but this,' and he rattled the pages, 'will ruin us. I should have bought a new tug.'

There was muffled laughter as he continued, 'Captain Smit, explain and justify what you are trying to do.'

'I'm not so good with my English,' said a much subdued Jan, who looked rather cowed in the presence of all the shore people, very different from the confident man he had seen on the tug last night, thought Tom.

'I discuss with my chief officer last night, he typed the list so he can tell you what I want.'

Tom had prepared himself for this and saw DB looking at him.

'The overall concept is of a salvage tug operating independently, able to perform salvage in remote parts of the world without outside assistance. For instance, a ship aground in the South China Sea on a remote reef, our tug arrives, can conduct a diving survey, lay ground tackle, has enough personnel to man pumps, a welder and fabricator to make things, enough gear and equipment for all eventualities. On re-floating, she's able to patch the bottom under water.'

'You are learning fast, Captain Matravers,' said Mr R. 'What do you say, Mr Brown?'

'I agree.'

'But the cost,' said Mr R, sharply.

'In relation to a new tug, not so much. The survey report was good despite the outward appearance,' said Mr Brown. 'We will have a good vessel, better than the competition in Singapore.'

'Do we really need such a big crew, more than twenty-five, enough almost to man two super tankers?'

'Yes,' said Jan, loudly, surprising everyone.

'The extra people, sir, are needed to make our concept of an independent salvage unit work,' put in Tom, quickly smoothing what some might have thought as rudeness on Jan's part. In their discussions last night Jan was emphatic it would not work unless they had the people. You could not always rely on the crews of the casualties and anyway, it might be an abandoned ship.

'Mr Bang?' Mr R queried.

'No problem, sir, I can find the people.'

Good for him, thought Tom.

'Two cranes seems an extravagance to me,' said Mr R. 'What do you think, Mr. Brown?'

'It would certainly make working the tug more efficient and enhance her value.'

Mr R did not seem very impressed. 'The more we do, the more you are pleased, Mr Dodd.'

Steve merely smiled and Tom could see his eyes sparkling mischievously. He and Jan had discussed this at length and would use it as a bargaining chip, Jan knowing the old man from past experience. The aft crane was crucial for making the tow deck more efficient to work with the towing gear and equipment in the aft hold, the forward one was not so essential. The derrick was fine, except in bad weather.

After much discussion it was agreed to go ahead with most of Jan's requirements and the concept of the independent salvage tug fitted in well with the old man's desire for expansion. Dispensing with the lifeboats would be no problem, Barry Todd, the superintendent, said; just put on more life rafts and have a rescue boat, he would clear it with classification. The tow deck needed reconfiguring and the fitting of dolly pins and a gob line winch. The dolly pins were to hold, when required, the tow wire amidships, and the winch to be able to pull and control the wire across the towing gunwale. Both the aft and forward hold to be enlarged to carry more salvage equipment, converting a ballast tank into fresh water, and other items. Jan and Tom were forced to give in on the second crane, the forward crane. The meeting broke up after two hours, with the old man exclaiming:

'Speed, gentlemen, speed. We need the *Pansy* to be re-christened *Sunda*, working, not sitting in the yard, spending money.'

Jan took Tom to the swimming club for what turned out to be rather a liquid lunch. They returned to find their tug stripped of all crew and swarming with shipyard workers.

'Good afternoon,' said Steve, 'I see you and Captain Smit have enjoyed your lunch.'

He laughed, his blue eyes dancing with merriment. Tom was sweating profusely in the afternoon heat after all the beer he had drunk, and Jan's shirt was wet through.

'I am off home,' announced Jan. 'See you at 0800 to-morrow. Lock up the cabin after you.'

'Your work list is very good,' said Steve, 'and the in-voices will reflect the numbers on it to make it easy for you to check. I can see I will be working through you rather than Captain Smit.'

He laughed.

'Don't worry, he will be watching you like a hawk,' smiled Tom. 'It's very much his baby and I suppose you could say he is using me as a front man.'

'Don't worry. I know Jan, we refitted the *Singapore*. This refit is going to take some months and she won't be able to move for over a month while the engine room is dealt with. She is too big for the slip, so will have to go to dry dock. You spoke well at the meeting and I'm surprised the old man agreed to so much. In general, work with the foremen and only come to me in emergencies or compete disagreements. Today is Tuesday, my wife suggests Thursday for supper, just us, you and one other.'

'That's very kind of you, I would be delighted,' said Tom, using his already wet handkerchief to wipe the sweat from his face. 'My god, it's hot in here!'

'You will have to get used to it, no air-con for some time,' said Steve as he left the cabin.

Tom locked the cabin and made an inspection round the tug, and finding he was in the way of the shipyard men, he drove back to the Orchid Inn and enjoyed a refreshing swim.

The days started to merge into one another as Tom and Jan were kept busy, monitoring the work and sorting out problems. The superintendent left them to it, expecting a daily report before going home. Barry Todd proved to be very amenable, approachable and helpful. He already had permission to cut away the lifeboats. He and his wife lived out at Sembawang and they asked Tom out to supper on the Saturday.

Thursday's supper was most enjoyable. Steve's wife, Maria, some Spanish blood, thought Tom was very good looking and a bundle of fun. The other guest was Sheila Turner, an unattached English girl in Singapore for six months, and she proved interesting and entertaining. Tom managed to arrange dinner with her the next day, which proved even more enjoyable, and Tom thought could lead to other things.

CHAPTER 4

The refit continued and time passed in a whirl of activity for Tom, both work and social, both of which were much more intermingled in Singapore than in the UK, and being an attractive, unattached bachelor, Tom was much in demand.

He was getting along fine with Sheila and they met for supper a few times, mainly at the Tangle Inn, until one evening, Tom plucked up enough courage to ask her to dine with him at his hotel. The restaurant was a fairly standard hotel-type restaurant, but pleasing enough in its way. The chairs had armrests and the tables had white tablecloths with proper napkins, the decor uninteresting, mainly pastel colours.

The dinner went well, the food was quite good and the bottle of wine acceptable. They laughed and joked, Sheila looking good in a colourful cocktail dress, quite short by Singapore standards, which drew envious glances from the usual group of men at the bar.

After dinner Tom said, 'Why not come up to my room?'

A fairly obvious invitation.

Sheila hesitated only a moment, before saying, 'Yes.'

They looked at each other as they travelled up in the lift to the first floor, and once inside his room, started kissing.

Tom gently steered Sheila to the bed, when Tom's pager went off.

'Sorry,' he said, as he rolled free and picked up the phone, dialling Cosel's twenty-four-hour number.

'Van will pick you up in ten minutes, we want you to join the *Singapore* and tow in a ship from the Malacca Straits.'

Tom was thrilled, all thoughts of sex flew out of his mind. Just, how to get rid of Shelia without upsetting her too much? Sheila was livid.

'Treating me like some cheap tart, don't bother calling me again!' she hissed.

He took her down in the lift and ordered a taxi, which arrived at the same time as the Cosel van. Sheila threw off his arm as he tried to help her in.

Tom was much too excited at the prospect of his first salvage and thought he would be able to make it up to her when he returned. When he reached Ops, he was given the position of the casualty anchored a hundred miles up Malacca Straits. He saw a green pin close inshore off the Malaysian coast.

'*Singapore* is underway now. You will go out in our high-speed launch *Cosel One* and meet her at port limits, Western Anchorage. She is steaming round at full speed from Eastern Anchorage. If you leave now, the boat is waiting for you at the new yard, you will arrive at the same time. Here is a Lloyds Open Form but there should be some on-board *Singapore*. Captain Hannibal is an experienced

41

master but Mr Brown thinks you should go,' said the duty ops man.

'Okay, thanks,' said Tom, feeling his shirt pocket for the notebook he carried at all times. He took it out and started the notes for his first salvage. The bright neon lights in Ops affected his eyes and he stood outside to let them adjust to the darkness. He walked through the unlit new yard, using a torch he had borrowed from Ops and found the *Cosel One*, engine running, alongside the radio barge, the Malay skipper welcoming him on board.

'Western Anchorage, Captain?'

'Yes, to meet the *Singapore*.'

'Okay.'

Tom stood next to him as he navigated out of the creek, the darkness almost hiding the banks into the main channel. The skipper called up port control and obtained permission while underway. Once in the main channel he opened her up to her full speed of 15 knots, which seemed much faster in the darkness. It was not long before they were through the anchored ships and on port limits, a flashing light close by and Sultan shoal on their port quarter. There was shipping traffic south-bound from the Malacca Straits, altering course to pass through the Singapore Straits and Raffles Light, while a heavily laden tanker was keeping to the deep water channel further south.

Soon after stopping, Tom saw the lights of a small vessel passing Sultan Shoal, moving fast. That's the tug, he thought, and was proved right as she slowed down. The

Cosel One went alongside the still-moving *Singapore*, and Tom stepped onto the towing gunwale, two Filipino seamen helping him onto the towing deck. He could feel the tug picking up speed as he made his way up onto the bridge, much smaller than the *Pansy*, now christened *Sunda*, although the christening ceremony was still to come.

Captain Hannibal, a middle-aged, heavily-set Filipino, welcomed him onto the darkened bridge. He settled himself into his Captain's chair, while the officer of the watch took a position. Tom could see an AB at the wheel hand steering in one of the busiest shipping lanes in the world. There were lights everywhere shipping bound south, fishing boats with a single bright light. He could see a tug, towing two barges on the port side of the *Singapore*, the white lights on the mast of the tug and a red light, and further aft, the two red lights of the barges. Captain Hannibal was keeping well inshore but far enough off to keep clear of the fish traps, the echo sounder running. Once into the Malacca Straits proper, the myriad lights settled down. Tom stayed on the bridge for an hour or so, then took up Captain Hannibal's offer to get his head down on the settee in his cabin.

The sun was rising over Malaysia when Tom returned to the bridge, refreshed and invigorated, a fiery orb over the dark jungle. Captain Hannibal was on the bridge with the binoculars pressed to his eyes. Tom followed the binoculars and in the distance could see a ship with accommodation amidships about two miles away.

'Starboard five.'

Tom watched the bow of the tug slowly turn and just before it pointed at the ship,

'Midships, port five, steer for the ship.'

'Steer for the ship,' repeated the helmsman, a smart Filipino wearing blue working shorts and white T-shirt, with a red baseball hat set at a jaunty angle on his head. He grinned as Tom walked past him, out onto the wing of the bridge, and joined Captain Hannibal.

'I will hold off and you can go across in the zed boat,' he said. 'Slow ahead!' he called out to the mate whose watch it was, a rather dour man of medium height with a sombre face.

The engine telegraph clanged and the beat of the single engine slowed; Tom noticed the vibration under his feet stop. The sun was high in the sky now and the day was quickly warming up with sky clear overhead, but cloud out to sea on the horizon, to the north.

Captain Hannibal circled the anchored ship, black hull and white accommodation, the derrick's masts and ventilators painted buff, and stopped abreast the bridge, a couple of hundred yards off. Tom waited on the tow deck as the black rubber boat was launched, then climbed over the towing gunwale as it dropped back to where he was standing, the Lloyds form in an envelope, tucked into his trousers. He jumped in and the boat driver twisted the throttle to full so the rubber boat almost leapt out of the water, throwing Tom onto the bottom. The Filipino driver laughed, his long hair streaming behind his head.

44

'Hold on, Cap!'

Tom did not know whether to be angry or not. He laughed as the Filipino bought the boat neatly alongside the pilot ladder on the casualty, hanging just forward of the bridge.

'I wait,' said the Filipino.

'No, go back to the tug,' ordered Tom.

'Okay,' and Tom stepped onto the ladder as the boat roared away attaining the plane in seconds.

'Mad bugger,' thought Tom, but at least he is alive and full of life.

Tom was met at the top by a surly-looking man who turned out to be Indonesian. He was led through the dirty and smelly accommodation up onto the bridge where a very fat European with a red face, which highlighted his white hair, was sitting in his captain's chair.

'Good morning, Captain,' said Tom, cheerfully.

'What's good about it?' growled the European. 'My useless chief engineer can't fix the main engine and I will get the blame for it.'

'Very sorry to hear it,' Tom commiserated. 'Just a simple signature and we can start the tow,' he suggested, producing his Lloyds Form and handing it to the captain.

'Lloyds Open Form, I don't need salvors, I need a tow,' his well-spoken English rather out of place from both the surroundings and the person.

Tom did not know if he was right or not but said, 'This is what was agreed as I understand it.'

'Okay, what the hell, in for a penny in for a pound! Where do I sign?'

Tom handed him his biro and, laying the form on the arm of the chair, the fat captain signed where Tom indicated. Taking the form to the table at the forward end of the bridge under the centre window he quickly filled it in and signed himself. He had carefully studied it last night and felt the weight of responsibility fall on his shoulders, for it imposed considerable onus on the salvors; ultimately it was a "no cure, no pay" contract and not many people operated this way. He carefully put the form back in its envelope and called up Captain Hannibal on his Motorola.

'LOF signed. Its calm enough, why not come alongside? Make the connection easier.'

'Okay, Cap.'

Tom had discussed towing with Jan and in calm waters like this it was the easiest way to connect.

'The tug is coming alongside for the connection, Captain, can we have your crew standing by? He will be coming on your port side.'

'Chief Officer!' barked the captain, his jowls wobbling, clutching a glass of what looked suspiciously like beer. 'You heard the Salvage man.'

A large, burly Indonesian, smoking one of their evil-smelling cigarettes, wandered into the wheelhouse from the chartroom and walked over to the port wing. He let loose a completely unintelligible barrage of Indonesian words to someone unseen, and wandered back into the chartroom.

'Bottom end of the market, this lot,' thought Tom, but no matter, it is my first salvage and first LOF.

Captain Hannibal brought the *Singapore* neatly alongside the casualty in the 69 position, the stern of the tug facing the bow of the ship. She was quickly made fast by the Indonesian crew who proved quite willing under Tom's leadership. The salvage bosun came on board with a couple of men and heaved up the heavy slip hook, which was made fast to the forward bollards. They then heaved on board the wire forerunner wire and made it fast on the large slip hook.

'You stay on board the casualty, Cap. I'll give you a man to watch the tow,' said Captain Hannibal when Tom walked back to where he was watching from his bridge wing.

'Ok, I think you had better have this for safe-keeping,' said Tom, handing over the envelope containing the signed LOF.

It was all new to Tom and so utterly different from his former life as Chief Officer on a cargo liner. Joining a moving tug at port limits from a fast crew boat, racing up the Malacca Straits in the middle of the night, being carried across the open sea to the casualty in a rubber boat, signing Lloyds Open Form; it was the stuff of dreams come true!

'Okay, Captain, heave up the anchor,' instructed Tom, back on the bridge of the casualty.

'Chief Officer, you heard the Salvage man!' shouted the European, sitting in his chair, his fat cheeks shaking, while still clutching what seemed to be a permanently full glass of beer. His face streamed with sweat in the increasingly hot day, the sun a molten bowl of steel shining into the wheelhouse. There was no reply but sometime later Tom saw the man wandering up the fore deck, still smoking his foul cigarettes. The anchor was soon aweigh and Tom signalled to Captain Hannibal.

Tom watched as the *Singapore* started moving off and once clear, turned sharply to starboard, the tow wire sliding along the towing gunwale until halted by the stopping bollard amidships, the tug turning fast, the propeller clear of the wire. As soon as she was parallel with the ship, the tug moved ahead, the main tow wire being paid out until when well ahead, the tow wire became tight and lifted out of the water. This was the critical time of starting a tow, to make the casualty move without putting too much strain on the gear and breaking it. The salvage AB left on board was on the forecastle, grease pot in hand, signalling all was well and the tow back to Singapore began. Tom carefully filled in his notebook with the times of all that had happened.

The tow picked up speed and Tom reckoned the *Singapore* was doing well to achieve a speed of about five knots with her loaded tow. There was a new officer on the bridge, a much younger man than the Indonesian mate, dressed in well-worn jeans and a not-too-clean sweatshirt.

'You the third officer?' asked Tom, it now being midmorning.

'Yes, sir.'

48

'Okay, well it would be good if you put a position on the chart every half hour so we can monitor the situation.'

'Okay.'

'Keep him occupied, lazy sod,' growled the captain, for once not holding the glass as he heaved his great bulk out of the chair.

'Been here all night, now I have someone reliable on the bridge I am off to my bunk. Call me when we reach Singapore,' and he waddled off into the chartroom, slamming the door as he entered the accommodation. Tom was quite happy to be left in charge and be rid of a man who seemed to be almost at the end of the line. Still, nothing to do with him, and he dismissed it from his mind.

The tow proceeded well and both the third officer and later the second officer opened up a little under Tom's gentle questioning and guidance, proving themselves reasonably competent, unused to regular position taking.

'Very difficult man,' was the only comment from the second mate.

Tom perused the log and noted she had been at anchor for three days, waiting for a tug. The nature of the engine problem was not entered.

Captain Hannibal came up on the radio later that evening, saying he had a message from base, informing them to tow the casualty to Sembawang shipyard, which meant passing through the narrow Singapore Straits. The Chief Officer, who was on watch, proved to be a surly, middle-aged man so Tom did not bother with him but worked out the tides himself for passing through the Straits where the current ran strongly.

'The tide turns in our favour about 0600,' he told Captain Hannibal on the radio.

'Yes, we should catch it nicely and make Sembawang in daylight,' he replied.

'Have you sent out a TTT warning notice to Singapore radio?' asked Tom.

'Radio Officer will be doing it shortly.'

'Okay, I will be on the bridge all night and your AB is fine, he has been fed. The wire forerunner is good and well greased, I've been up to have a look a couple of times,' said Tom.

It was a long night and Tom cat-napped in the captain's chair. Captain Hannibal kept well over to the eastern side of the Malacca Straits, clear of the north-bound traffic. It was a clear night and the casualty followed well with no one steering.

Just after daylight, they entered the narrow Singapore Straits, passing Raffles Lighthouse and Singapore on their port side, past eastern anchorage, full of a huge range of anchored ships with Indonesian Batam island on their starboard side, and so to the entrance of Johore Straits where the pilot met them and boarded the tug. Tom insisted a man was on the wheel from daylight, which greatly assisted the manoeuvrability of the tow in the confined waters.

It was late afternoon when the Sembawang harbour tugs came bustling downstream to meet them. Tom joined the

50

salvage AB on the forecastle and when given the instruction by Captain Hannibal on the radio, they slipped the tow, the AB wielding the seven pound hammer he had standing by. The wire forerunner slithered out of the fairlead and dropped into the muddy water, the *Singapore* turning away to starboard, recovering the towing gear.

Tom returned to the bridge and found the casualty captain ensconced in his chair, clutching a glass of beer in his hand. The pilot was instructing the tugs and put her alongside the berth without too much trouble, although the Indonesian crew were slow with the lines.

'Safe and sound now, Captain,' said Tom, after the pilot departed.

'I thought we were going to Singapore,' growled the captain, his face ruddy in the fading daylight.

'Change of orders last night,' replied Tom as the *Singapore* came alongside to pick up the slip hook and lashing wires. He walked out onto the bridge wing to watch.

'I will bring the termination letter shortly,' said Tom, retuning to the wheel house.

'I will be in my cabin.'

A short time later Tom went into the captain's day cabin with the letter typed up by the *Singapore*'s Radio Officer, to find the captain at his desk, glass in hand, talking with his agent and the shipyard personnel.

'Ah, the salvage man,' he said loudly, 'let's get rid of him.'

Tom walked up and handed over the letter and copy, which he had already signed.

'What's this, "satisfactorily completed"?' the captain asked, his pudgy fingers holding his pen, raised in the air, his jowls wobbling.

'Well, nothing went wrong and you are safely alongside a safe berth in a safe place.'

'Okay, okay,' and he signed, retaining the copy.

Tom left elated and climbed aboard the *Singapore*.

'Well done, Captain, a good job well done,' said Tom, very pleased with his first salvage as Captain Hannibal manoeuvred his tug clear of the casualty and set off down the Straits to Eastern anchorage.

'What happened to Immigration?' asked Tom.

'No bother, I have an open-dated port clearance so there was no problem leaving. Ops will have informed them of our return to Eastern anchorage via Sembawang. When you are picked up I will send the crew list ashore if the immigration don't board. Cosel keep good relations and they are understanding of our work. If they come on board, I will put you on the crew list, if not, I won't. Presumably you have your passport with you?'

'I see, yes, I have my passport.'

It was after midnight when the anchor was let go in the anchorage, as near to Clifford Pier as possible. Tom had not been idle and used the time to write his report, based on the evidence he had seen in salvage cases when working in London with the marine lawyers. The crew boat picked him up and took him to Clifford Pier, where he caught a taxi back to his hotel. He dropped into bed in the early hours, exhausted.

It was late morning when he arrived at the office and dropped off his paperwork with Ops, then returned to the *Sunda*, to be greeted by Jan.

'On holiday, are we?' Jan greeted him, laughing, beer in hand, sitting in his cabin with papers strewn all over the table.

'My first LOF,' Tom laughed. 'Well, it was Captain Hannibal's LOF really, he didn't need me. However, I learned a lot and have done all the paperwork.'

'What's that funny hunting word you English use? "Blooded"?' Jan guffawed, handing Tom a cold beer. It was a little early for him but he could hardly refuse. They discussed the progress of the refit and walked round the tug, inspecting the work.

'I will take you out to lunch at Jurong Pier to celebrate your salvage "blooding",' Jan announced as there was a call on the company radio, which Jan had had transferred to his cabin.

'DB wants to see Captain Matravers.'

Tom went ashore by the smart shipyard gangway and walked through the busy yard in the morning heat; the sun was hot and the sky was clear. His shirt was soon wet through.

'Captain Matravers, your first LOF,' said DB, 'sit down.'

He had the papers, including the Lloyds Form Tom had dropped off in Ops, in front of him. 'This looks quite good to me, our lawyers should be happy. Well done. The old man wants a word.'

Tom went to the next office and spoke with Mr R's secretary, an aloof and unfriendly lady, who disappeared inside his office. A short time later she opened the door and ushered him in.

'Sit,' said Mr R, pointing to the chair in front of his large desk, the tug position chart on the wall behind him.

'I have briefly looked at your paperwork. It appears good, and if all our masters did half as well, we would reduce our lawyers' fees,' Mr R laughed. 'Still, it's no more than I expected from you. How are you getting on with Captain Smit?'

'Very well, thank you, sir. He has taught me a lot already and the refit is going well.'

The old man's face clouded.

'The cost, the cost! You will have to find me a major salvage to pay for it,' he laughed. 'Anyway, well done.' He stood up and shook Tom's hand, 'Keep up the good work and get the *Sunda* finished.'

Tom left the office in a slight daze, unused to praise, and went back to the *Sunda* where he met Jan coming down the gangway, his bulk blocking anyone coming in the opposite direction.

'Lunch,' he announced. 'Need to get there early, otherwise we will have to wait for a table.'

Tom followed Jan to the car park, where getting into his car was something of an event. When he finally squeezed himself in, it had a distinct list to starboard.

Lunch was mainly prawns, squid, crab, and was a lively and liquid affair. Jan regaling Tom with salvage stories. After lunch, Jan decided to go home.

'To beat the traffic,' was his excuse, and he dropped Tom off in the car park.

Tom decided to do the same, enjoying a refreshing swim in the hotel pool. He was the only swimmer, although there were a couple of women sunning themselves, who ogled him. He rang Shelia's number from the bar telephone only to be told she was away. So that is the end of that, thought Tom.

CHAPTER 5

Tom was immediately awake on hearing the telephone ring. He was lucky, having the ability to go from sleep to awake almost instantly. He picked up the telephone receiver, fumbling in the darkness.

'Salvage, Nipa shoal, van will pick you up in twenty minutes,' said the crisp voice of the duty Ops man.

Tom quickly dressed and picked up his small emergency bag, which contained, among other things, money and his passport. He was in reception, which was open to the elements, when the van arrived. The early morning tropical coolness was pleasant, belying the heat of the day to come. The dawn faded quickly into daylight as he was driven out to Jurong, and the air was much warmer when he walked into Ops.

'Car carrier, loaded, about 15,000 dead weight,' briefed Ishmael, who was sitting at his desk, as though he never left it, various Lloyds publications spread out before him. 'Salvage Master has gone out in *Cosel One*, *Sunda* to sail as soon as possible. It's high tide, Captain Smit will be here shortly. We have given you crew from the small tugs in the new yard. Chief Engineer, Second Engineer and Radio Officer are on board.'

Tom was impressed at the speed things were happening. 'We have a problem,' he said, 'the tow deck is full of equipment.'

'Get rid of it, dump it on the quayside, but be quick, don't forget we have competition. If the Salvage Master obtains the Lloyds Open Form, it is important you are there and he is not made to look a fool waiting for your arrival. The *Singapore* is towing a ship in from the Indian Ocean, as you know.'

Tom felt galvanised; problems were to be overcome, not talked about.

'Okay,' he said, and walked quickly down to the *Sunda*. Pedro, the tall, rather thin, dark, boatswain, had already organised the scratch crew and they were landing equipment, using the newly installed crane, proving its worth and efficiency.

'Good work, bosun,' said Tom, as he walked up the gangway. 'We need a clear tow deck.'

'Okay, Cap,' grinned Pedro, the Filipinos and Malays working with a will, the prospect of salvage and a bonus a spur. It was fully daylight now.

On the bridge, the cook handed Tom a cup of tea. The acting second officer was clearing the chart table of equipment left by the shore workers, not yet on board, who were installing a second radar and other equipment. He stepped out onto the bridge wing to check that the radar scanner of the old machine was clear, then returned inside the wheelhouse to switch it on. As he waited for it to warm up, Jan

57

appeared, looking bright but serious, his normal bonhomie missing.

'Make sure the tow deck is completely clear, Tom,' ordered Jan, 'nothing loose must be left. Throw everything ashore, clutter on the tow deck means an accident, and I don't tolerate accidents, especially if preventable. As soon as it is clear, get the towing gear ready.'

'Understood,' said Tom, leaving the bridge by the outer companionway. He walked along the clear boat-deck, with its rubber boat and launching crane in place of the lifeboat, and down onto the tow deck.

'Throw all this rubbish ashore,' said Tom pointing to a heap right at the aft end. 'The deck must be completely clear.'

'OK,' replied Pedro.

The *Jurong* appeared alongside and Pedro handed the crew member on her aft deck a mooring line with an eye in it, which he put over the towing hook.

'*Jurong* secured. Another five minutes to clear the tow deck, Jan,' said Tom into his walkie-talkie, as he heard and felt the big diesels start, one after the other, puffs of smoke appearing out of the still un-painted funnel. The chief has been quick, thought Tom, and wondered what scratch crew he had with him. It was amazing how everyone one jumped to it with the prospect of a salvage, and things happened quickly.

'Let go aft and send a man forward to let go,' ordered Jan over the radio.

Tom repeated the order.

Shortly afterwards, the *Jurong* started towing the *Sunda*, stern first, clear of the wharf and out into the creek. Although high water, Jan obviously thought it was safer not to use the main engines too close to the shipyard and risk his propellers. Tom found Jan on the port bridge wing, walkie-talkie in hand, directing the small harbour tug. Towing the big tug stern first was no easy matter, she wanted to sheer all over the place and there was not much room. The second mate was at the wheel, almost as tall as himself. Tom checked the radar was working, set up on the one and a half mile range. The chart for Singapore Western Anchorage was on the chart table. As soon as the *Sunda* was in the main channel, Jan dismissed the *Jurong*.

'Full ahead, both engines!' he ordered.

Tom, apprehensive at using the bridge controls for the first time, checked the rev counter and clutched in. He pushed the single control lever for each engine forward slowly and the *Sunda* rapidly picked up speed. After a few minutes, the engines were at full power, black smoke pouring out of the funnel, and the tug was already creating a big wash. The black smoke soon stopped. Jan was still on the bridge wing binoculars raised to his eyes, his hand pointing.

'Steer for that beacon,' said Jan.

'Okay, Cap,' replied the second mate, spinning the wheel and settling the tug on the new course.

The *Sunda* was soon into the anchorage proper, racing past the anchored ships, causing the smaller ones to roll with her huge wash. Heads appeared on bridge wings, wondering why the tug should be running at such speed. Sultan Shoal was soon abeam as she entered the main strait proper, crossing the lines of traffic in both directions, passing close ahead of a large container ship which provoked an angry voice on the VHF which Jan ignored. He was standing inside the wheelhouse at the centre window. The sun was on their port side, well up in the sky, heating the day.

'There she is,' said Jan, pointing at a car carrier stationary ahead of them. As they came closer, they could see her bow high out of the water.

'Well aground,' commented Jan, 'will keep Paul our Salvage Master happy. It will be a good excuse for him to lay ground tackle, it's what might be called his thing.'

They were now rapidly closing the stricken ship and Jan moved over to the bridge controls, slowly pulling the two levers back, slowing the big tug.

'*Sunda*, this is Mike 4. LOF signed. Connect up astern,' said the voice of the Salvage Master over the company radio.

'Answer him, Tom,' said Jan. 'I don't want to talk to him.'

Tom acknowledged the Salvage Master's instructions.

'Right, Tom. We may only have a scratch crew and usually it is better not to mix Malays and Filipinos, but it is a salvage and only for a short time, so should be okay. Thank heavens we have Pedro, the bosun! He is very good and will get the best out of all of them. Launch the zed boat, the rescue boat, take Pedro and three men with you and the slip hook and lashing wire. When you have secured the slip hook and backed up the bollards, send Pedro back to the tug and I will manoeuvre in stern first, to make the connection. You will have to use the casualty crew because we don't have enough men here on the tug. Once connected, come back here,' said Jan, very much in command, crisp and clear with his instructions, stroking his luxuriant moustache.

'Understood, Jan,' acknowledged Tom, leaving the bridge.

The newly-installed crane proved its worth and the rubber boat was quickly launched and loaded. Tom drove the boat himself to what appeared from sea level, the huge car carrier, the high vertical sides very tall above the water. Underneath, the reef was clearly visible when they reached the pilot ladder hanging from an opening amidships. It was hot now in the mid morning sun, but Tom did not feel it, being far too busy and suppressing his excitement.

He handed over the control to an AB who said he could drive the boat, and climbed the pilot ladder followed, by the bosun and the other two AB's. The enclosed car deck appeared huge and cavernous, despite the luxury cars. A crew member showed Tom onto the bridge while the bosun and AB's made their way aft. The Salvage Master, Captain

Paul Rogers, was a tall man, over six feet, rather thin, with an unsmiling long face and prominent nose, with black hair parted in the middle.

'Welcome,' said the Salvage Master. 'this is Captain Roland,' and he introduced a thickset European. 'Captain Matravers will be my assistant during this salvage.'

This was news to Tom and he wondered what Jan would say. Tom shook hands with the grim-faced Captain, which was not unsurprising given the circumstances; he would have some explaining to make to his owner.

'Once the divers are out of the water and have reported, I will make the final decisions, but it looks like ground tackle. Offload as much fuel as possible consistent with stability, and discharge some of the cargo,' said the Salvage Master in his rather toneless voice, betraying a hint of an accent from the Southern Hemisphere. 'I want the *Sunda* connected as soon as possible.'

'The bosun should be aft now, the slip hook and gear are in the zed boat,' reported Tom.

'You go and get the *Sunda* connected and report back to me. I have been assigned the owners' suite on the next deck and that will be my headquarters,' ordered the Salvage Master.

'Very good, Captain Rogers,' replied Tom formally, and left the bridge. He found Pedro, easily distinguished by his height, directing some of the ship's crew he had rustled up from somewhere and they were in the process of heaving up the slip hook and wire lashing, using one of the

62

mooring winches. Once it was on board, Tom told the zed boat driver to return to the *Sunda*. He spoke on the radio to Jan.

'The Salvage Master wants you to connect as soon as possible. He wants me to remain here as his assistant.'

'Okay,' replied Jan, the annoyance coming through his voice on the radio. 'Will speak to you later. When you are ready send Pedro and the men back, keeping the best AB for yourself. I am short-handed here and it is a big tug. You organise the ship's crew to heave the forerunner on board and our AB can connect it.'

'Very good, Jan, all understood,' replied Tom.

Pedro organised the ship's crew, who were working with a will under his leadership, directing them, lashing the slip hook to the aft bollards and backing them up to those at the forward. It was not long before Tom was able to call up Jan and tell him they were ready. Pedro obtained a heaving line and had it ready, handing it to the AB, chattering away in Tagaloc. Tom watched Jan manoeuvre the *Sunda* off the stern of the car carrier. She looked huge, high out of the water because there was little fuel on board and the hull was still unpainted. His radio crackled.

'The current is running towards Singapore so I will come in your starboard quarter. Be quick, I don't want to be set too far to the north or onto the reef.'

'Understood. Pedro is on the way back.' He had climbed down on the rope ladder hanging over the stern, and Tom could see the zed boat going alongside the tug as she manoeuvred, stern first towards the car carrier.

The AB with the heaving line climbed up onto the rails, helped by two of the ship's crew, and stood waiting held by his two helpers. The *Sunda* came in faster than Tom thought prudent. When close in under the stern, Jan stopped her with a great swirl of water from the two propellers in what Tom thought must have been a full ahead movement, black smoke pouring from the funnel. The AB just dropped the heaving line onto the tow deck below him and in a trice Pedro picked it up and made it fast to the messenger line.

'Heave!' he shouted, his voice shrill from the urgency of the situation.

Led by the AB who jumped down off the rails, the crew heaved the line on board and rushed it to the drum of the mooring winch. The messenger tightened as the drum turned and with tension on the line, the forerunner moved along the tow deck and up into the air, watched by Tom. As the eye neared the fairlead, he signalled to the winch driver to slow down, but it slipped through without catching and Tom stopped it opposite the slip hook. The AB slipped the eye over the hook, closed it and secured it with the safety locking pin.

'Okay, Cap,' grinned the AB.

'Forerunner secured,' reported Tom into the radio, as the *Sunda*, now opposite the stern, turned to port and headed up tide.

'That was quick, well done,' said the voice of the Salvage Master from the radio.

Then quite quietly, but clearly audible to anyone listening carefully, a voice said, 'Prick.'

Oh dear, thought Tom, all is not so rosy underneath, bad blood somewhere. He continued watching as the tow wire lengthened and the *Sunda* appeared a little smaller as she increased the distance from the casualty.

'*Sunda*, this is Mike 4. Anchor off and await instructions,' ordered the Salvage Master.

'Roger,' said a Filipino voice.

The forerunner tightened, the slip hook held firm as the lashing wires tightened themselves, then slackened as Tom clearly heard the anchor cable on the tug running out. He left the AB to watch the connection and found his way up onto the bridge through the accommodation. The Salvage Master was standing on the starboard bridge wing, hatless under the midday sun, looking at the big tug.

'Fine sight, even better when she is painted in the new colours,' he said, as Tom joined him. 'Jan is a very good tug master. The divers are making their inspection now.'

'Yes, most impressive,' said Tom, feeling the heat on his bare head. He must obtain a hat he thought.

'I want you with me on board the casualty, there is a spare bed in the owners' suite. Go back to the *Sunda* and collect enough gear for two or three days. Jan will moan and groan but he is connected now and will be fine. I have

65

arranged with Daniel Bang to send out a temporary replacement.'

Tom called up Jan and asked him to send over the zed boat to pick him up. He made his way to the pilot ladder amidships, not fancying trying to climb down the ladder hanging over the stern, which was free to swing, twist and turn.

'He is a prick,' boomed Jan, as Tom came onto the bridge of the *Sunda*. Jan was ensconced in his captain's chair, beer in hand. 'He steals my chief officer without even asking me,' shouted Jan, taking a swig from his can. 'Have a beer, lunch coming up.'

'I'll collect my kit,' said Tom. 'He says for two or three days. A temporary replacement is being sent out from Singapore.'

Jan grunted as Tom left the bridge. When he returned Jan was tucking into a chicken curry, a fresh beer unzipped.

'There's yours,' he said, pointing to a tray on the wheelhouse table containing the same.

Tom started eating, the tug was at anchor with the tow wire slack. It was hot, with the sun high, almost overhead, in a cloudless sky. The sea was calm, reflecting the bright sunlight, the water shimmering in the heat. The car carrier loomed huge and somehow incongruous with her bow high up in the air, the forepart clear of the water, part of the reef visible at low water, the light beacon just off her starboard bow. It seemed to Tom he had entered a different world where nothing was ordered or routine; life was full of surprises and diverse problems to be solved, exciting and different.

'Mike 4 and I do not see eye to eye,' said Jan, in a low, uncharacteristically sombre voice. 'I know him of old and for what he is, he knows it, but he also knows I won't do anything which will harm or hurt the company, but be warned, Tom, be warned.'

Tom's heart sank and he wondered what was behind this apparent bad blood. Captain Rogers seemed to be okay, a bit dour, but he was thrilled to be at the centre of things and be the Salvage Master's assistant.

'What do you mean, Jan?' he asked, worried.

'I said be warned. He will be nice to you, your best friend or mate, then stick a silver knife into you, especially if he thinks you are a threat to his position. I am safe and secure, a tug master, and am happy as I am. I have no wish to go further, I am no threat. You, however, are an unknown quantity, fresh, new, it's known the old man has seen you. Don't forget we are a small company, you're obviously well-educated, a master mariner and you have worked ashore with lawyers. The best way to find out and assess you is to keep you close by and if he considers you a threat, beware. The fact that I am your captain, he has dismissed, without even the courtesy of asking. He knew I would not make a fuss, would not do anything to hurt the company. Just be warned, be on your guard. Enough.'

He paused and then his mood changed. 'Second mate, fetch two beers from my fridge.' The jovial tug master was back.

'Enjoy and learn,' he guffawed, 'but keep me informed. Best of luck.'

Tom finished the second beer and left. He looked back at the big tug, with Jan waving from the bridge wing, and tried to throw off the sombre and pensive mood he felt, after what Jan had said. It might be a new world, he thought, but there was not much change in human nature and behaviour.

CHAPTER 6

Nothing like action, Tom thought, as he climbed the pilot ladder, knapsack on his back, and made his way through the hot car deck to the accommodation. The artificial lighting was dim after the bright sun outside and the glare from the calm sea. He found the Salvage Master at the writing desk in the owner's cabin.

'Lunch with Jan, I see,' he said, looking up from his paperwork, making Tom feel guilty about the beers he had drunk.

'Not to worry. Now, here is the plan,' he continued, unsmiling, in his rather toneless voice, with its hint of an accent, either from Australia or New Zealand, just discernible.

'I have calculated she is so far out of her draft that technically she can't re-float without cutting her up,' he gave a short snort. 'But of course, she will, I just don't know when. We will discharge as much of the fuel as possible, ballasting until we are ready. We will discharge from the top decks, stability may be a problem. The divers have reported, here is the sketch, you will see she is aground to just abaft amidships over half her length. The rudder and propeller are in deep water and undamaged.'

'The *Coselversatile*, our salvage and mooring vessel, will be here this afternoon and lay ground tackle. The fuel barge, which has heating coils, will also arrive this afternoon and go alongside the port side. The ship's crew are all ready to discharge the fuel.

'We will have a re-floating attempt at high water but it is just for show to keep the captain happy. The fuel discharge should take twenty-four hours or so, which will give us plenty of time to discharge the cars and possibly lorries onto the barges, which you will put alongside on the starboard side. So it looks like an attempt tomorrow evening. I don't like night time re-floatings, especially with all this kit around, so will probably delay until the next morning.

'We can expect an owners' rep, surveyors and other hangers-on to come out but hopefully through Cosel. We are in Indonesian waters and they have to clear out of Singapore immigration and clear back in on return. It is much easier if they come out on our crew boat, it gives us control of them.

'The Indonesian Navy will be here sometime. I am waiting for the salvage permit, which is being flown up from Djakarta. I already have the permit number. Our agents were efficient this morning for once and obtained it quickly before our competition had a chance. I have primed the Master to hand out cigarettes and booze as cumshaw when the Navy turns up. It is very important to remain on good terms with the Indonesians, they can stop us working at any time they feel like.

'My salvage ship, *Coselvenom*, will be here shortly and we will then have a full salvage crew on hand. I will tell the chief officer to anchor her off, she had an engine problem, now fixed, as no doubt you heard on your radio.'

Tom had a busy afternoon. The *Coselvenom* crew came on board, led by a very handsome, very competent Filipino, Juan Ventur. Tom and he hit it off immediately, which made working together much easier. Juan was an experienced salvage man having worked for the company for some years. The fuel barge turned up, towed by two small tugs, one forward and one aft. Tom put her alongside the casualty on the port side without incident. Juan, with a fitter, stayed on the barge to work it for the fuel discharge. Juan had tanker experience, which made him doubly useful.

A large, flat-top barge arrived and Tom put that alongside on the starboard side, opposite the vehicle midships loading and discharge position. He kept the small tugs with the barges in case of emergencies and needed to be moved. The fuel discharge started later in the afternoon with Juan in charge. Tom and two AB's who could drive, soon loaded the first barge, packing them as close as he dared. They were not lashed, relying on the calm weather. The barge was towed off to anchor by the two small tugs, while they waited for the second barge to arrive.

At 1800 the Salvage Master held his show re-floating attempt, Tom being on the bridge with him, and as expected, there was no movement of the casualty. They had not even bothered to move off the fuel barge, continuing with the discharge of fuel.

The *Coselversatile* arrived on site later that evening after dark, having been engaged on a mooring at Malacca. She was manned with a Malay Captain and crew. A bald-headed Englishman, Wayne Dawson, was in overall charge. He turned out to be very knowledgeable as well as speaking fluent Malay. He explained to Tom, who came over in the zed boat, how he would anchor the *Versatile* with the bow facing the stern of the casualty. The main wire would be run from the 100 ton pull winch to a slip hook secured on the casualty on the opposite side to that of the *Sunda.* Immediately with the powerful winch there was a 100-ton pull. Ground tackle blocks laid out on the fore deck would increase this by another sixty or seventy tons, which made it easier to control than using the big winch alone.

DB brought out various surveyors and interested parties in the *Coselone*, the fast crew boat, during the afternoon, and except for the owners' rep, departed back to Singapore that evening. The Indonesian Navy gunboat departed in the afternoon with happy officers clutching cigarettes and bottles of whisky. It was scheduled to return the next day to pick up a copy of the salvage permit, which had not arrived from Djakarta when DB left Singapore.

'Busy day,' commented Tom, as he and the Salvage Master discussed the day's progress that night in the owners' cabin, while enjoying a cold beer sent over by Jan.

'Very satisfactory, something usually goes wrong but it has been a good day. I see you have been keeping notes. I expect a full report when this is all over,' said the Salvage

Master. 'You can call me Paul when not on duty,' and he gave a rather thin smile, which did not reach his eyes. 'We are going to have to watch stability with almost no fuel and no ballast but still plenty of cargo. I've told the mate to work it out and am awaiting the result.

'The fuel discharge will continue all night, Juan is a good man and we can leave him to it. Another flat-top will be out in the early hours so we can continue the car discharge at daylight. A third barge may or may not arrive on time. The *Versatile* is connected on the port quarter giving Jan lots of room to swing around. We won't be making a re-floating attempt at all tomorrow. I want to finish the fuel transfer and have the barge clear before any attempt. She might come off with a bit of a rush, a bit like launching a ship on a slipway. Once they start to move off, they go.'

He chuckled, then continued coughing on the cigarette he was smoking. 'Get your head down and berth the flat top at first light.'

It had been a long day and Tom was asleep as soon as his head hit the pillow.

The next day was not so frantically busy and the discharge of more cars and lorries was completed by noon. The two loaded barges at anchor added to what seemed to Tom the almost surreal scene: the reef showing at low water with its beacon, the car carrier with its bow stuck up in the air close by, the cars and lorries sitting on the two flat tops, the large, business-like, ocean-going tug, *Sunda*, anchored off with the tow-wire over her stern. The salvage

73

vessel, with her horns pointing at the casualty, was rather like some marine monster, also attached by a wire, and the fuel barge still alongside. It was another hot day and the calm sea shimmered and shone rather like a mirage in the desert.

The fuel discharge was completed that evening and Tom un-berthed the barge with the two small tugs anchoring it close by the car barges. All was ready for the morning re-floating attempt at 0700, just after daylight, when the de-ballasting would be complete. The Salvage Master told Tom to station himself aft with Juan and his men, and to be ready to slip the *Versatile* and *Sunda* if necessary.

'It will be good experience for you.'

Tom would much rather have been on the bridge where the Salvage Master directed the operation. However, he could follow most of the action from the radio traffic.

It was a cloudy morning when the attempt began. The wire to the *Versatile* was bar taut out on the port quarter, the horns emphasising the monster-like appearance in the early morning light, with a human figure perched on top of the starboard horn. The *Sunda* anchor was aweigh and she was towing out on the starboard quarter, the tow wire taut but most of it in the water, looking magnificent in the rapidly brightening day. Tom was looking forward on the starboard side through his binoculars at the beacon. There were white marks painted on it, residue from some previous salvage, and he could see it was not yet quite high water.

'*Sunda*, this is Mike 4, tow full power,' ordered the Salvage Master. All traffic on the company frequency was suspended until the salvage attempt was over.

'Roger, Mike 4, tow at full power,' replied a Filipino voice, Tom's temporary replacement, he thought. Tom could see an increase in the turbulence around the stern of the ocean-going tug, caused by her two big propellers, and the tow wire lifted, the centre still just in the water. The stenhouse slip hook came off the deck as the lashing wires tightened themselves round the bollards. An AB was standing by each slip hook with a seven-pound sledgehammer, ready to slip either vessel.

Suddenly, there was the deep cough of a powerful diesel starting and the stern began to vibrate as the casualty main engine came to life. Power was quickly built up to what Tom thought must be full astern and the vibration and noise from the propeller was considerable. It was fully daylight now, the sun well above Batam Island, when Tom heard on the radio, 'Commence salvage yawing,' and could feel the tension the Salvage Master was under.

'Commence salvage yawing,' replied the Filipino voice.

The *Sunda* turned to starboard, towards the *Coselversatile*, healing sharply the way she was turning. The tow wire came out of the water with the increased pull and began to hum, water droplets spurting from the wire. Tom stepped away and Juan laughed.

'Don't worry, Cap, it won't break,' embarrassing Tom as the rest of the salvage crew smiled.

The *Sunda* crabbed her way towards the *Versatile* quite quickly, the current being with her. When just past amidships, Tom saw the *Sunda* turn rapidly to port, the tow wire humming even louder and the pitch of the sound increased, causing even Juan to step back. The *Sunda* heeled to port and started moving sideways, away from the anchored salvage vessel.

'High water, Juan,' Tom called over the noise, looking through the binoculars at the beacon, the wash from the propellers was running forward along the side of the ship.

Quite suddenly, Tom heard what appeared to be a loud crack. He flinched, not knowing where the noise came from. Juan looked startled and then the casualty started to move and heel over to starboard. The wire to the *Sunda* was extremely tight, humming away, but that to the *Versatile* was slack. Wayne Dawson on the horn saw what was happening and frantically signalled to his winch-man, but the winch was not fast enough to pick up the slack.

Tom urgently called into his radio.

'Mike 4 *Versatile* wire slack, shall I slip?'

There was no answer.

The casualty was moving fast now and heeling more to starboard, sliding down the reef. Tom wondered about stability with the increasing heel, and if the *Versatile* was not slipped quickly, there might be a disaster. The *Sunda*, meanwhile, was still towing to port, pulling the stern away from the salvage vessel, while the main engine of the casualty still appeared to be going full astern. It seemed essential her wire was slipped or it would pull her under when the tension came back on it.

'Slip *Versatile*!' came the firm voice of Jan over the radio. Juan heard it and signalled to the AB standing by the safety locking pin to pull it out. The man wielding the hammer gave the iron ring round the hook a mighty hit, which moved, allowing the hook to open and the wire slithered out through the fairlead. The vibration and noise ceased as the main engine stopped and the voice of the Salvage Master ordered, 'Cease towing!'

The tow wire immediately slackened and most of it went under water. The casualty rolled to port and steadied almost upright and Tom heaved a sigh of relief that she was stable.

Tom was back on the starboard side where he could see the beacon, now some distance away, indicating they were well clear of the reef. He found his hands were shaking as he looked through his binoculars.

'Slip *Sunda*!' ordered the Salvage Master, and shortly afterwards the forerunner slipped over the stern. The vibration began again as the main engine was started ahead, and then stopped. Tom could hear the rattle of the chain when the anchor was let go.

'*Sunda* to anchor. *Versatile* dismissed,' said the Salvage Master.

Tom shook hands with a grinning Juan and walked over to the other side where he could see the *Coselversatile* quite close by, recovering his pulling wire and, by the look of it, heaving up his stern anchor. He needed to be quick or when the casualty swung to the current, she would hit her.

Tom left Juan to organise returning the slip hooks and lashings to their respective vessels and made his way up onto the bridge. Captain Rogers was on his own, looking as though the successful re-floating had been unsuccessful.

'I've told the captain and owners' rep we will reload here but they want to go straight into Singapore. They don't seem to understand or realise we are in Indonesian waters. It would cause all sorts of problems with the barges now loaded with cars and fuel, they would have to be entered as such and the cargo would become trans-shipment cargo. Anyway, get the fuel barge first as quickly as possible and then the car barges.'

Tom called up the *Sunda* and arranged for the zed boat to collect him and Juan. They went to the fuel barge, Juan bringing his fitter with him, and while Tom directed the two small tugs for the berthing, Juan readied the pump room to reload the fuel. It all went well, and once berthed and the fuel pipe connected, the fuel was pumped back into the casualty.

Tom left Juan to it and brought the first of the two flat tops alongside. By noon the two barges were discharged with no damage to any of the vehicles and they were towed back to Singapore by the two tugs, the two fuel barge tugs remaining in case of an emergency. The sky had cleared and it was another hot day, the sea reflecting the glare from the sunlight. Tom was now wearing a hat he had found himself and sunglasses.

'Nothing more for you, Tom,' said the Salvage Master, still unsmiling, when Tom reported to him. 'Return to the *Sunda* and tell Jan to escort the casualty to Singapore when we leave. The captain has seen sense so it will be tomorrow when the fuel barge has finished. Juan can do the un-berthing. The divers report no serious bottom damage, just scratches and a few indents. They were lucky. Give me your report as soon as possible,' and he turned away as the casualty captain called him.

Tom felt rather deflated as he made his way down to the pilot ladder and back to the *Sunda*, his mini fleet dispersed. He received a very different welcome from Jan, who was jovial, his usual beer in hand, laughing and joking. Two huge curries appeared and Tom was soon in a better mood.

'I've got to write a report for the Salvage Master,' Tom said when he finished his chicken curry, feeling bloated and desirous of an afternoon nap.

Jan suddenly became serious, his bonhomie gone. 'Make sure you keep a copy and send another one to DB. Don't ask questions, just do as I say, it's for your own good.'

Tom, although surprised, said nothing.

'Understood?' queried Jan, looking at Tom.

'Yes, thank you, Jan,' replied Tom, studying Jan's unusually hard-looking face, ruddy and smooth with its usual sweat line on his forehead, his grey hair slightly over-long and unruly, the moustache of which he was so proud, luxuriant on his upper lip, covering most of his mouth.

'Why did he not slip the *Versatile* earlier, leaving me to give the order? He knew you, being new, would not take it on yourself to slip but wait for the order, which should have come from him. He could see what has happening from the bridge as well as I could. I gave the order because I could see a disaster in the making, it's almost as if he froze, even I cannot believe it was deliberate. It is very odd because in general, whatever I think of him, he is a good salvage master.' He paused and his face changed, 'Enough, Cosel has another successful salvage under its belt, we have beaten the competition and it's *Sunda's* first. A celebration is called for, we won't be moving until tomorrow. Second Mate, three beers from my fridge, one for you,' and he laughed, a deep belly-laugh, dispersing any gloom Tom might feel from his serious warning.

CHAPTER 7

'This is my daughter, Hilda,' said Mr R, introducing Tom. 'Hilda, this is Captain Matravers.'

'I have heard a lot about you,' she said in a quiet voice. She was small and petite, with black hair. Her face had lovely, smooth sallow skin but her nose was too small, making her face look bigger than it was. Her eyes were a deep, smoky blue, at odds with her black hair, with hidden depths, and were watching him, appraising, sizing him up. It made Tom feel quite uncomfortable.

Mr R moved off, leaving Tom tongue-tied and wondering what on earth to say, his usual *sang froid* deserting him. The rest of the party were all chatting away, drinks in hand, the morning hot as usual in the tropics, even though it was Christmas Day. All the people Tom had met in the last few months were gathered for this annual party, together with surveyors and other business associates of Mr R.

'The rising star,' said Hilda, a mischievous twinkle in her eyes.

'Now you are embarrassing me,' said Tom, blushing. Taking the bull by the horns, he continued, 'As you know so much about me, perhaps you can tell me what you do?'

He smiled.

'Nothing,' she answered seriously. 'Spend the old man's ill-gotten gains.'

Tom looked shocked but quickly smiled.

'And you believed me,' she laughed, but the laughter did not reach her eyes, which were still searching him out.

Tom laughed too and the ice was broken.

'Actually, I work for a fashion designer who is completely disorganised. He's a brilliant designer but not much use at anything else so I am his anchor, arrange and order his life, a completely different world from salvage, tugs and barges.'

They chatted away in the garden, a tree shading them from the hot tropical sun, until Mr R came and took her off to meet some business acquaintance.

Tom gravitated to the salvage people. Jan was in good form, with his wife and three children. Time passed quickly, and the buffet food was good. Tom was enjoying himself and only drinking soft drinks, aware that they were on salvage stand-by. The *Sunda* was at anchor in Eastern Anchorage and they could be on board and away in less than an hour. The refit was finished. She had been dry docked, completely re-painted, fully equipped and was ready for anything.

Tom went inside to find the lavatory and when he came out, he found Hilda sitting on the sofa.

'It's cooler in here,' she said. 'Come and sit next to me.'

Tom did as she bid and they started a serious conversation about Singapore politics and the rights and wrongs of Lee Kuan Yu. The conversation was going well, when Tom's pager went off and he looked around to find the phone, spotting it on a table near the bar. As he stood, Hilda said, 'Work comes first,' with a glint in her eye.

'But, of course,' he said, 'and in your father's house too.' He smiled as he walked away from the sofa and over to the phone.

'Collision, two tankers Malacca Straits,' said the voice of the duty ops man. Ishmael was outside in the garden with the party. 'I can't raise Ishmael on his pager.'

'Okay, I organise,' said Tom, his brain racing. He knew he must get Jan and himself away as soon as possible, and maybe Jan's wife could run them down to Clifford pier. It was how to tell the old man and DB, without alerting the other salvage men at the party that something was up.

'Hilda, I wonder if you could help? Could you get your old man to come in here without alerting anyone? There are lots of salvage people here and I don't want to alert them that something is going on.'

'Involved in a salvage?' she jumped up. 'How exciting,' and she gave a big smile, transforming her rather plain face.

A short while later Mr R came in alone. On seeing Tom, he asked, 'What's up?'

'Collision, Malacca Straits, two tankers. I was just try-ing to see how I could get Jan away without alerting the Salvage Association people something was up, so we get a head start over the competition.'

'Get his son to pretend he is ill and wants to go home. He's done it before. I will fix this end and get Ishmael to the office. Quick, quick we need the contract!' hurried the old man, alive and alert despite his advancing years.

It was early afternoon and most people had eaten and been drinking since mid-morning, so were not as vigilant as they might have been. Tom was able to put the old man's suggestion into practice and it was not long before Jan was driving the car like he drove his tug, with his family holding on for dear life and his wife, Gerda, gritting her teeth. They made Clifford pier in record time, the roads clear on this Christmas Day holiday, and found the zed boat waiting for them, the tug alerted by Ops.

The second mate, Jesus, had used his initiative; the anchor was aweigh and the engines running as they climbed aboard. The crane was already lifting the zed boat out of the water as they made their way onto the bridge. Jan clutched in and pushed the two engine control levers forward, the propellers stirring up mud from the bottom. The tug was soon moving fast, Jan himself steering, weaving the big vessel through the anchored ships, with Tom at the engine controls. By the time they were at port limits, the *Sunda* was at full speed, her huge wash causing the smaller ships to roll, and a few fists had been waved at them.

'We haven't reported to port control,' said Tom, as Jan handed over the wheel to an AB, giving him a course to steer that would take them past Raffles Light.

'Ishmael will fix it,' replied Jan, opening a can of beer brought up by the mess man and settling himself into his captain's chair. Tom put down the beer he had been given, unopened.

'This could be the big one,' said Jan, as he took the can away from his lips. 'Get Pedro organised with the fire fighting equipment and check the monitors. Make sure the towing gear is ready. I will stay up here. It will be dark before we reach them. The *Singapore* was in Western Anchorage so has a head start on us and may reach the casualties first. There is a new captain. Captain Hannibal is on leave, and I don't know the new man. I don't know why they did not give the chief officer temporary command, he would have been okay.'

The *Sunda* had been fully operational for a couple of months, during which time they had made two abortive runs out into China Sea. The refit had been completed a couple of weeks after the car carrier salvage. Jan had worked on Daniel Bang and secured most of the crew he wanted, denuding the *Singapore* of her best men. The Second Mate, Jesus, was ready to be promoted and the Third Mate would make a good Second Mate, so they had good officers. The two divers were experienced, ex-Philippine navy divers and proved to be reliable and resourceful. There were some good ABs and one of them was the zed boat driver who had caused Tom to fall during his first salvage, and proved to be an excellent boat handler. The Chief Engineer had a good team in the engine room and Tom thought all in all, they would be able to give a good account of themselves in any situation.

Six hours after leaving Singapore, Tom could see two fires burning ahead, one much bigger than the other, the radar indicating they were some six miles away. It did not look as though there were any other smaller vessels nearby indicating tugs, but there were three larger echoes, suggesting ships standing by. The *Sunda* was shaking and vibrating, almost as if she knew the urgency of the situation, and doing just over sixteen knots, a magnificent speed for the tug; the Chief Engineer had worked wonders. The distance rapidly reduced and the stern light of a small vessel appeared ahead, and from the radar echo, suggested it might be the *Singapore*.

Using the company radio, Jan made contact. It was indeed the *Singapore*, so Jan told the captain to tackle the smaller-looking fire while the *Sunda* would deal with the large one. He should make contact with the captain and agree Lloyds Open Form, agreement on the radio being quite sufficient. If they wanted to abandon ship, then they could move onboard his tug.

Twenty minutes later, Jan slowed down the big tug approaching the larger fire. It was a large tanker and she appeared to be in ballast, high out of the water. The fire was raging in the accommodation, and it appeared their communications were knocked out because there was no answer to Jan's call on VHF channel sixteen. He circled the ship as the two monitors on the foremast and one on the after mast were manned and started, the powerful fire pump making a high-pitched whine, adding to the noise of the fire.

'They have abandoned,' said Jan, his voice strained with the tension. 'Fires on tankers are dangerous and on tankers in ballast, even worse,' he continued.

Tom's nerves were screaming, the sound and sight of the burning ship bringing back memories. It was like a reality flashback, and it was taking all his willpower not to scream. He wanted to hide, but knew if he gave in he was finished; not just as a salvor, but as a man.

'I am going alongside the starboard side, the windward side, so the flames are blown away from us rather than towards. Use grapnels to make light line moorings. I don't want anyone on board until we assess the situation. If the flames go forward and she is not gas-free, then there could be an explosion,' said Jan grimly, his voice loud, his face appearing yet more ruddy by the light from the flames.

At first, nothing came out when Tom opened his mouth, but taking a deep breath, he managed, 'Understood, Jan.'

I have to overcome this fear, he thought, I cannot let Jan or, worse, myself down, in front of the crew.

Pedro was manning the foremast with an AB, so Tom went down onto the main deck and organised the crew, the ever-resourceful Pedro having already issued the grapnels. Jan brought the *Sunda* smartly alongside the starboard side of the tug to the starboard side of the burning tanker, in the 69 position, the fenders crunching as she touched the high side. The crew were quick with the grapnels and she was lightly secured. Tom could already hear hissing from the steam, produced as all three powerful monitors poured hundreds of tons of water into the burning accommodation. Tom returned to the bridge to see the mess man climbing the foremast, carrying water to the fire fighters. The heat from the fire made the wheelhouse extremely hot. Suddenly, there was a deep rumble from inside the burning ship and Jan literally screamed.

'She is going to go, stand clear!'

Rushing to the engine controls, he pushed the control levers firmly right forward. 'Man the wheel, Tom!' he shouted. 'Steer straight ahead.'

The engine revolutions and propeller pitch rapidly increased as black smoke poured from the funnel, adding to the smoke from the fire. The big tug surged ahead, breaking the lines to the grapnels, leaving them trailing in the water. The rumble grew louder and then there was a massive, ear-splitting explosion and sheets of flame seemed to lick the tug as she gathered speed past the high side. Although Tom could not see it happening, the deck of the tanker seemed to open up, the two sides folding to the side of the ship, leaving a gaping hole in the middle. There was another explosion and the ship split in two, the aft end beginning to sink as the *Sunda* cleared the stern,

'Hard a-port!' shouted Jan, and the tug heeled over as Tom spun the wheel. 'Midships, meet her.' Tom swung the wheel back and then to starboard. and the swing slowed. Jan brought the engine levers to neutral and then astern.

The tug was now facing the sinking tanker, the aft end capsizing with great clouds of steam as the fire was extinguished and it disappeared into the sea, the darkness hiding the final end. The forepart, with no apparent fire, was slowly sinking by the stern, the water rushing forward through the breached tank bulkheads and within minutes that, too, had gone, the bow high in the air. One minute, a large and substantial object; the next minute, it was gone. It was a shattering sight and experience, and Jan, Tom and Jesus said nothing, shocked and subdued.

Jan suddenly walked forward and pushed the levers forward. 'Steer for the other ship, Tom,' he said roughly, hiding his shock and picking up his binoculars. 'I don't see the *Singapore*.

'There she is,' said Tom. 'She seems to be standing off. Take the wheel, Jesus.'

The *Sunda* reached the other ship, a loaded tanker with a fire in the forward tanks.

'Jesus, call up the *Singapore* and ask why he is not fighting the fire!' ordered Jan, as he manoeuvred the *Sunda* close enough to the fire so the forward monitors could reach the flames. 'Tom, call up the tanker and offer Lloyds Open Form.'

'Ship on fire, this is the *Sunda*, we are fighting your fire and offer our services on the terms of Lloyds Open Form,' said Tom, the VHF tuned to channel sixteen, the emergency and distress channel.

There was no answer and Tom repeated his message.

'I am consulting my owners,' said a voice.

Jan grabbed the microphone from Tom and said, 'Don't be a fool, you have just seen one ship blow up! Anyway, I am claiming salvage, in any event.'

At that moment, Jesus, who had been talking in Tagaloc on the company radio, still steering the *Sunda*, said, 'Something wrong on *Singapore*. The chief officer says they can't fight a tanker fire.'

Jan exploded.

'Launch the zed boat,' he shouted, then in a calmer voice, added, 'Tom, go across and take charge. If necessary, depose the master and take command, logging it.'

Tom's fear and shock disappeared. The sight that caused the flashback had gone and action cleared his head, the past forgotten in the excitement of the moment. He left the bridge. The burning tanker looked huge from the zed boat, the *Sunda* small in comparison as her monitors poured water into the flames.

'Wait!' ordered Tom to the boat driver as he climbed on board the *Singapore*, shocked to see the fire monitor unmanned. He quickly made his way to the bridge, where he found the chief officer.

'Captain not very well, he say cannot fight fire,' he said, pointing to a figure slumped in the captain's chair.

'What's wrong, Captain?' Tom asked, walking over to the chair.

The smell of alcohol caught Tom's attention as a voice mumbled, 'Monitor not working.'

'Is that true?' he asked the chief officer, whose face he could just discern from the light of the flames.

'No.'

'This man is sick, I am taking command. Get him below, out of the way. Start the fire monitor, alert the crew, get moving. Mr Gonzales, you should have told us. Send the second and third mate up here, move it!'

Tom's firm voice and orders galvanised the man and in short order two ABs and the mess man carried the un-protesting captain off the bridge as Tom manoeuvred the *Singapore* closer to the tanker. The company radio microphone in his hand, he told Jan what he had done and asked for instructions.

'Don't forget to log the takeover,' said Jan. 'As you can see, I am on the windward side, although there is not much wind, but I am not made fast and bow on. You go alongside aft of the fire but be ready to pull off. We must not let the fire move aft, if we can contain it to the single tank it will be good. We need to get some men on board, I don't see any of the ship's crew. Send the zed boat back.'

'What's your name?' asked Tom of the smaller of the two officers.

'Rudi,' he answered.

'Tell the zed boat to return to the *Sunda*. Go down and tell the bosun we are going alongside the tanker starboard side to. Use grapnels at first and get a man on board to secure the mooring lines.'

'Okay, Cap.'

The single monitor on the foremast was manned and the whine of the fire pump could clearly be heard, although not as loud as that on the *Sunda*, as a satisfactory amount of water gushed forth.

Tom was a natural boat handler, as he proved with the tug. He could just feel the right thing to do, although if asked, he would not have been able to tell anyone what he was doing, he could only describe his actions after the event. He angled the tug so that when he went astern, the tug straightened up and came alongside parallel to the hull. The loaded tanker freeboard was such that an agile AB was able to leap from the bridge onto the tanker, catching hold of the rail. The *Singapore* was soon made fast, with the monitor fighting the aft part of the fire, the water streaming off the deck of the tanker.

Tom saw the *Sunda* alter course and she, too, went alongside, the lines being taken by the *Singapore* men. Hoses were soon snaking on board and shortly afterwards, half a dozen hoses poured water into the fire from the other side of the deck, some lashed to the deck fittings. There were now four monitors fighting the fire and the flames appeared increasingly subdued. Tom had climbed aboard the tanker, leaving Gonzales in charge of the tug.

He made his way aft and saw both lifeboats turned out and lowered to boat deck level. When he came onto the boat deck, he saw the boat on the starboard side was loaded with luggage, some men sitting on it.

'Where's the captain?' he asked a rough-looking character dressed in jeans and a sweat shirt, the deck lights lending the fellow an unhealthy, pale look.

He pointed upwards towards the bridge. Tom carried on and in the wheelhouse found the captain sitting in the captain's chair, with another man standing beside it.

'Good evening, Captain, I am from Cosel Salvage and offer our services on Lloyds Open Form. As you can see, we are fighting the fire with our two tugs.'

'No sign. My owners say no sign.'

A swarthy face looked back at Tom, the light of the flickering flames on the foredeck rendering it redder than was natural.

'Very good. As you heard on the radio, my company will claim salvage anyway. Are you willing to help us in any way?'

'My crew say fire not their job and want to abandon ship,' sighed the captain.

'They can go onboard the two tugs if they like,' offered Tom.

'No good, you are too close to the fire.'

Tom walked out on to the starboard bridge wing, where he could see the two tugs alongside with tons of water being poured on board the burning tanker, cascading off the deck, down the side of the ship, some of it onto the tugs. It looked as though they were gaining on the fire.

'Captain won't sign LOF, says he awaiting his owners' instructions,' said Tom, into his radio.

'No problem, we will just claim salvage. What about the crew?'

'They say fire is not their job.'

'Even better for us, it means we will get a better award, provided we get this fire out. The salvage master is on the way with the *Coselvenom*, with more foam and men. We need to make a foam attack to get this fire out.'

'Okay, I am on my way back, the lifeboats are loaded with luggage.'

Tom heard Jan laugh.

He made his way back to the *Singapore*, the heat increasing as he came nearer to the fire. The sweat was soon pouring off him and he realised he should drink more water. He crossed over to the middle of the deck where there was a stack of water bottles, and just as he was picking one up, there was a loud explosion.

Tom fell on the deck, as did those with the fire hoses, the bottle rolling free from his hand. When he pulled himself together and looked up he saw flames shooting aft out of the forecastle, and then a whole series of small explosions. It must be the paint store, he thought, as he watched the forward *Sunda* monitors swing round and pour water into the forecastle. He stood up, ashamed of his weakness, and walked back to the rails. The AB's also stood up, laughing and joking.

The radio crackled and he heard Jan's voice.

'Move forward, *Singapore*, closer to my stern and lift your monitor so it is more onto the flames.'

'Okay, Cap,' came Gonzales' voice.

Tom waved two of the AB's across and told them to move the mooring lines of the *Singapore* as she moved forward. The flames in the forecastle seemed to be increasing, despite the amount of water being aimed through the door. He climbed back on board the tug and made his way to the bridge. He heard a noise and looking aft, saw the lifeboat being lowered, full of the crew.

'They are abandoning ship,' said Tom into the radio.

'To hell with them!' replied Jan. 'We are going to have to make a foam attack and try and get the fires out. Something must be feeding the fire in the forecastle,' said Jan over the radio.

'Okay, just the monitors?' asked Tom.

'Just the monitors,' said Jan. 'Start the foam in five minutes from now and tell the hose people to keep their hoses away while the attack continues. If successful, we won't need them.'

Tom told the chief officer to go on board and tell the firefighters what was happening while he spoke with the chief engineer. The flames provided illumination, but when they were out, they would need some lighting on deck. The deck lights had gone out some time before and now the tanker was being abandoned by its crew it would be up to the salvors. Tom saw the water jets from the *Sunda* change to white at the same time as the *Singapore*, the foam entering the forecastle from the forward two monitors and smothering the flames. In short order, the flames went out on deck, blanketed by the aft monitor of the *Sunda* and the single monitor from the *Singapore*. He saw Gonzales enter the forecastle, then indicate with his torch one of the hoses to be brought in.

It was dark now the flames were out. There were no deck lights on the abandoned tanker suggesting the crew had shut down the generators before they left. The only lighting was from the deck lights of the tugs, and there was a quietness after the roar of the flames, the only sounds coming from the tugs. Tom switched on the searchlight that was on top of the wheelhouse and saw that Jan had done the same. He saw Gonzales come out of the forecastle and, shielding his eyes from the glare of the searchlights, gave a thumbs up signal.

So the fires were completely out, thought Tom, and felt a huge surge of exultation. They had succeeded and he had not failed, he had overcome that moment of panic and fear, fought off the flashback brought on by the fire on the first tanker and been able to fight a second fire in charge of his own tug.

CHAPTER 8

Tom saw the jets from the *Sunda* monitors droop and stop and, brought back to earth himself, rang down to the engine room and told them to stop the foam and fire pumps. He climbed on board the tanker and made his way forward along the deck, stopping opposite the bridge of the *Sunda*.

'Have a beer,' laughed an ebullient Jan, as he threw a can at Tom, who managed to catch it, the cold tin a sudden shock to his hands. Tom drained it in one; it tasted like nectar. The accommodation of the tanker was faint in the darkness, the smell of crude surrounding them reminded him of the danger they were all in.

'*Coselvenom*, now the fires are out, will be here shortly, I have her on the radar at six miles. The Salvage Master will take charge,' and he gave a mirthless laugh as he took a swig from his can. 'If it was me, I would connect up and tow her to Singapore, an abandoned loaded tanker. We would get a nice bonus. I have told the divers to dive at daylight, we need to know what the damage is forward.'

'Any news of the crew?' asked Tom.

'Not worried about them, they are quite safe in their lifeboat. No one has been on the radio to say they have been picked up. The crew of the first tanker were all picked up, lucky they abandoned quick enough. I have cancelled the SOS.'

At that moment, Tom saw a lifeboat emerging from the darkness, full of men approaching the *Sunda*.

'Speak of the devil!' exclaimed Tom, loudly. 'It's the captain come to reclaim his ship.'

'Good, I will get him to sign LOF before the Salvage Master arrives and claims the glory.'

Jan disappeared into the wheelhouse and shortly afterwards appeared on the after deck to welcome the captain and his crew.

Tom saw Jan shake hands with the captain and then almost drag him along and up to his bridge. The rest of the crew made their way across the tug, helped by the salvage men, and climbed aboard their ship, leaving the lifeboat loaded with the luggage alongside the tug. Tom went on board the *Sunda* to find Jan and the captain in heated argument about the LOF.

'I no sign!' shouted the captain, his sallow face flushed with anger.

'You sign. I risk my crew and my tug to save your ship and you run away!' boomed Jan, his moustache quivering with rage, his clenched fist raised as though about to strike. 'I claim salvage!' and he brought his fist down on the table.

Tom wondered how best to break what looked like fisticuffs, when Jan saw him and shouted, 'My legal man, he will explain!'

'It is much better you sign,' said Tom quietly, trying to defuse the situation, the second mate trying to make himself invisible in the corner as Jan disappeared. 'If you don't sign, we will arrest your ship and claim salvage through the courts, all very expensive and unnecessary for your owners. Just sign and it is all taken care of through Lloyds, no courts, just an arbitration in London.'

Tom felt he was in some sort of fantasy-land, divorced from reality. Here he was, in the Malacca Straits, in the middle of the night, standing on the bridge of a tug alongside a tanker where they had just put out a major fire, a lifeboat alongside, talking about arbitration in London, while ships passed, some quite close, their navigation lights bright in the darkness; but he knew this was reality, not fantasy, and very important.

Jan reappeared, carrying an armful of cold beers, followed by the mess man carrying glasses and some biscuits.

'A nice cooling drink,' said Jan, thrusting a filled glass at the captain who, looking distraught, took it and drank. The mess man handed Tom a glass but Jan just opened a can and drank. The captain munched on a biscuit and seemed to have calmed down.

'You can't move until we have had the divers down,' continued Tom, 'and I suspect the forepeak is damaged. You will have to be towed. Our Salvage Master is arriving in the next few minutes. Much better you sign and save a lot of trouble. You have the option of an easy, well-known procedure through Lloyds or an expensive court action.'

'My owners say no sign,' said the worried captain, appearing much calmer.

'That was before you abandoned your ship. We are now what is known in legal terms as 'salvors in possession' and the situation is entirely different. Don't forget, we are here to assist you but we prefer a contract,' Tom said, his voice quiet.

'Okay, I sign but you help me.'

'Of course,' said Tom, and Jan slapped the captain on the back, handing him another beer.

A voice came over the company radio. 'I am coming alongside, move the lifeboat.'

Jan grabbed the microphone, beer in hand, and said, 'Go alongside the *Singapore* or better still, the tanker, the fire is out. The lifeboat is full of luggage.'

The Lloyds Form was lying on the chart-room table where the captain signed, followed by Jan, who was grinning from ear to ear. He slapped the captain again on the back and said, 'Get your generators started, Captain, so we have some light and can inspect the fire damage.'

The captain left the bridge, climbed on board his own ship and made his way back to the bridge.

'My LOF the *Kinos*,' said Jan proudly. 'I could not bear it if that prick claimed it,' he laughed. 'Ricky!' he shouted. 'A message for you,' as he scribbled on a piece of paper.

A rather pale-faced, middle-aged Filipino appeared from the radio room and took the proffered paper. 'Send it quick,' ordered Jan.

Tom and Jan climbed aboard the tanker to find the tall, thin figure of the salvage master walking towards them, his figure illuminated by the searchlight of the *Singapore*.

'Are your spark arrestors in place on the funnels of your tugs?' he greeted them.

'Of course,' replied Jan, curtly.

'LOF has been agreed between the office and the owners,' he rather drawled in his flat, toneless voice, the southern hemisphere accent more apparent than usual.

'I've signed with the captain,' retorted Jan.

Tom thought it was a strange way to greet two colleagues who had just put out a major fire on a loaded tanker.

'We won't need yours, Jan,' said Captain Rogers, as he walked forward to look at the fire damage.

Jan looked livid, his face clearly visible in the searchlight and Tom could see he was holding himself in check.

'Don't worry, Jan,' said Tom, 'your LOF binds the cargo much better than one signed by the owners only. We had a case about it.'

'Thank you, Tom,' said Jan, and then shouted, 'I've told Singapore.'

They followed the Salvage Master, who neither turned around, nor said anything when they caught up with him. The deck lights came on, making it much easier to see their way amongst the pipework. The AB's, who had been manning the fire hoses, were now reclining, waiting for orders.

Tom could see the forecastle was badly damaged. The door was blown out and the deck plates were badly buckled and torn from the explosion. Further forward, he could see the collision had twisted and bent the plates. The foam blanket looked good and there was no sign of any fire, although the strong smell of crude oil lingered, reminding them of the danger they were in at all times. It only took a spark to cause an explosion.

Tom looked out to sea and saw the darkness was fading with the coming daylight. A new day, Tom thought, and immediately felt invigorated.

They entered the forecastle but the damage prevented them going in very far; the foam blanket, however, looked good.

'I am going onto the bridge to talk with the captain. Tom, you come with me,' ordered the Salvage Master.

'Tom is Captain of the *Singapore*, the new man is sick,' said Jan. Captain Rogers looked surprised.

'He can still come with me until we decide what to do.'

'Connect up and tow to Singapore,' said Jan forcefully.

The Salvage Master ignored Jan and started walking aft along the now brightly-illuminated deck. Jan nodded to Tom, who followed Captain Rogers. On the bridge, Tom introduced the captain, who looked much better, to the Salvage Master, who started asking questions and demanded to see the general arrangement plan and cargo plan. The *Kinos* was loaded with 150,000 tons of crude oil bound for

Japan, and she was fitted with an inert gas system. The tanker was quite modern, only a few years old.

'Once we have the divers report,' said Captain Rogers, 'we will decide what to do. I know an owners' rep is on the way.'

Tom, standing in the wheelhouse, saw the sun, a golden orb, rising above a distant Malaysia, heralding in the day. The damage on the forecastle was clearly visible from the bridge and Tom studied it through the binoculars. He gladly accepted the captain's invitation to breakfast but the Salvage Master declined, saying he was too busy. Tom was ravenous and thoroughly enjoyed the excellent eggs and bacon.

Back on the bridge, Tom found the Salvage Master in deep discussion with the senior diver from the *Coselvenom*, who handed him a sketch of the underwater damage. It was extensive, with the forepeak open to the sea and the bulbous bow all torn and twisted, one of the plates hanging down below the bottom of the ship. There was no sign of any oil, so the freshwater tank abaft the forepeak must be intact.

'I am pretty sure oil has leaked into the freshwater tank from the cargo tank, which was on fire because of the explosion and fire in the forecastle,' said Tom, when Captain Rogers finished talking with the diver.

The captain joined them on the bridge. Captain Rogers said, 'It is quite clear we will have to tow you stern first to

Singapore. You better hoist, you're not under command signal, Captain.'

'I talk to my owners first,' said a worried captain, his face drawn with black bags under his eyes, emphasising his sallow skin. He was not a large man but he seemed to be shrivelling under the weight of the disaster that had struck his ship. The chief officer, a burly younger man, shook his head.

'Not to worry, Captain, you are in good hands,' said Tom.

'She will have to be dry docked, the damage is too great for the divers to tackle,' said the Salvage Master, in quite a lively voice. 'That means a full discharge,' and his eyes lit up at the prospect.

'Tom, we will make preparations to tow by the stern to Singapore. Rig two Stenhouse slip hooks, one on each quarter.'

'Understood, Captain Rogers,' said Tom, and left the bridge, making his way forward to confer with Jan on board the *Sunda*.

'Okay, I tell Pedro to fix. Have a beer,' and he rang down to the mess room.

Tom was sitting comfortably in the chair on the port side of the bridge. Jan had arranged to have two captain's chairs, one on each side of the wheelhouse. Jan was well ensconced on the starboard chair with a convenient ledge to rest his beer can.

'Could do with a cigar,' Jan laughed, 'that would upset our Salvage Master. Still, even I can smell the crude.'

At that moment, they both heard the distinctive 'thrump thrump' of rotor blades slashing the air, heralding the approach of a helicopter. Jan rushed out onto the bridge wing, hotly followed by Tom.

'He can't possibly land, there is the smell of crude. I've had the divers searching the fire area for a hole or leak on deck. There is not much wind but what there is blowing aft and a good chance of an explosive mixture somewhere. Go and hold the Salvage Master's hand, Tom,' said Jan, an urgency creeping into his voice.

'*Kinos*, *Kinos*, this is helicopter Charlie Echo, permission to land,' said a voice on VHF channel sixteen.

'Negative, negative,' was the Salvage Master's response, high pitched with tension, or was it fear, thought Tom.

'Go,' urged Jan and Tom quickly climbed aboard and made his way up to the bridge of the tanker where he found Captain Rogers in something of a state, and the captain of the *Kinos* looking at him rather oddly.

The helicopter hovered above the bridge, making it difficult to hear, but Tom caught the words 'winch down.'

'I don't want that thing anywhere near this ship,' said a visibly worried Captain Rogers. Tom saw him in a very different light, his voice still high pitched with the strain.

'Why not send out the *Sunda* to stand off the ship and the helicopter can land on her tow deck? There's plenty of room,' suggested Tom, quietly.

'Good idea,' said a relieved Salvage Master, and in a calm, clear but toneless voice, gave his instructions to the tug and helicopter.

It was not long before the *Sunda* was standing off. Tom was not sure he would have done it quite the way Jan manoeuvred the tug, which appeared to have been simply putting both engines on full ahead. The tug had suddenly shot ahead, her bridge almost touching the damaged forecastle of the drifting tanker. Tom watched the helicopter land, the rotors appearing very close to the accommodation, but it was an illusion because Tom knew there was plenty of room. Four figures jumped out onto the tow deck of the tug as the rotors slowed, and had stopped turning by the time the zed boat with the people left the tug.

The four figures turned out to be the owners' rep, Lloyds classification surveyor, Cosel's dive master – the bald-headed Wayne Dawson – and the Salvage Association surveyor. The Salvage Master, who seemed to know them all, introduced the captain of the *Kinos* and said, 'We can use the owner's suite which has a table.'

'Nice one here,' said Wayne. 'Well done getting the fires out, the damage forward from the air looks extensive. I see the *Sunda* seems to have some burnt paint on the side.'

'The first tanker blew up when we were still close, although we were moving off,' said Tom tautly, momentarily reliving the moment of panic and fear.

'A bit hairy, eh?'

'Bit too hairy for my liking,' laughed Tom, relieving his own tension.

Some time later they were sitting around the table in the owners' suite, the Salvage Master and Lloyds Surveyor in chairs, the rest on the L-shaped settee. The Salvage Master came into his own with the general arrangement plan and diver's sketch spread out, explaining the damage as he saw it and the necessity for a dry docking, thus requiring a full discharge.

After considerable discussion, it was finally agreed. The Salvage Master's eyes gleamed and he almost became animated at the prospect.

'I think this will be the biggest tanker job Cosel has ever done,' whispered Wayne, who was sitting next to Tom.

'I think the LOF should be terminated as soon as possible,' said the Salvage Association Surveyor, Mike, a tall, clean-shaven man with a pleasant, well-worn face, 'and the cargo transfer done under contract.'

'No,' said Captain Rogers emphatically. 'I know you are trying to save underwriters' money but I don't think Cosel would agree to do it on contract. It is salvage, the ship is badly damaged, you need us with our salvage expertise and equipment. She needs towing to the transfer location and towage to the dry dock. You need salvors, not contractors.'

'We can always put it out to tender.'

'The only people who can do this sort of thing with a damaged ship are our competition,' pointed out Captain Rogers, 'and they would be expensive, even if they would agree a contract, knowing we are on LOF.'

'I tend to agree with the Salvage Master,' said the owners' rep, an overweight Englishman with white hair and a red face. 'It will take time to bring in anyone else. Cosel, I was told, already have an option on a suitable tanker and have the necessary Yokohama fenders and equipment. I think we will leave it with Cosel and the cost can be fought over at arbitration in London. What about the damage, Mr Dawson?'

'Very extensive, as you can see from the sketch. I spoke with the senior diver on the *Sunda*... Ah, here is the diver in charge,' as a tall, thin Filipino appeared, dressed in jeans and a sweat shirt. 'The main problem is the plate hanging down from the bulbous bow. Nicky?' and Wayne waved his hand in the direction of the smart-looking man.

'It is too big for us to cut underwater with the equipment we have on site,' said Nicky, pointing at the sketch. 'The forepeak is open to the sea, although there is no oil leakage, and the hole is too big and the surrounding plates so mangled and twisted, it would prevent us putting on more than a temporary plywood patch, which would not survive the ship going ahead. To do more than that would need more

108

divers, fabricated steel plates from ashore and vastly more equipment than we have here. It would take a long time and be dependent on good weather, it can sometimes get rough in the Malacca Straits. Remember the *Seawise*, Cap?' Nicky's accent, somehow enhancing his excellent English, suggesting he had lived outside of the Philippines at some point in his life.

'Time, gentlemen, time is money for us,' said the Englishman. 'We need to get the ship back into commission as quickly as possible. She is on a good time charter and there are penalties for delay, although no doubt our lawyers are busy declaring *force majeure* at the moment.'

'So, we are agreed, tow by the stern to a designated transfer area, full discharge and tow to dry dock,' said the Salvage Master, summing up.

'We can discuss the situation of termination of the LOF after the full discharge. I expect she may be able to proceed under her own power in ballast,' said Mike, the Salvage Association Surveyor, his pleasant face now serious.

'I suggest the transfer be done just outside Singapore port limits, Western Anchorage, which is close to our base,' said Captain Rogers.

'Can the two tugs tow this large, loaded tanker stern first? It will be very difficult,' pointed out Mike.

'I have discussed this with our Towing Master, the slip hooks are in place now,' Tom put in, surprising Captain Rogers. 'As you know, he is very experienced and he says there is no problem, providing we have a good, manoeuvrable harbour tug on the bow to assist in steering. She will tend to yaw.'

'*Coselhare*,' said the Salvage Master.

'Makes sense,' said the Englishman.

'I agree,' said the Lloyds Surveyor. 'I have been talking with Nicky and Wayne.'

'I don't disagree,' laughed Mike, breaking the tension, and the meeting broke up.

Tom escorted the four men back to the *Singapore*, where they boarded the waiting zed boat, the long-haired driver behaving himself, driving the boat at a respectable speed. Tom watched the helicopter take off and disappear in the direction of Singapore. Another new experience for Tom to add to those already packed in during the last twenty-four hours of this Christmas and Boxing Day. Never in his wildest dreams did he think he would participate in such drama with such success. They still had a difficult tow ahead of them and he suddenly remembered the sick captain; he wanted him off the tug. He walked along the deck and climbed on board the *Sunda*, when Jan brought her back alongside.

CHAPTER 9

'Have a beer, it's lunchtime,' Jan greeted Tom.

'Thanks,' said Tom. 'It's agreed we tow back to outside Singapore Western Anchorage.'

'Good, and the harbour tug?' asked Tom.

'*Coselhare*.'

'Excellent, she's a good tug. This will be a big award. Luckily, we have you to write it up, in addition to our Salvage Master. The old man will be pleased, let's hope nothing goes wrong,' Jan laughed, and drank from his can.

'The drunk captain,' said Tom seriously. 'I don't want him on the *Singapore*, he could cause trouble.'

'I agree, send him across in the stretcher. He won't cause trouble on my tug,' said Jan.

'Right, I will arrange. Presumably we will start as soon as the slip hooks are ready, although the *Coselhare* won't be here until this evening?'

'Better we start. If we tow slowly, we will be all right,' said Jan.

'Pedro should have completed securing the slip hooks,' said Tom. 'I'll go and check and report to Rogers.'

'I will stay here and receive the drunk. I should think we will make about three knots, more with the tide, less against it. It's 1300 on Boxing Day, so by the time we are

111

connected it will be mid-afternoon,' he paused. 'So we arrive early morning, day after tomorrow, and we can adjust to make it daylight. It's good. We go down the East side of the Malacca Strait and the *Coselvenom* can lead. Ricky can send the TTT to Singapore Radio, no problem. I have been looking around with Juan and we can forget about the anchors, they are jammed good. The divers have patched and sealed cracks on deck. Check if there is a stern anchor.'

It was a long speech for Jan and he laughed. 'Perhaps I will make a Salvage Master!'

'Right, thanks for lunch and beer.'

'Any time.'

Tom climbed back on board the drifting tanker to find his bosun and Pedro with some salvage crew, returning from aft.

'Slip hooks secured,' reported Pedro, head and shoulders taller than the rest of the men, his smooth face wet with sweat in the afternoon sun.

'Well done. Now, Pedro, we have a bit of a problem on board the *Singapore*. Her captain is sick. I would like you to help Jose here strap him into the stretcher and bring him over to the *Sunda*. Captain Jan will take care of him.'

'What's wrong with him?' demanded Juan, who had joined the group.

Tom moved Juan away from the group, although he suspected the crew of the *Singapore* already knew, and said, 'Drink.'

Juan looked shocked.

'Okay. I will take charge,' said a shaken and angry Juan. 'Don't tell Captain Rogers it is drink.'

Tom made his way aft, the sun hot on his bare head. He had forgotten his hat, and the heat was reflecting off the steel deck plates, the sea calm and glimmering. He found the hooks well secured and backed up to the forward bollards. Pedro had done a good job.

Walking back to the tugs, he saw the stretcher, with its load strapped in, being heaved up the side of the ship. The captain was sweating profusely, his arms pinioned by the straps, moaning piteously. Tom was shaken and felt sorry for the man, knowing he was finished at sea. The crew carried him along the deck and he was lowered onto the tow deck of the *Sunda,* where Jan was waiting with his mess man and cook, who carried him inside. Tom felt for Juan, sensing he had been humiliated, that one of his people – and a senior one, at that – had let the side down, just as Tom would have been if it had been a European.

Tom climbed up to the bridge on the outside, passing the lifeboat which had been used by the crew and their luggage. It had been hoisted and stowed in its davits by the ship's crew. He found the Salvage Master, Captain Kios and Nicky, the diver, pouring over the chart of the Malacca Strait.

'Nicky here reckons the plate hanging down has added another twenty feet to the draught. We don't want to hit bottom, although if we knocked it off, it would solve a lot of problems.' He gave a chuckle, which Tom had got to know, was his effort at a laugh, 'So we will follow the deep water channel to Singapore. It adds a little distance but no matter. We cut across at the bottom to the anchorage,' and he pointed to a large cross in pencil, some miles outside Port Limits.

'Understood,' said Tom. 'Jan says the anchors are jammed and unusable, however there is a stern anchor, although lighter than the main anchors.'

'No problem, I will have *Coselversatile* lay a mooring for us,' said Captain Rogers. Captain Kios looked surprised and said, 'That is very good.'

'The slip hooks are all secured and ready,' reported Tom.

'Good, we can start. You arrange with Jan which side you are taking.'

'*Sunda* starboard, *Singapore* port side,' said Tom. 'Jan suggests the main engine is on immediate standby for emergencies but please, in no circumstances, use it without informing him first.'

'Right. He is the tow master,' agreed Captain Rogers. 'Juan, my chief officer, will drive the *Coselvenom* and lead, to warn any ship that approaches too close.'

'Captain Jan wants his third mate, Alfredo, to be in charge of the party, standing by the slip hooks. He wants three men, one at each hook and one standby. He requests two of your men and he will supply one AB.'

'Okay, agreed. Suggest you make fast first, as you have a single screw and no bow thruster,' he chuckled, his thin lips curving into a smile. 'Gives you a bit more room. *Sunda* is more manoeuvrable.'

It was a hot Boxing Day afternoon and as remote from snow-covered England, with its Christmas trees and coloured lights, excited children and stressed out parents, food and drink, day of sales, as Tom could imagine. He walked along the deck of the fire-damaged casualty with Juan and spoke with Jan from the deck of the tanker before returning to the *Singapore*.

Once back on board his tug, he called for tea, took a minute or two to put himself in command mode, and with Juan and his men letting go the lines, neatly manoeuvred the *Singapore* clear, with an ahead movement to kick out the stern and clear of the *Coselvenom*, then full astern. The tug moved off smartly, with a gentle, increasing curve to starboard. When clear, and the bow pointing at the tanker, he went full ahead and hard a-starboard, until parallel with the side of the ship. He slowed down off the port quarter and put the stern of the tug close to the stern of the *Kinos*, where Juan just tossed the heaving line onto the tow deck. The towing connection was quickly made and Tom slowly moved ahead, paying out the tow wire to almost its fullest 1,500 feet extent. The *Sunda* followed and was soon connected on the starboard quarter.

Tom and Jan had discussed the tow and agreed the *Singapore* would tow at a steady speed while Jan, in charge of the towage convoy, would increase or decrease power as necessary, in an attempt to control the loaded tanker. It was still some hours before the *Coselhare* was due to arrive.

'Increase to half speed, Tom,' ordered Jan over the radio.

'Course sou' sou' west,' came the voice of the Salvage Master.

Tom slowly increased to half power, watching his wire, which remained satisfactorily in the water. The *Sunda* paid out, most of her wire ending up well ahead of the *Singapore*. The *Kinos* took a long time before she started to move, and took a sheer towards the *Sunda*, and Tom saw the tow wire slacken and go deeper into the water as Jan slowed his tug. The sheer stopped in time and the tanker altered course, heading towards the *Singapore*. Tom saw the tow wire tauten as Jan increased power. It was hot in the wheelhouse, with the doors open, Tom darting out frequently to check on his tow, and inside checking the compass.

'We will keep it slow until the *Hare* arrives,' said Jan on the company radio, his disembodied voice filling the hot space.

The yawing was quite gentle at slow speed and the tugs settled down into towing routine, the towing gunwale regularly greased as the wire swept across it, the AB with the duty keeping his head well down. Tom soon began to catnap, the previous thirty hours without sleep and almost non-stop, high stress action catching up with him.

'Why don't you sleep, Captain?' suggested Gonzales.

'No, I'll stay up here and catnap, thanks. However, I am going to have a shower and shave, etcetera,' said Tom.

'No problem, everything good.'

Tom returned half an hour later, clean and refreshed, and calling for more tea. Daylight faded quickly as the sun went down over Sumatra, and the warm, tropical night set in. It remained calm, the tug gently moving in an almost imperceptible swell, the tow steady as a rock, except for her incessant yawing. The proper towing signal lights were displayed on the tugs and the Salvage Master had arranged for temporary side lights to be fitted while the casualty was making stern way.

There was an increase in radio traffic when the *Hare* appeared and was made fast to the bow of the *Kinos*, Jan increasing the speed of the convoy. The yawing increased at first but the *Hare* master, under Jan's guidance, soon had the hang of it and quite good steerage control was made. The convoy made about three knots as Jan predicted.

The night progressed peacefully enough as they were overtaken by all southbound traffic, mainly heavily laden tankers bound for Japan. The cloud increased at sunset and there was now spectacular lightning to the north. Just after midnight, a rain storm hit, with strong gusts of wind whipping up the smooth sea, and visibility was reduced to less than half a mile.

'Ship ahead of me, you can see my searchlight, alter course to starboard. You are in the southbound deep water channel and I am leading a damaged, loaded tanker under

117

tow,' said the strained voice of Juan over the VHF channel sixteen.

There was no answer.

'Alter course to starboard, you are standing into danger,' he repeated, his voice raised in apprehension, and a little time later the rogue ship, a small coaster, appeared out of the reducing rain, dead ahead of the two tugs, looking as though it was about to pass between the two and hit the tanker.

'Switch on the searchlight, second mate!' shouted Tom, 'Point it at the idiot.'

The *Sunda* searchlight found the coaster first, bathing it in light, revealing it to be a tired-looking thing, loaded to the gunnels with a deck cargo. It was only at the last minute that it altered course to starboard, just missing the bow of the *Sunda*, and disappeared into the night.

'Anyone get her name?' asked the calm voice of Jan, but there was no answer.

'Can do without that, 'said Tom into company radio microphone, his heart racing.

'It happens,' said the laconic voice of Jan.

Tom sent the lookout off to make tea. The night seemed longer now that he was too apprehensive to catnap. The general noise of a tug at sea seemed to set in louder, the steady beat of the engine noisy for the size of the vessel, the click click of the eco sounder, the glow from the radar, and the occasional order from Jan on the radio to the *Coselhare*. The *Singapore* kept a steady course and speed while the tow maintained her continuous yawing. He occasionally left his chair to stretch his legs, walk out onto the bridge wing and sniff the damp Malacca Strait air, and look up into the sky, which was now clear of the rain storm, the stars shining brightly. The waning moon was falling. The lights of the ships on the port side bound north were clearly visible in the distance, those bound south behind them.

When Gonzales, the chief officer, took over the watch from the second officer, Tom felt more comfortable and was able to catnap. It was soon dawn, the daylight and a shower enlivening and invigorating him, despite forty-eight hours with no proper sleep. The *Kinos* appeared much larger in the daylight than just the lights in the dark, the yawing continuous but controlled by the *Coselhare*, which he could occasionally see if she was out on the port bow of her tow, the master earning his salary and bonus.

The day passed quickly enough, remaining fine but hot, the sea glassy calm, the swell gone.

The second night seemed much longer, with no excitements, the tow having gained its own momentum and rhythm, and it became almost routine, although Tom knew he should remain alert, an emergency could occur at any time without warning. The third day dawned, and by now it was seventy-two hours without sleep, and Tom was tired. He wondered and marvelled at Jan's stamina, his calm voice occasionally giving an order or advice on the radio, as he controlled the unwieldy tow.

They made the turn to pass across from the deep water channel to the anchorage off Singapore, which meant crossing the northbound traffic stream. Singapore Radio was repeating the navigational warning TTT and by agreement, Jan's radio officer, Ricky, reissued it over the VHF radio channel sixteen every fifteen minutes, warning all vessels of the convoy, *Coselvenom* still leading.

Tom saw the container ship coming up astern down the Malacca Strait moving very fast and assumed she would leave the convoy on her port side. She must have been doing more than twenty knots, thought Tom when, to his consternation the container ship, *Zeus*, her name clearly visible, passed the *Kinos* closer than was normal or sensible. She altered course round her stern to pass between the two tugs and their tow. Tom could not believe his eyes and wanted to shout and scream but realised because the *Zeus* was going so fast, there was nothing she could do but carry on. If she altered course to starboard she would hit and roll over one of the tugs, if she went to port she would hit the tanker with an equally catastrophic result.

Jan's calm voice came over both the company radio and VHF channel 16.

'Slow down *Singapore* or you will take off his propellers. Let her pass over your tow wire.'

Tom had seen the tow wire from the *Sunda* slacken and sink further in the water. He slowed right down and the container ship passed safely between the tugs and tow, her wash causing his tug to pitch quite heavily. Tom's heart was racing with the fear of what seemed to him another near miss with death, and he felt his hands shaking. The mess man appeared with a cup of tea, for which he was exceedingly grateful. Jan informed Singapore Radio what had happened but there was no response from the *Zeus*. No doubt the owners would have something to say to the master when the complaint came through.

'We are coming up to the Cosel mooring buoy,' said Jan. Tom, who had seen the *Coselversatile* some time before the container ship incident, was impressed at Jan's continually calm voice as he gave orders to the various tugs bringing the tow to the buoy, using her main engine to slow down the tanker, and slipping the *Sunda*.

'Very neat, Jan,' congratulated Captain Rogers, as the first line was run to the mooring buoy by one of the small harbour tugs that had been standing by, although Tom could not see it. The *Singapore* remained connected aft while the *Hare* was slipped and used as a pusher tug, the control of the operation having passed to the Salvage Master when the *Sunda* slipped.

It was almost noon when the order was given to slip the *Singapore* and Tom went alongside the *Sunda*, the sea being flat calm with only the occasional residual wash from ships passing a good distance off. The *Hare* was connected to the stern of the *Kinos* to keep her off the buoy.

The lightening tanker, the *Buron*, slightly bigger than the *Kinos*, was due to arrive the next day, having been diverted from her voyage to the Persian Gulf in ballast, so there was a little down time before the cargo transfer started. Tom took the opportunity to go on board the *Sunda* and talk to Jan before seeking his bunk.

'Well done, Tom, a difficult tow. Well done, with only two near misses, and thankfully the Salvage Master kept quiet.' He guffawed. 'Have a beer, lunch is on the way.'

'How's the sick man?' asked Tom, drinking from the cold tin he had been handed.

'DT's, delirium tremens, he has been shouting and screaming so we had to keep him strapped in the stretcher. Not a nice job for the mess man to look after. Look, there is the *Coselone* taking the surveyors and hangers on to the *Kinos*. She will take him ashore. He is finished, he should never have been employed.'

He took a swig from his can, shaking his head.

'Captain Rogers called me on the radio and said I should help him as his assistant for the cargo transfer, as I did with the car carrier. It would be good experience for me.'

'I heard and agree.'

'If the *Singapore* goes to sea, Gonzales, who should be okay, will need a good chief officer.'

'I've already spoken to Daniel Bang on the radio telephone, and he's sending one out as soon as possible.'

'I'm dead on my feet, and after that curry, can barely stay awake,' said Tom, drowsily.

'Here's the *Coselone*, so we can get rid of the drunk,' said Jan, looking equally tired, his chubby, unshaven face drawn and black bags under his eyes. They watched the stretcher being passed over to the crew boat, with Jan shouting down to bring the stretcher back.

'Right, I'm off to my bunk,' said Tom.

'Hold on a minute, Tom, I need to talk to you about ...' and his voice trailed off and his head fell on his chest, 'Perhaps now is not the right time, we are too tired, but it is important. Go to bed and I will talk tomorrow, although it will be a busy day.'

CHAPTER 10

Tom wondered what on earth Jan could mean, but he was so tired, he was out like a light as soon as his head hit the pillow. He woke early the next morning, before dawn and started on his report, having forgotten all thoughts of a talk with Jan. He was in the wheelhouse when the sun rose over Singapore, feeling ready for the coming day, and he enjoyed an early breakfast, eating it on the bridge wing. Captain Rogers had told him to report on the *Kinos* at 0800.

'Thought a good sleep would do you good, especially as you will pilot the lightening tanker *Buron* alongside the *Kinos* for the transfer,' said Captain Rogers when Tom reported onboard.

Tom felt he had been kicked in the stomach, and glad he had only eaten a comparatively light breakfast.

'No problem is there, Tom? You look as though you have seen a ghost?'

The Salvage Master was testing him, Tom thought; rise to the occasion, this is your opportunity. He had a Master's certificate, so was even qualified to do it; always a first time for everything.

'No, Captain Rogers, it's nice and calm, should be no problem. Do we have any assisting tugs?' he asked.

The Salvage Master smiled, his thin lips pressed together, his long face crinkling a little.

124

'Two small harbour tugs and the *Coselhare*. I am sure you have noticed but the *Singapore* has a towing hook. Get Jan or do it yourself. Connect the *Singapore* in place of the *Hare*, using the *Kinos* mooring lines. All she has to do is tow straight astern to stop the tanker swinging while you are docking the *Buron*. The chief officer should be able to look after that.'

'Gonzales is OK. What time is the *Buron* arriving?'

'About noon. Inspection will take a couple of hours, then bring her alongside. Why don't I tell the captain our pilot will board and you bring her to the anchorage? Give you a chance to see how she handles. I don't expect you have handled a ship that size before.'

'No,' said Tom tightly, 'it will have been helpful to bring her to the anchorage.'

'Good. I will arrange that and you can use the *Sunda* zed boat as the pilot boat,' he chuckled. 'All good experience for the future.'

Tom spoke to Jan on his radio, who agreed to connect the *Singapore* and send across his clean clothes.

'Harbour tugs are towing three Yokohama fenders and a barge with hoses and transfer equipment and will be here shortly. The barge is to be made fast on the port side and the fenders on the starboard. I will lead the forward mooring party and Juan the aft, made up from the *Kinos* crew, who are cooperating, and the salvage crew from my salvage vessel, the *Coselvenom*. The tanker specialist on our behalf for safety and the transfer is Captain Chris Jules. He is still in bed, having arrived from London last night,' reported the Salvage Master on the company radio.

'All sounds good to me,' said Tom, pretending nothing out of the ordinary was happening. 'I'll go and pick the anchorage with a view to the docking afterwards and prepare myself.'

Tom watched from the bridge, Jan connecting the *Singapore* to the casualty. It seemed Jan only had three speeds full ahead, full astern and stop but if was very effective and quite spectacular in its way. He used two mooring lines to the towing hook. He noted the long-haired boat driver, returning Jan to his own tug, drove at a very sedate speed, with Jan sitting bolt upright. A metal ladder was produced by Pedro for him to climb on board, which Tom had not seen before.

Later in the morning the harbour tugs delivered the loaded barge, which Juan made fast amidships and immediately set his men to work. The Yokohama fenders towed in a single stream were made fast on the starboard side, one at each end and one in the middle. Juan seemed to be everywhere and Captain Jules and the *Kinos*' chief officer were ullaging, measuring the cargo in the tanks.

An hour before the *Buron* was due, Tom left the work on deck and went up to the owners' suite, where he found Captain Rogers busily writing. He changed into the whites his tailor had made for him, with the *Cosel* logo embroidered on the left breast, feeling somewhat embarrassed and self-conscious.

'Thought I would look the part and give confidence to the master,' he said, as Captain Rogers looked at him.

'Very smart, maybe it's time we put our people into boiler suits.'

Tom felt relieved and made his way down to the barge on the port side where the *Sunda* zed boat was waiting.

'Very smart, Cap,' laughed the long-haired Filipino, whose name Tom had discovered was Rene, and who was dressed in jeans a long-sleeved shirt and baseball Cap.

'Don't get me wet, Rene, I am the pilot.'

'I know,' said Rene, 'no problem,' as he increased to full speed and the zed boat sped across the calm, sparkling water, occasionally jumping over the residual washes of passing ships heading towards Raffles Light. Tom felt refreshed by the hot, noontime air rushing past his face. The tanker seemed a long way off at first, but it was not long before they saw the pilot ladder on the starboard side, the bottom wooden step close to the water and Tom rather dreaded the long climb to the deck of the tanker in ballast. She was still moving ahead as Rene neatly put the zed boat alongside, with two rubber fenders over the side to protect the boat, and Tom stepped onto the ladder.

It was a long climb up the vertical wall of the ship's side, the red boot topping first, then the grey painted side flaked with rust, facing him. He was met at the top by the chief officer, who took him up to the bridge and was glad of his whites, the Captain of the *Buron* was resplendent in a starched white uniform and cap.

127

'Tanner is my name, Jack Tanner,' he said, in a well-modulated English voice, holding out his hand which Tom shook. He pointed out to the captain where he proposed to anchor and that he would be the pilot for the docking after the inspection.

'Very good,' said Tanner, 'all yours,' and Tom gave his first order on someone else's ship, feeling the weight of responsibility.

'Half ahead.'

It was not long before Tom felt confident and started to feel the ship, adjusting to the time it took for anything to happen after giving an order. She responded quite quickly for her size being in ballast, and he was no longer daunted by the foredeck, which had at first seemed to stretch out to infinity. He steamed past the *Kinos*, watching for other traffic and when well clear, ordered hard a starboard. It took time but she started to turn and he judged correctly when to stop the swing. Once turned and heading in the same direction, he anchored astern and to the south of the moored *Kinos*. The tide would not turn until evening so all he had to do was pick up the anchor and steer alongside.

Rene brought a party over in the zed boat, which included the Salvage Master, Captain Jules and Juan, who proceeded to make a tank inspection with a couple of other men, dressed in white boiler suits. They were checking to make sure the tanks were empty. Tom remained on the bridge, despite Captain Tanner's invitation to his cabin and a drink. He was tensed up, tormenting himself with all the

128

things that could go wrong in the coming docking, until he pulled himself together and wrote up his notes. The Salvage Master signed the delivery certificate when the inspection party came up to the bridge.

'I will let you know when we are ready to receive you,' said Captain Rogers, Juan smiling at Tom and giving him a thumbs up. The party departed, leaving Chris Jules, who would supervise the hose connection on the *Buron*.

Tom ordered the anchor to be heaved up and proceeded at dead slow. It was not long before the all clear was given by Captain Rogers.

'*Singapore,* this is Mike five, increase to half power. I am coming alongside now.'

'Increase to half power,' replied Gonzales on the portable radio, and Tom could see through his binoculars the increase in turbulence at the stern of the tug. He had studied the Yokohama fenders, huge, black oblong things made of rubber covered in motor car tyres, and saw that unless he made a complete hash of it, they would keep him well off the *Kinos*. There was almost no wind and what little current was ahead. Although it was hot on the bridge with the wheelhouse doors open, Tom was too tense to notice.

The biggest ship he had ever sailed on was a 15,000 deadweight cargo ship and the *Buron* was more than ten times her size. The time already spent on board allowed him to become familiar with the size and he felt quite confident he had the feel of her. He saw the company yacht dwarfed by the *Kinos*, with Mr R and DB on board, emphasising the importance they placed on this operation, which he knew was the largest so far undertaken by Cosel.

He approached the *Kinos* at an angle, the *Coselhare* standing by forward and the two harbour tugs aft, ready to push or pull, having been connected by mooring lines. Tom achieved the correct angle and when the bow was half-way along the *Kinos*, he went astern on the engine, which caused the bow to swing slowly to starboard. By the time the bow was opposite the bow of the *Kinos*, the *Buron* was stopped and parallel to the *Kinos*. The mooring parties were efficient and quick. The *Buron* was made fast fore and aft while being pushed alongside by the Hare which Tom had moved amidships. The spring wires were made fast amidships to stop her moving forwards or backwards.

'Very good, Captain,' said Captain Tanner. 'You did not really need the tugs. I am impressed,' and he walked forward and shook Tom's hand.

Tom felt elated and allowed himself to feel a little proud he had made a success of his first large tanker berthing, albeit in ideal conditions; he decided not to tell Tanner it was his first. He thanked the tugs for their assistance and told Gonzales on the *Singapore* to reduce power and then swap over with the *Coselhare*.

'Have a quick beer in the comfort of my air-conditioned cabin,' offered Captain Tanner, a tall, dark-haired Englishman who looked fit and trim and very smart in his whites, quite unlike Captain Skios on the *Kinos*. He led the way to his day room, which stretched most of the width across the whole accommodation, and the portholes gave a good view of the foredeck. He could see Juan and his men with the crew of the two ships and Captain Jules connecting up the cargo transfer hoses. A pilot ladder led over the side of the *Buron* and another one on the *Kinos* and someone crossing the Yokohama fender using it as a bridge between the two vessels.

'Here's to us,' said Captain Tanner. 'Call me Jack,' and he raised his glass. Tom responded, looking away from the portholes as they drank. Tom sat down in one of the comfortable easy chairs. The day-room was well appointed, with a clean blue carpet and matching curtains and covers on the chairs.

'I expect this lot to take about thirty hours, no point rushing it. There shouldn't be any problems, your Captain Jules knows his stuff,' said Jack, looking at Tom, and then said, 'I know you. I was two years ahead of you at school. You sailed, very young to be in the team.'

'Well, well,' said Tom, somehow pleased to be recognised. 'Small world, but in those days, you were so far ahead that you were some sort of god,' and he laughed. 'What are you doing in, how should I say, an outfit like this?' He waved his hand around as though encompassing the whole ship.

'Command, one word, command, my friend. Do you think I would have got command at my age in a UK company? Shipping is dying, there is no future in British shipping. As far as I am concerned, any command is better than no command.'

'I agree,' said Tom, thinking of the thrill when he took over the *Singapore*, 'even a tug!' He laughed 'And at school, all we thought about was passenger ships.'

'Mike five, this is Mike four, where are you?' The voice of the Salvage Master crackled over the portable radio around Tom's neck.

'Mike four, this is Mike five, am still on the *Buron* with the captain.'

'I want you here, please,' the voice emphasised the word 'please'.

'Got to go,' said Tom, finishing his beer and rising from his comfortable chair.

'Come over any time for a beer and a chat,' said Jack as Tom left the cabin and made his way back to the *Kinos* via the Yokohama fender. It felt extremely odd to be clambering over a fender, albeit a large, floating one between two large tankers, one high out of the water.

Juan waved and shouted, 'Almost ready.'

He found Captain Rogers in the control room with Captain Jules, the *Kinos*' Chief Officer and Captain Skios.

'We are about to start, just waiting the word from Juan,' said Captain Rogers, giving Tom a look that suggested he did not approve of Tom's dilatoriness in returning.

Tom found the complexities of the piping system and operation of the tanker daunting and tried to concentrate, but was still buoyed up by his berthing. Tanker operations were so alien to him. When dealing with dry cargo, you could see what was happening, the cargo was visible. Here, it was in pipes or sealed but vented tanks, and one could see nothing. If, however, a mistake was made and there was a spill or burst pipe, then it became an environmental problem, although in the tropics crude oil dispersed quite quickly, but certainly a real and potential hazard of fire and explosion. Tom gave up trying to concentrate and decided he would have a session with Chris Jules when the transfer had settled down.

'1700, commenced cargo transfer,' intoned Captain Jules and Tom entered the time in his notebook, as did the Salvage Master.

'I suggest you stick with Chris,' said Captain Rogers, as he left the control room.

'Your doggy, Chris,' laughed Tom.

It was an interesting evening with Chris. He missed the setting sun being in the control room, but he learned a lot. He did not think he would ever like tankers the smell of crude and, for him, the perceived, ever-present danger with his recent experience of what could happen if things went wrong. The exploding tanker was still very fresh in his mind and Tom shuddered when he thought about it, vigorously thrusting the images from his mind; he did not want another flashback.

'Tom,' said Chris sharply, 'you were away with the birds. Look, this is what...' and he gave an explanation of

133

some point of tanker practice. It was after supper and Tom had had a long day.

'The Chief Officer and Pump Man know their work. Juan is good, so we should not have any problems and his party will deal with the mooring lines as necessary. The weather is set fine. I am off to bed.'

Tom found Captain Rogers in the owners' suite. 'John has gone to bed.'

'Yes. However, one of us should be around and go out on deck to keep the men alert. I will take the first watch, you get your head down.'

CHAPTER 11

Although Tom had a broken night's sleep, he felt fit and well at breakfast on the *Buron*, having accepted Jack's invitation. They reminisced about the past, long after the saloon had emptied of all the other occupants, and stopped only when Chris Jules came on the radio to call Tom back to the *Kinos*.

The morning sun was bright, the heat reflecting from the steel deck and Tom felt it, while inspecting the mooring lines with Juan. It was quite a walk, round the whole ship. He was enjoying a cup of tea and glass of water on the bridge when Jan called on the company radio.

'Get yourself back here. Zed boat will pick you up, pilot ladder, port side. Ship on fire Western Anchorage.'

Tom froze and did not reply.

'Did you copy?' asked Jan, fiercely.

'Understood, on the way,' replied Tom as firmly as he could, making a huge effort to control himself and move.

'I heard, I agree,' confirmed the voice of the Salvage Master.

Tom made his way on deck and walked quickly, the heat forgotten. Never run, he kept telling himself, to the pilot ladder. As he climbed over the rail, the Zed boat arrived on the plane, Rene's hair streaming out behind him.

He stopped the boat perfectly at the foot of the ladder, rocking a little in its own wash. Tom climbed down the ladder and stepped on board. Remembering what had happened in the Malacca Strait on his first salvage, he sat and held on as the grinning Rene immediately put on full throttle to the powerful outboard and the boat leapt away on the plane. He passed ahead of the *Kinos*, past the mooring buoy and towards Sultan Shoal light, which was clearly visible. The *Sunda* was already underway at some speed, a white moustache of a bow wave building up forward.

'Follow me!' ordered Jan on the radio. Rene, with his legs wide open, wedged inside the boat, sitting on the petrol can, heard and said, 'It's okay, Cap, I can put you on board, no problem.'

It's madness, thought Tom, but he did not want to lose face, so gritted his teeth. It was calm as the zed boat raced parallel to the tug, her speed increasing all the time. Rene, no longer grinning, but with a face set hard in concentration, black hair streaming behind his head almost like some biblical figure, except for the baseball cap, closed the gap. When inches away, with the two rubber fenders just touching the huge rubbing strake of the tug, Tom knew they were finished if the hull of the rubber boat ended up underneath; the boat was running at exactly the same speed as the tug. Jan was watching from the bridge wing, immobile, like some huge statue.

'Now, Cap!' shouted Rene, his voice high-pitched with the strain. Tom, taking a huge breath, stepped onto the rubber side of the boat and clutched at the four arms waiting to help. In a second he was over the towing gunnel and standing on the tow deck, which vibrated beneath his feet. His whole body shook with delayed fear and current exertions. Rene gave a whoop of delight, or perhaps it was relief; accelerated away, the boat seemed to leap into the air as it overtook the tug.

'Mad but very good,' laughed Jan, as Tom made it to the bridge. 'You need this,' and thrust a cold beer into his hand.

They crossed the invisible port limit line into Singapore and started to pass the first of the anchored ships. Their wash was by now huge, as the *Sunda* thundered along at full power, vibrating and shaking, the aerials rattling. The Chief Engineer must have over-ridden the governor, thought Tom. The rev counter was past the red line on the gauge mounted on the bulkhead, the tug was running at more than seventeen knots.

'Let Ops worry about clearance, this is an emergency,' said Jan, looking ahead through his binoculars. 'There, look,' he pointed, while giving a helm order to the man standing at the wheel to steer around a ship dead ahead.

Tom could see smoke billowing up into the sky as the *Sunda* passed another ship close by, an angry man on the bridge waving his fist. They rapidly approached the smoke

137

and then, between two coasters, they saw the old-fashioned, twelve passenger cargo ship that was on fire and Jan started to slow down.

'Port side to!' Jan shouted to Jesus on the foredeck.

Pedro was already manning the forward mast fire monitors with an AB, and they were giving a good jet of water, the fire pump humming, the pitch higher than the slowing engines. He is approaching too fast, thought Tom, as Jan pulled the engine levers back past the vertical and down, altering the pitch of the propellers into the astern position and increasing the power. The whole tug shuddered and shook as though having a fit and black smoke poured from the funnel. The *Sunda* stopped opposite the burning accommodation and Pedro directed the monitors onto the fire.

'Quick, get the hoses on board the casualty!' urged Jan, as Tom stared into the fire, the crew making fast the tug alongside. Steam hissed into the air from the water engulfing the fire.

'Move!' shouted Jan, but Tom still stood there, apparently transfixed by the flames flickering out of the portholes on the boat deck.

'It's the screaming,' he mumbled, 'it's in my head.'

He was back on another burning ship, inside the passenger accommodation on the tween deck and there was a man running towards him, screaming, covered in blood. More people were passing him, women and children, screaming, their mouths open in panic.

'What did you say?' shouted Jan over the noise of the fire, the fire pump, the monitors and the idling main engines. But Tom did not respond.

Jan hit him open-handed across the face. The helmsman looking shocked.

'Tom, come back!' and he hit him again.

Tom responded, became alive again, the flashback to another time, another place, another ship, receded. His eyes refocused and he saw Jan looking at him with a strange face; was it contempt? Tom thought. His fist was raised as though to hit him again.

'It's okay, Jan!' he shouted. 'I am okay now, sorry, I am okay now,' and Tom ran off the bridge, down onto the main deck where the crew were already dragging the fire hoses and nozzles across the ships side and into the accommodation, Jesus directing.

Tom felt utterly humiliated, drained, and his face felt on fire where Jan had hit him. He knew he had to redeem himself, not only in his own eyes but those of the crew as well. He threw himself into action, entering the burning ship without breathing apparatus, followed by an AB with a hose. The lower cabins were intact but when they climbed into the main passenger area, it was all but burnt out. The fire seemed mainly out, extinguished by the powerful monitors. They were met by Jesus and more men who had come through the aft door. It was a matter of extinguishing small pockets of fire with the hoses. It seemed to have all happened in minutes, but time passes quickly when in extreme danger.

Tom went out on deck and shouted up to Jan, who was watching from the bridge wing, to turn off the monitors. Jan signalled to Pedro, who swung them away from the casualty. The captain and some of his crew, who had been sheltering on the forecastle, came aft and he shook Tom's hand.

'Thank you for saving my ship,' he said.

'Are all your crew accounted for?' asked Tom, who saw the rest of them moving aft from the forecastle.

'Two missing, we must search for them,' urged the captain, regaining his confidence now the fire was out.

'Okay, Pedro,' said Tom, who had joined him, leaving an AB with the monitors, which were still running. Jan was taking no chances.

'We must make a search, cabin by cabin.'

They found the two corpses in a burnt-out passenger cabin. Tom froze again. The charred bodies were fused together, as though they had been burnt while making love, and so badly disfigured, it was difficult to realise they had once been human. Tom felt himself spinning in a vortex and knew he was in deep trouble if he did not fight this thing, which was beginning to destroy him. He felt himself sinking further into the spinning tunnel, fire and black charred corpses flashing past him, the images so vivid they were real, like the two before him, wisps of smoke still rising, filling his nostrils with the smell of cooked human flesh. It was beginning to overwhelm him and all reality was leaving him when, as though from a great distance far above, he heard the voice of Pedro, calling.

'Cap, Cap!' as he shook him. 'Cap, Cap, are you okay?' and the voice seemed louder as Tom, fighting with all his strength, felt himself rising, slowly coming back into the present, until at last, with a final effort, he shook himself free of the images and tunnel, sweating and shaking.

'I am okay now, Pedro,' Tom said. 'Tell the captain.'

Tom and Pedro made their way back to the main deck and told the captain, who was visibly distressed when he heard of their find. The port official he was talking to immediately spoke into his radio. A port authority tug was now alongside on the opposite side to the *Sunda*.

An AB handed him a radio and Tom spoke into it, keeping his voice calm and as normal as he could.

'Jan, Mike five, two corpses, fire out.'

'Good, well done. I am sending Ricky down with the LOF. Get the Master to sign it. DB should be here shortly to take over, they want us back at the *Kinos*.'

'Understood, Jan.'

Ricky appeared and handed Tom the LOF on a clip board with pen attached. Tom held it clear of his body, his clothing wet from the fire-fighting. He saw that it had been completed in the name of the ship, *Queen*, and Jan had signed it. The Captain, an Asian dressed in jeans and a

141

sweatshirt was still talking to the Port Official. Tom waited a little before he interposed.

'Excuse me, Captain, I wonder if you would sign this?' and proffered the clip-board, indicating where the captain should sign.

The Asian took it and signed.

'Thank you, again,' he said, bursting into tears, which fell onto the paper. Tom quickly took back the clip-board before the signatures were made illegible by the tears and patted him on the back.

'Ah, hullo, Tom,' said DB, looking fresh and cool amongst the fire-fighters now taking the hoses back to the tug. Tom felt extremely hot and dirty.

'Well done, quick response and I see you have the LOF. I will take that.'

He checked it and saw it had been signed by both the master and Jan, folded it and put it into his shirt pocket.

'I will take over here. We want you back at the *Kinos*. *Singapore* will take over from the *Sunda* here and *Cosel-hare* will take *Singapore's* place on the *Kinos's* stern.'

'Understood,' and Tom made his way back on board the *Sunda*, where Jan handed him a beer but said nothing, looking very bleak. Jan shouted at Jesus that they were leaving and as the *Singapore* approached, the lines were let go and Jan left in his usual manner with full ahead.

Tom knew something was desperately wrong because Jan said nothing on the short passage back to the anchorage off the two tankers, the *Kinos* higher and the *Buron* lower

142

in the water. The sun was well past the meridian and beginning to fall as Jan almost shouted.

'Talk, Tom, talk!'

The tug swung to the tide, the anchor holding. The only sign anything was happening on the two tankers moored side by side close by was the changing height of each, the *Buron* now much lower in the water with the cargo loaded, the *Kinos* high above her with cargo discharged.

Jan addressed Tom with an intensity that shook him.

'Talk. You are lost, Tom, if you don't.'

'What do you mean, Jan?' asked Tom, feeling foolish because he knew he was playing for time, his thoughts in turmoil.

'I am not a fool, Tom. You are the first man I have ever hit in my life and it was not because I don't like you. Pedro tells me you froze on the *Queen* when you saw those corpses. Fire and corpses, Tom, talk to me.'

The company radio crackled.

'Mike five...' and Jan leapt up, moving very fast for such a large man and spoke into the microphone.

'Bog,' and he switched off the radio, indicating to Tom he should do the same with the portable one round his neck.

'Listen, Tom,' said Jan in a quieter voice.

'Go away!' he shouted at the second mate, who appeared in the wheelhouse.

'Listen, Tom,' he repeated, 'you almost froze just before the tanker exploded, but it was not just fear, which can be controlled. I mean, I was frightened, anyone would be, but for you it was the beginning of panic. Now the *Queen*, so not once, but twice.'

Tom felt as though his heart had stopped. His life, his very self, was disintegrating around him and he had to hold on to the bridge table to stop himself falling. He remained silent as he shuffled to the vacant chair on the port side, his head spinning, filled with unconnected thoughts.

'I performed okay, Jan, on the *Kinos* fire and the *Queen*, it was only a momentary thing,' he said in a small voice.

'Not good enough, Tom, I had to hit you. *In extremis*, we cannot afford weakness, we are leaders, our men's lives depend on us. We don't have the luxury of panic or fear, it must be overcome.'

Tom felt terrible and near to tears. He saw Jan staring at him, his face hard and strong, all bonhomie removed, willing him to talk, but he was not sure if he should say anything. He knew it was a flaw, a weakness in him, which he thought he had overcome with the exploding tanker, but the *Queen* had shown him it was worse than he hoped. The flashbacks, the spinning vortex, had shown him up to himself but he had not realised how perceptive Jan was in seeing the flaw, despite the intense activity at the time. Pedro had confirmed it.

He felt so tired, he felt himself sinking again. The flashback was returning and he knew he had to make a supreme mental effort or he was lost. He must to shut out the screaming, it was the screaming in his head which seemed to unnerve him. With a huge mental effort, with a strength

144

he did not know he possessed, he said, 'I was blown up as a cadet. Many lives were lost, some were burnt. We were told not to talk about it and I have not.'

'Ah,' and the breath hissed out of Jan like a deflating tyre. 'I knew something was wrong but it had to come from you, it was no good me asking questions,' and he picked up the internal phone by his chair. 'Cold coffee,' he barked.

'Well, thank the good lord you told me. I thought I had lost you, and you would go the way many others have after a trauma, or in your case, traumas. Suicide, drink or the lunatic asylum. Oh, I have seen it,' and he laughed, but it was a mirthless laugh, his face remained hard. 'Now, listen carefully, I will only say this once.'

He paused while he opened a can of beer given to him by the mess man, who brought one over to Tom.

'It is only just being recognised how important it is for some people who have survived extreme danger and seen awful scenes, to talk about it. I went through a war, Tom, and saw things no man, let alone women or children, should ever see. But thank heavens I married an advanced, thinking wife and we have talked about it and been able to put it all behind us! You have not been able to do so. In fact, you were told to do the very thing which would make it worse, not talk about it. Rest assured, if you do nothing, it will overwhelm you *in extremis,* like the tanker blowing up or the corpses on the *Queen*, and will ultimately destroy you. And worse, in my thinking, you will be a liability to your men.'

He took a long draught from the tin, while appearing to collect his thoughts, and went on.

'It is not a normal event for a tanker to blow up along-side one's own vessel, and few people experience such a thing, and very few go through a shipwreck, so you have done well to get this far, instead of walking inland as far away from the sea as you could reach. However, if you are to remain a salvor, and from what I have seen so far you could be a very good one, you must address your problem. Now is not the time, in the middle of a major salvage, and you are wanted over there,' and he waved in the direction of the two tankers, a heat haze rising above them.

'But you must talk it through with someone. If not me, then someone else. A priest is quite good, a Catholic one, use the confessional. It is essential. If you don't, it will finish you. Once done, you will know if you have to do more or have been able to put it behind you. The flashbacks may reoccur but they will not be so intense and eventually they will stop. You owe it to yourself and the men you may lead in the future.'

He was silent and then said, 'You are good, Tom, very good, and will make a fine salvor, but you must repair the flaw, the darkness, within you.'

Tom was silent, feeling humbled but grateful. He realised that what he thought was his epiphany was the only the beginning of what could be his epiphany.

Jan got up and switched on the radios, indicating Tom should turn on his as well, which broke the silence and brought Tom back to the present.

'Don't delay, Tom.'

'Mike five, this is Mike four, is something wrong? You should be over here now, I need you,' said the quite agitated voice of the Salvage Master.

'On the way,' said Tom brightly, and he sprang out of his chair.

The fast ride over with Rene seemed to finally clear his mind and he knew what he must do.

CHAPTER 12

He left the grinning Rene, who always seemed to be cheerful, enjoying his work, at the bottom of the pilot ladder. He had brought the zed boat perfectly alongside. The heat hit Tom as he reached the top of the ladder, now quite a long climb up the black hull, with more than half the cargo transferred.

'I have to go ashore,' said Captain Rogers when Tom found him, in quite an agitated state. 'You are in charge, I have to go ashore. I expect to be back before midnight.'

After what had just occurred on the *Queen*, followed by the conversation with Jan, Tom felt it was too much, until he told himself that it was just what he needed; others' confidence in him would restore his own.

The operation was proceeding smoothly, the two ships had their own captains, there was Captain Jules and Juan for tanker expertise; what more did he want? He berthed the *Buron* successfully and despite what he experienced, he had not actually failed with the fires. He shook himself free of the past in order to look to the future. With all this expertise at his fingertips, he felt he could handle any emergencies.

'Fine, Captain Rogers, I will look after it for you. I hope nothing is wrong,' but the Salvage Master was silent.

He left the cabin and Tom could hear him climb the stairs to the bridge. Tom followed shortly afterwards and saw the *Coselone* approaching the port side. Captain Rogers was not on the bridge and Tom saw him on the black foredeck, the tall figure slightly stooped as though carrying a load on his shoulders. He climbed over the rail onto the pilot ladder. A little later, he saw the black crew boat pull away and increase speed, making a big wash for her size, and head towards Sultan Shoal where, he presumed, she would clear in at immigration.

Tom felt quite comfortable with his new responsibility. He would not have to do anything unless something went wrong. It was afternoon and hazy, the skyline of Singapore barely visible. All traffic seemed to be giving their area a wide berth.

Tom went down to the air conditioned control room, where Captain Jules was talking to the chief officer, and then out on deck where he found Juan, resting with his men. They were all covered with a variety of clothing, including headgear that seemed more suitable for cold weather, but it was to protect themselves from the sun. Tom told Juan he thought it would be a good idea if they lowered the gangway. The *Kinos* was now high out of the water and there were going to be people boarding early next morning when the transfer was finishing.

That evening, after supper, Tom called Jan and asked if he would come over.

'Not climbing that pilot ladder, Tom, unless it is an emergency. I am strictly a tug man.'

'No worries, the gangway is lowered.'

'Okay, then, I will be over shortly.'

Tom met Jan at the head of the gangway, his bulk seeming to take up the whole width, masking the mess man who was behind, carrying a bag. Tom led the way to the owners' suite where Jan immediately opened the fridge, which was empty, except for bottles of water.

'Where's the cold coffee, Tom?'

'Dry ship,' said Tom, apologetically.

'Well, Tom, just as well I brought my own supplies,' said Jan, laughing, taking the bag from the mess man.

'Wait in the zed boat with Rene,' Jan said to him.

Jan opened a can and settled himself down onto the grey settee, pushing the Salvage Master's papers out of the way. He put the can on the table but did not offer Tom one.

'I'm waiting,' said Jan quite coldly, his mouth, although partly hidden by the moustache, a hard line.

'You said, no you told me, I must talk, and I have taken this opportunity while the Salvage Master is ashore and on neutral ground, to do just that. I have never told anyone everything, although I gave evidence at the official enquiry.'

Tom spoke non-stop for two hours.

Jan was silent, just the occasional pop as he opened another can from his dwindling resources. Tom felt utterly drained and exhausted when he finished, with his arrival as a survivor on the tanker at Bahrain, where he again had to deal with the corpse. He was seventeen years of age at the time.

'Thank you, Tom, well done. You have nothing to be ashamed about, but now you have revisited the fire, the burnt corpses, the hours in the water alone, the dead man in the bottom of the lifeboat, and how you felt, there is every chance the flashbacks will go. More importantly, if involved again with a fire, you will know what to expect and forewarned is forearmed. You may never again have to deal with a fire. Most people go through their entire sea careers and never have an accident, let alone a fire, although we are more likely than most. The *Queen* is only the third fire I have fought. You already have two and your youthful experience,' and he guffawed, his face relaxing into the one Tom knew.

Tom felt somehow cleansed, as though talking about the events as a teenager had allowed his soul to come to terms with it all. No wonder the Catholics were so keen on confession! He felt almost renewed, the past was behind him now, not with him.

'My God!' exclaimed Jan. 'Look at the time! It is well past my bedtime, and my bag is empty.'

He spoke into his radio and a little later the mess man arrived and cleared the empty blue cans into the bag and tidied the table. He led the way, Jan following, whistling a tune Tom did not recognise. Tom saw them safely into the zed boat, Rene proceeding as before at a sedate speed.

As Tom made his way to the control room, a voice on his radio asked, 'Mike five, this is Mike four, why is the gangway down?'

Tom looked at his watch and saw it was nearly midnight, saying into his radio, 'Jan came for a visit and I thought it easier for the surveyors in the morning.'

There was no reply and Tom thought it prudent to meet the Salvage Master, so returned to the gangway where the *Coselone* was just coming alongside. Captain Rogers passed Tom without a word. He followed him to the owners' suite, where the Salvage Master sniffed the air.

'I would have guessed Jan had been here. We are running a dry ship and this place smells like a no smoking pub at closing time.' His lips curved into a thin smile.

'Everything okay?' asked Tom.

'My son had an accident and is in hospital, but will live,' was the rather curt reply.

'I am sorry,' Tom commiserated, although he did not know Captain Rogers had a son.

'Call me at 0400, we have a busy day ahead of us.'

Tom was up when the transfer was completed at 0830 and the various inspections took place. White boiler-suited men seemed to be everywhere.

Captain Jules and Juan were on the *Buron,* calculating how much cargo had actually been transferred and would be carried to Japan. The *Kinos* was fully inserted, her tanks filled with gas, which meant there could not be an explosion, and would proceed to Sembawang once the divers completed their survey.

Tom felt confident as he stood on the bridge of the *Buron*, wearing his Cosel whites, while Tanner was resplendent in his, looking very much the Master with his Captain's cap. The *Singapore* was connected astern of the now light ship *Kinos*, while the *Coselhare* was connected forward to the *Buron*, both tugs with the ship's mooring lines, which could be easily slipped from the tug's towing hooks. He knew the loaded *Buron* would behave in a very different way when loaded than when he berthed her light. He had been over to the *Singapore*, urging Rene not to get him wet, and briefed Gonzales. Captain Rogers was forward with a mooring party and Juan aft; they were singled up and were awaiting his orders. It was near noon and hot on the bridge wings, the white paint reflecting the bright light, the long, grey-coloured foredeck stretching a long way, while the figures on the forecastle were diminished by the distance.

'Let go all fore and aft.'

Captain Tanner looked surprised but did not demur.

'*Singapore*, this is Mike five, commence towing as we discussed.'

Tom could see the increased turbulence and the mooring line to the towing hook tighten as Gonzales steered to starboard, pulling the stern of the *Kinos* away from the stern of the *Buron*. He ordered the *Coselhare* to tow and pull the bow off the moored *Kinos*.

'Slow ahead, Captain.'

'Slow ahead it is,' said Jack, moving the engine telegraph lever forward with a 'ting', a second 'ting' of the telegraph bell indicating the engine room had understood the order and put the engine on slow ahead. Tom could see the rev counter needle slide round the dial mounted on the forward bulkhead of the wheelhouse.

At first, nothing happened, except the gap at the stern increased, which Tom watched from the port bridge wing. The aft Yokohama fender floated free, revealing the blackpainted hull of the *Kinos*. The sterns were well clear of each other.

'*Singapore*, tow straight.' Tom could see the tug alter course.

Looking forward, he saw the bow slowly move away from the *Kinos*, and the *Buron* inched ahead, the speed increasing, the hull well clear of the *Kinos*, the fenders all floating free until the bridge passed the bow, the mooring party, except the Salvage Master, waving. Tom dismissed the tugs and the mooring lines used for towing were let go, the mooring parties heaving them on board the *Buron*.

'Very good, Tom, very neat,' said Jack, signing Tom's chitty, acknowledging the pilotage and the time of departure, 'and the best of luck to you in the salvage world,' he continued, shaking Tom's hand.

'Thanks, Jack, and no doubt I will read in some future Nautical Magazine of your promotion to some important shore job.'

They laughed and Tom walked off the bridge as Captain Tanner took control, looking ahead, giving a helm order and course to the helmsman, who was dressed in jeans and a rather dirty sweatshirt, in sharp contrast to his captain.

The *Coselone* was now alongside the *Buron,* her hull tight against the grey hull of the moving ship and Tom stepped on board the firm platform of the crew boat from the pilot ladder. Much easier than the zed boat, he thought, as the skipper pulled away. Chris Jules and a couple of surveyors he had not met were already on board, sitting in the air-conditioned cabin.

'Well done, Tom,' congratulated Chris, 'that was good. In fact, the whole operation has gone well, which is as it should be. There was not too much of a problem with the tanks that had been on fire, we were able to put the cargo in separate tanks on the *Buron.*'

The *Coselone* headed back to the *Kinos*, where Tom and Chris stepped off at the gangway. The launch departed back to Singapore via Sultan Shoal immigration. Once on deck, Tom could see the *Buron* disappearing at speed down the deep water channel that by-passed the narrow Singapore Straits. Ships that pass in the night; he thought of his meeting with Tanner.

Tom was pleased with himself. Last night's talk with Jan was fading into the shadows of his mind, as he made

155

his way outside the accommodation to the bridge. The air-conditioning in the wheelhouse made his shirt stick to his sweaty body and he wiped his face with a handkerchief. It was another hot day and Tom was glad of the closed doors and cool wheelhouse.

Captain Skios, in sweatshirt and jeans, welcomed Tom. 'All yours, pilot.'

Tom felt confident and it only took three engine movements to clear the mooring buoy, slow astern, stop, half ahead and follow the *Sunda* through the Singapore Straits. The plate hanging down was not causing any difficulties. The divers had reported it was still connected tightly to the hull.

The passage to Sembawang was uneventful, Tom simply followed Jan. It was early evening when the Lloyds Open Form was terminated with the *Kinos* alongside the shipyard wharf, a very low-key affair after such momentous events. A signature and a handshake and that was it. Tom felt huge relief, knowing the salvage was a huge success and Cosel would be paid. After all, it was a "no cure, no pay" contract and the company had been at risk until the final signature.

Tom joined Jan on the bridge of the *Sunda*, now alongside the *Kinos*, the crew picking up the last of the salvage equipment and the towing slip hook, which had been made fast forward in case of emergencies. Jan was his old, ebullient self, congratulating Tom on his ship handling abilities, the ever-present can in his hand. They departed shortly afterwards, Jan simply pushing the engine levers to full ahead and the tug shot along the *Buron*, narrowly missing the overhang of the forecastle.

The passage back to Eastern Anchorage was made at full speed; the thought of fuel economy was the last thing from Jan's mind.

'It is Cosel's biggest salvage so far,' Jan said enthusiastically, 'and we did everything. Your piloting was fantastic. Let me tell you a little secret: our esteemed Salvage Master could not put a rowing boat alongside, let alone a large tanker. If you had not been there, he would have got Chris Jules to do it or get a pilot from Singapore.'

He threw the empty blue can out of the wheelhouse door and over the side, as he opened a red can.

'Don't like anchor beer so much,' he said, drinking. 'I warned you once and I do so again. I am safe. I am a tug man, he cannot touch me, but you have shown yourself to be potentially much more, and if he thinks you are a threat, he will knife you. Enough,' he guffawed. 'Life is for enjoying.'

Jan weaved his way amongst the anchored ships at a speed Tom thought reckless, but Jan had been around a long time and knew what he was doing. Suddenly, ships' sirens started sounding, and fireworks with what looked suspiciously like distress rockets and flares, illuminating the sky.

'Has someone started a war?' asked Tom, as the anchor was let go, the engines going full astern, and the bottom mud stirred.

'No, it's the New Year,' and Jan enfolded him in a huge bear hug. 'Happy New Year, Tom.'

CHAPTER 13

The New Year's Day party was a much bigger and grander affair than Christmas Day. The old man was celebrating and he showed some style when he wanted to. The sitting room, which was very large, with a high, white ceiling and polished, light brown, wooden parquet floor, was laid out as the food and drink area. The tables, covered with white table cloths, almost groaning with food, kept cool and fresh by the air-conditioning, despite the French doors being open onto the green, beautifully manicured lawn. Handsome young waiters in tight black trousers, and good looking girls in black mini-skirts, both highlighting their white shirts or blouses with red bow ties, served champagne or whatever drink anyone fancied. The trees, a darker green at the far end of the lawn, were draped with tinsel, which glinted in the tropical sun, and the flower beds were colourful with newly-opened flowers, the earth freshly turned.

The old man greeted each guest personally, standing in the French windows, dressed in a black and white silk shirt. His black trousers, like those of the waiters, were well-pressed, and he was looking very smart, far removed from his usual, dowdy self. His thin, normally unruly wisps of hair were well-groomed. He was cheerful and full of life, belying his small stature and greater age. Hilda stood next to him, acting as hostess, and Tom wondered where the mother was, never having seen her before, although he knew she was alive.

Hilda looked fabulous, her black hair, piled on top of her head made her look taller, elongating her face, and enhancing her smooth skin while minimising her small nose. She was almost beautiful, the cheongsam enhancing the effect, and when she smiled, Tom was bewitched by her perfect white teeth, glimpsed between her subtly made-up lips. He stood there, staring at her, until he realised what he was doing and blushed, looking away in embarrassment. Hilda noticed and gave an even more bewitching smile, which suggested a hint of triumph, or was it his imagination?

Mr R had been effusive in his welcome and Tom, unused to such overtly familiar behaviour, felt uneasy and somehow out of place. He finished the cool, amber, bubbling liquid from the tulip-shaped glass he was holding and took another one from the waiter standing close by, who smiled at him, obviously noting his embarrassment.

There were many people Tom did not know, although he knew all those who worked for Cosel, as well as some of the nautical surveyors. He wandered over to the marine group, who all turned at his approach and wished him a happy and successful New Year.

'Man of the moment,' laughed Steve, his blue eyes twinkling. He was dressed in a blue silk shirt which matched his eyes, white trousers and white shoes, while this pretty wife smiled next to him, her flower-patterned frock in stark contrast to her husband's plainness. Tom

160

wondered if it was deliberate or coincidence as he replied, smiling.

'Hardly. Captain Rogers was the Salvage Master and Jan was in charge of the fire-fighting and Tow Master.'

'Ah, but we know, my spies have told me all,' and he laughed again, looking at Tom while Wayne Dawson, his bald head shining, and Dan Brown, laughed with him.

'No secrets in Cosel,' said Dan, who was wearing a shirt covered in brightly coloured flowers, which seemed out of place from his normal, rather dour, self.

'Well done,' said Barry Todd, the Marine Superintendent, his beard and moustache hiding his lips while his head was almost bald, shaking Tom's hand.

Tony House was dressed completely differently from the bright shirt he wore on the sea trials of the *Jurong*; he was wearing a blue silk shirt with white dots, a burgundy-coloured cummerbund, fawn trousers and tan shoes. Tom wondered if it was deliberate as nothing seemed to match, but the overall effect was quite startling.

'Well done, indeed,' he said. 'I wonder if my spies are the same as everyone else's but they all seem to say the same thing,' and he shook Tom's hand vigorously. 'We must meet up for a quiet drink.'

At that moment, the large figure of Jan, his moustache neatly trimmed and normally unruly greying hair well groomed, wearing an outrageously-coloured dragon shirt, red, gold and black, with white trousers and white shoes, appeared in the French windows, flanked by his wife. She

161

was dressed in a much more sober, rather plain, yellow frock, along with their three children. Someone clapped and it was taken up by the Cosel group, then the whole party on the lawn, everyone smiling, the old man appearing behind the children.

Jan looked quite astonished and grabbed a foaming mug of beer from a waitress holding a tray. The old man squeezed his way through the children and raised his hands into the air.

'I just want to say thank you to the salvors, Captain Smit and Captain Matravers, and sorry Captain Rogers is not able to be here. Cosel is on the move,' and there was renewed clapping. 'I was going to wait to make an announcement, which will make the salvage world sit up and take notice of our company. No doubt they already realise we are a force after the successful conclusion of the *Kinos* only half a day ago. The success makes now as good a time as any. We are buying what, when she was built, was the largest tug in the world, the world's first super tug, delivery in six months, Southampton, UK.'

The effect was more than the old man could have wished for. Some of the Nautical fraternity literally had their mouths open as they all clapped and some shouted, 'Well done, Mr R, you are really putting Singapore on the salvage map.'

'An even more successful New Year to Cosel!'

Tom noted that even DB looked surprised, and wondered.

'The buffet is open,' finished the old man. 'Enjoy!'

Jan, still looking embarrassed, with his proud wife on his right, his children obviously adoring him, moved over to the Cosel group.

'I have never been so embarrassed in my life,' boomed Jan, his mug already empty, looking for a waiter.

'Hush, hush, dear, you were secretly thrilled. Anyway, your wife and children are proud of you,' said Gerda, smiling.

Jan grabbed another mug while Peter, Jan's eldest, took a glass of champagne for himself and handed *Coca Cola* to his younger siblings. Jan was about to remonstrate with the twelve-year-old, but thought better of it.

'Learn to drink sensibly, Peter, drink it slowly and enjoy,' he said, while emptying his own mug. Gerda held on to his arm as Jan started talking to Dan and Steve. Tom listened, while scanning the room for Hilda.

Looking at one of the beds full of red flowers, he noticed a figure wearing a white frock. The contrast with the colours was startling, and he started to walk towards the figure. She – for it was a woman – turned and he stopped, in shock. It was Shelia, and she was smiling at him. Tom looked round but could not see Hilda, so continued walking.

'Happy New Year,' she said, kissing him on both cheeks.

'And to you,' he said, pleased to see her. 'I thought you had left Singapore.'

'I did but I came back, as you can see. I'm glad to see you again, despite the last time we parted,' she laughed, as Tom blushed, squirming with embarrassment.

'I came to understand later that in your scheme of things, a salvage is more important,' and she hesitated, 'than any female,' and she laughed again, her face crinkling with amusement.

'Quite a party Mr R is throwing,' said Tom, waving his arm at the crowd on the lawn, some sitting with full plates at the numerous white, wrought iron tables scattered under the shade of the trees.

'Why are you here?' asked Tom.

'Because I was invited,' she said, quite coldly.

'Sorry, I mean you are not a salvor or marine-orientated,' he said quickly, to cover his confusion, and not wishing to upset her.

'Well, some people have a social life and have friends outside their work, you know,' she said, looking into his eyes, her own twinkling, the colour in her peach-like cheeks not entirely due to make up.

'My word, she is pretty,' thought Tom, as he thought back to the night in the Orchid Inn.

'Actually, Hilda invited me. I got to know her through my job in advertising and I am sure even you know that fashion needs constant promotion and advertising.'

'And did she mention me?' asked Tom after some thought.

'Well, that would be telling, wouldn't it, Captain Matravers?' she laughed merrily, a little tinkle, like a brook running over stones.

They were still standing by the flowers, fresh glasses supplied by the attentive young man who had surreptitiously been looking at Shelia, until Tom gave him a look that made him move away, when Tom saw Hilda in the French windows. He started to turn but she had spotted him and waved, moving slowly across the beautiful lawn towards them.

'So you know each other?' asked Hilda, gaily.

'We have met before,' answered Shelia, looking at Tom, 'but I didn't mention it when you were telling me about him.'

'Let's have some lunch and I'll join you and we can all catch up with each other. I am sure Tom has lots to tell us since Christmas Day,' she chuckled. 'My father can't stop talking about it.'

She turned and left them, walking towards Mr R, who was talking to a bunch of people who were quite obviously not marine. Business associates of one sort and another, bankers perhaps, thought Tom, Tony's colourful clothing standing out amongst them.

'To the buffet, Shelia, I for one, am starving,' suggested Tom, guiding her across the lawn with an easy familiarity. 'I still can't believe it was only Christmas Day when I was last standing on this lawn. So much has happened in such a short time.'

The buffet was the most impressive Tom had ever seen: lobsters not crayfish, he noticed; Belon oysters from France; a huge salmon, flown in from Scotland; big prawns, partly shelled; a York ham; a side of beef, rich and red inside; a huge turkey, guinea fowl, duck; all with chefs ready to carve for them, along with an assortment of salads with different lettuce, every conceivable salad vegetable, and numerous dressings. There were opened bottles of red and white French wine for those who had consumed enough champagne, which they were encouraged to take, or a waiter would bring over to them.

They all met at a table in the shade of a tree, for the afternoon sun was hot, their plates piled high. The three of them made a jolly party, turning some heads, but Tom did not notice, too engrossed in playing the host to his two pretty guests.

'Now, you can't run away! I want you to tell us all about your exploits,' said Hilda, her eyes betraying a hint of mischief. 'I've listened to my father talk about the business of salvage, which I find fascinating, and how the latest two salvage operations will transform the finances of the company. Now I want to hear what happens on the frontline.'

'Yes, do,' said Shelia, brightly. 'I used to sail, so have some knowledge of the sea.'

'Are you sure?' said Tom. 'It's not the usual party talk.'

'It is here,' laughed Hilda.

'Well, stop me if I bore you,' said Tom, suddenly making the decision to talk. 'Where to begin?'

166

He stopped and thought.

'Christmas Day, of course, just seven days ago. And you, Hilda, were in at the beginning, when I asked you to get your father into the sitting room because I had been paged, and now I am in the same place, almost at the same time as then, a full circle. But it encloses much, and as Hilda has just said, may transform the finances of the company.'

'And you, Captain Matravers, have changed a lot in that short time,' said Shelia seriously. 'Something happened to you out there. You are more assured, more self confident, perhaps? You hold yourself slightly differently, you are more grown up. It's quite noticeable to me, more interesting,' and she gave him a wicked little smile.

Hilda looked surprised and Tom, too, for different reasons. He did not think Shelia was so perceptive but maybe he did not know too much about women's thought processes. He certainly felt different and it seemed months had passed, rather than just a few days, so much had happened to him, not just physically but mentally, too. The difference from being on board a salvage tug and this glittering party was so immense, he felt it was almost as though a different person was involved, as if there were two Tom's. The champagne and wine and the proximity of these two attractive women seemed to open his mind.

Their glasses were topped up by a waiter and Tom launched into his account, starting with Hilda manipulating her father into the sitting room without alerting the nautical guests that anything was happening.

'It started with Jan's mad drive to Clifford Pier. He drives his car in the same way as his tug, full ahead or stop, there's no in-between. I suppose his family are used to it, but it frightens the life out of me. The children think it's exciting and fun, while Gerda just grits her teeth and bears it,' he laughed, 'but it is exciting.'

He tried to articulate not just the excitement but the sense of purpose in taking risks, the big tug proceeding at full speed out of the anchorage, through the narrow Singapore Straits and the race through the night to beat any competition. It was difficult to describe the fear approaching the burning ship, the empty tanker, and the subsequent explosion and sinking, missing out his momentary hesitation, but emphasising Jan's bravery, courage and leadership in extreme danger. He was so carried away, he lost all sense of time, caught up in his recollections, until he came to.

'Sorry, I must be boring you.'

'No, no,' said Hilda and Shelia together, their rapt attention evidence that he had managed to convey some of the drama, and they were with him. He refilled his glass, long empty, and continued with his taking over the *Singapore* and finally extinguishing the fire on the *Kinos*.

'It's not so exciting now,' he said, as a waiter removed the empty bottles and replaced them with full ones, but he described the skill and stamina of Jan in controlling the difficult tow to Singapore, highlighting the drama of the

168

coaster in the middle of the night and the container ship crossing the tow wires.

It was late afternoon when he reached the fire on the *Queen*, hesitating when it came to how he froze, glossing over it and missing out altogether the horror of the burnt, intertwined corpses. It was difficult to generate any excitement in the cargo transfer and if there had been, it would have reflected badly on the salvors. He could not possibly tell them of his conversation with Jan, although he mentioned the Salvage Master's son in hospital, a personal tragedy. He described feeling almost exalted at the berthing and un-berthing, and his personal sense of achievement.

The daylight was failing as he told them of the build-up in tension during the final passage to Sembawang, where he was acting as pilot, following the *Sunda*; so much had been achieved, but it was all still 'no cure, no pay' and Cosel would not earn one cent until the casualty was safely moored alongside the wharf and the termination letter signed.

He was so engrossed in his account, he did not noticed the old man joining them, sitting just behind the two women, with the same spellbound attention. Tom was covered with confusion and embarrassment; what he might say to the women, he would not have said to a man? He wondered how much Mr R had heard.

'Sorry, sir, I got carried away,' he apologised. 'I must go, everyone seems to have left. I have overstayed my welcome,' and he stood up.

169

'Not at all, Tom,' said Mr R. 'I just wish I had been here when you started. If you can keep these two non-seafaring ladies quiet for hours with your story, it must be good. Let's hope you can do the same with the Lloyds Arbitrators so they give us the awards we deserve,' he laughed.

'It's later than I thought,' said Shelia. 'Tom's story made me lose all sense of time. I found it absolutely fascinating. I wonder, Mr R, if I could take you up on your offer for your driver to take me home?'

'Of course, my dear,' he replied, putting his hand on her knee.

It was almost dark and someone inside the house switched on the fairy lights draped over the trees, transforming the darkness into a fairyland of coloured light. It was quite magical.

'I wonder if I could go with Shelia, and your driver drop me off at Clifford Pier?' said Tom.

'Of course,' said Mr R, and Hilda looked at Tom with a questioning look, which Tom ignored.

A figure came out of the French windows as they made their way back to the house. The light from the sitting room showed this to be a small woman, and from her walk, an elderly one.

'Catherine, meet Captain Matravers and Miss Stirling,' said Mr R, tenderly.

'Good evening,' said a quiet, well-modulated voice, and Tom saw an elderly lady with almost translucent skin and white hair.

170

'They are just leaving, mother,' said Hilda, taking her mother's arm and leading her back into the house.

Shelia and Tom held hands in the luxurious car, her head resting on his shoulder, then quite spontaneously kissed each other, arousing a desire in Tom, honed by the wine and his talking. The car stopped outside an apartment block.

'Come in for a drink, Tom.'

Sheila's voice was light and breathless.

'Thank you,' he replied, loudly, so the driver who was getting out of the car could hear. 'Just a quick one and I must get back to the tug.'

They got out of the car and Tom said to the driver, 'I'll get a taxi from here, thank you,' dismissing him.

They rode up in the lift, not touching one another, but the sexual tension was electric. Once inside the flat, Tom said sharply, 'The telephone,' and Shelia pointed.

Once he had told ops the telephone number of the flat, they touched and it set them on fire. They ripped off each other's clothes as Shelia guided him into the bedroom, where they finished off what they had begun all those months earlier, the afternoon enhancing the natural passion of two young people on the verge of love, Tom reaching a place he had never been before, his whole body full of feeling, his head a kaleidoscope of colour and bright lights.

CHAPTER 14

Tom awoke in his bunk on the *Sunda* and thought with dread of the day ahead. The euphoria of New Year's Day, both the party and the night with Shelia, had disappeared, to be replaced by a feeling of uselessness and lack of confidence. It had all happened so quickly and it was all due to one man.

Tom had done his best with the salvage reports and he knew in his heart of hearts that they were good, but the lawyer rubbished them, saying he was no good and would never make a good Salvage Master. He felt trapped because he had no option but to work with the man. The relationship with Shelia, which had started on such a sexual high, was turning sour and he knew it was all his fault. The union achieved on their first night together had not reoccurred, however hard he tried. He was out of balance, out of kilter with himself, and felt like resigning. The glittering future that seemed mapped out before him, paled into insignificance against the daily meeting with the lawyer.

It was not so bad when they worked in the office, but now he was working, well, it was drinking really, in the hotel, the whole thing turned into a disaster for Tom. He tried drinking with the man but that did not work, except to make Tom ill. He tried not drinking and that made the man even more unpleasant.

He got up, showered and dressed in his shore-going gear, dark trousers, white shirt and tie; the man even criticised his choice of tie, so Tom bought some more, plain and un-patterned. Miguel, the mess-man, brought his breakfast on to the bridge wing and laid out the table with a white tablecloth, cutlery and china.

This is the highlight of my day, he thought, looking around at the anchored ships and the Singapore skyline. And it's downhill all the way from here. I am going to have to do something, but he said that every day for a week and done nothing.

Perhaps I don't really have the courage for all this, then thrust such thoughts from his mind.

'Captain not well today,' said Miguel, his round, smooth face looking concerned.

'I am not the captain, Miguel, I keep telling you. Captain Jan is the captain.'

'But Captain Jan not here, so you are the captain,' and he gave a girlish giggle.

'Bugger off and get me some more toast and don't burn it!' laughed Tom, feeling a little better.

'Yes, Captain,' and Miguel scuttled off.

It was a pleasant start to the day and it would have to be a very good hotel which could better it. Freshly cooked eggs and bacon tasted so much better in the open, the early morning sun not yet hot. Tom admired some of the myriad ships around, almost a history of shipping for the last thirty years from small tugs and barges to a Straits Steamship passenger ship, from ex-Dutch coasters, and costal tankers to large, modern cargo ships, including, unusually, a small feeder container ship. At the South China Sea end, three new LPG carriers, were laid up. Only half a mile away he could see the competition tug, the black-hulled *Misssisippi* whose Master he sometimes met in the Clifford Pier bar. The man on watch was instructed to keep watch on the other tug and to inform him and base if she moved.

'Tea, captain,' chirped Miguel, who poured from the fresh pot of tea he brought with him.

'Your shoes, captain,' and he put Tom's well-polished, black shore-going shoes on the deck.

'Thank you, Miguel, I don't know what time I will be back,' said Tom.

'Girlfriend will be happy,' smiled the mess-man, but Tom ignored him and said curtly, 'Tell the bosun I want to leave at 0830 and Rene to behave himself. I don't want to arrive wet.'

'Okay, Cap.'

The company radio squawked and Alfredo, the third mate, answered. He came out of the wheelhouse and said, 'Ops say go to office.'

'Okay, Alfredo,' said Tom, thinking that in time, the young Filipino would make a good officer and salvor. He had initiative, an essential ingredient that Tom thought he, himself, was lacking at the moment and resolved to do something about the situation with the lawyer. He felt his spirits rise a little.

174

'You keep dry,' grinned Rene, his hair as long as ever, when Tom climbed into the zed boat. The surrounding brown water was uninviting and Tom stood at the bow wearing gloves, holding onto the painter. Rene, as usual, departed at speed and Tom literally rode the boat ashore, bending his knees as she bounced over the wash of numerous country craft and launches, which caused quite a chop on the otherwise smooth sea.

He climbed the green, seaweed-covered, concrete steps at Clifford Pier, giving Rene a cheery wave as he backed the boat away and set off at full speed, weaving his way through the approaching boats. The van was waiting for him and he read the Straits Times on the forty-minute journey to the office at Jurong.

The lawyer was late, which was not unusual, and when he did arrive in Mr R's car he went straight into a meeting with the old man. He was in a foul mood when he finally came into the office assigned to him, a small room with the curtains drawn to shut out the bright sunshine. His secretary had been typing away since Tom arrived, while he read Lloyds List.

'Mr R says I have to finish with you within the week. Have you been talking to him?' he snarled.

'I have not seen Mr R since the New Year's Day party, where he personally and publicly thanked us. The *Kinos* terminated the day before and that is three weeks ago. You have my report,' replied Tom firmly beginning to become angry.

Keep your temper, Tom kept telling himself, sipping his third cup of tea.

'Well, someone must have said something, he wants the arbitration yesterday.'

'Of course,' Tom pointed out, 'he wants the money.'

'He shouldn't be buying any more tugs until the arbitration is over, it puts me under a lot of pressure,' the lawyer complained.

'We have done the car carrier,' said Tom, quite curtly, 'and I have signed my statement. The *Kinos*, as I said, is written up, as is the *Queen*. It should not be too difficult to finish.'

'If your reports were any good, which they are not,' growled the lawyer.

'Listen, Mr Dickinson, I have compared my car carrier statement against my report and it is almost word for word, with the occasional addition, so don't tell me my reports are no good. You don't really need me,' said Tom, beginning to flare up.

'Why, you little punk, you little prick, you little squirt with a poncy accent! Don't forget who got you your job. I put in a good word with Mr R and it won't take much to get rid of you.'

'What do you want, a commission, ten percent of my salary and bonuses?' Tom shouted, getting out of his chair and standing up, leaning over the table. Susan, the secretary, left the room.

176

'You rotten little bastard!' shouted the lawyer, heaving his not inconsiderable bulk out of his chair so the two men were standing inches apart, glaring at each other. Tom almost flinched at the stale smell of drink, but knew if he backed down now, he was finished as far as this person was concerned; he would be a slave.

'If you worked at the hotel instead of propping up the bar and making a fool of yourself and letting us down, we would have finished by now!' shouted Tom, almost beside himself with rage, staring the lawyer in the eye, the eyes bloodshot and red-rimmed.

The lawyer shouted back a string of obscenities and made as if to hit him, but Tom did not move, almost daring the infuriated older man. Suddenly the lawyer dropped his eyes and sat down. Tom, with a surge of triumph, knew he had won.

'Third World War,' said Mr R loudly. Tom had not heard the door open and turned round, looking a little abashed at the stern-looking old man, but held his ground.

'I think the position has been resolved, sir,' he said, looking directly at Mr R, who turned and shut the door.

Robert Dickinson, like all bullies, had backed down when confronted, but Tom thought he had probably made an enemy and would have to watch his back. He also wondered about the Salvage Master, who was yet to give his evidence. He suspected he just copied out the salvage reports, altering a few words here and there, as he did with Tom's car carrier report.

177

Tom sat down and looked at the somehow diminished figure in front of him, the neatly parted sparse fair hair, the round, chubby, slightly puffy white face with its bloodshot eyes and red eye lids, the thin lips, the bull neck above a plump, unfit body. But it was the hands that stood out. They were quite delicate for such a coarse man, the fingers, which never seemed to stop moving, as though permanently playing some obscure musical instrument, were long and slender. He could not quite visualise Mr Dickinson in charge of a tug, or any ship, for that matter, although it was said he was a Master Mariner.

'Come on, Robert, let bygones be bygones,' cajoled Tom, who knew it was in his own interests to finish the work. 'Let's get on with it and then you will be rid of me.'

'Get Susan back,' barked the lawyer.

The rest of the morning was spent with the lawyer, who pulled himself together, dictating from Tom's report and the log of the *Singapore* to the pert little Chinese lady, Susan, who seemed to let his occasional rudeness wash over her. She arranged and brought in lunch, which consisted of a sandwich and tea.

At the end of the day, just after 1800, the lawyer said, 'Be at the hotel at 0900 sharp tomorrow,' and was whisked off with Mr R in his luxurious, chauffeur-driven car.

Tom returned to Clifford Pier in a van, wondering where his future lay. He rang Shelia from the pay-phone on the pier but she was out. He felt very flat but extremely thankful he had had it out with Robert, who once had

178

seemed such a friend. He decided to have a few beers in the pier bar before going back to his tug.

'Well, well, the competition,' said a cheery voice, looking up from the bar where it appeared he had been for some time; the Captain of the *Mississippi*, anchored half a mile from the *Sunda*.

'Congratulations on the *Kinos* and I don't know how I let you get the *Queen*,' continued the fresh-faced Scotsman, his burr muted by years in the East.

'We were in the right place at the right time,' said Tom, taking the bar stool next to him. 'I'll have a Tiger, please.'

When they first met they became quite friendly, though competitive rivals. Frank Ings was a tall young man with a full head of red hair, fit and athletic, handsome in a rugged sort of way, who came to Singapore as a young second mate and stayed ever since. The *Mississippi* was a good rival for the *Singapore*, but no match for the *Sunda*.

'How long before your mob brings out a bigger tug to compete with the *Sunda*?' asked Tom, opening his third beer.

'Don't know,' replied Frank, his speech beginning to show the length of time he had spent in the bar. 'It can't be too long, especially as there is a rumour you have bought the one and only UK super-tug.'

Tom thought long and hard before replying but came to the conclusion it would do no harm, the old man had announced it publicly.

'It's true.'

Frank sat up.

'Well, I'll be damned, Cosel really is on the move! My mob were very angry with us that we didn't get a look in on the *Kinos*. The *Mississippi* was – how should I say it? – temporarily *hors de combat* at the crucial moment.'

'We know,' laughed Tom.

'You won't be so lucky next time,' said Frank, seriously.

'How about a curry?' asked Tom. 'I've had a difficult day and I'm starving.'

'Heard your lawyer was in town,' Frank chortled. 'Let's go to that roadside place for a coolie curry, very tasty and down-market.'

Tom returned on board late that night a little the worse for wear, Rene driving at a sedate speed consistent with his state. He almost fell into the black, murky water when trying to climb on board the tug, a passing country boat causing a wash that upset his already unsteady balance.

'Happy night?' asked Miguel on the bridge the next morning, as Tom nursed a cup of coffee.

'Shut up, Miguel. Go and get my breakfast,' he ordered, as the mess-man left the bridge, giggling.

Tom was at the Goodwood Park Hotel right on time but he need not have bothered, Robert Dickinson did not appear until 1100, his eyes looking more bloodshot than ever. He sat at the just-opened bar, nursing a beer.

'Susan is typing,' is all he said, so Tom read an out-of-date Daily Telegraph. No work was done all day and Tom

180

resisted Robert's attempt to get him to drink with him. Eventually, mid-afternoon, Tom left, saying he would be at the hotel at 0900 the next morning and suggesting they do some work, they might get a salvage and Tom would be gone.

'Bugger off, you little prick!' mumbled Robert, draped over the bar, much to the disapproval of the barman, who could do nothing unless he fell off the bar stool.

Tom had a date with Shelia that night.

'Well, you seem in a better frame of mind,' she said as they sat down to an early evening drink in the Ming Court lounge bar, sinking into the cream-coloured armchairs, the pianist playing cheerful tunes.

'Confrontation over, I won, but I have an enemy,' said Tom, briskly.

'Let's hope your better mood lasts, you were such fun to be with,' said Shelia, smiling. 'Tell me about your lawyer.'

'I would rather not,' said Tom, and they went on to talk of other things, enjoying each other's company again. A good dinner with wine in the hotel bistro, which was really quite good, and the evening ended in bed with a much more satisfactory outcome.

'I am busy with business for the next two days,' said Shelia from the bed, her blond hair flared out over the pink pillowcase, 'but free on Friday.'

'Dinner at the Mandarin, they have a seafood special in their small restaurant. I will book, say seven-thirty? Meet me in the lobby bar at 1900.'

'Yes, Sir!' said Shelia, giving a mock salute from the pillow as Tom bent over her, his hand fumbling below the bed clothes, his lips glued to her as he made his farewell.

Mr Dickinson was in a better mood.

'On the wagon bloke,' he greeted Tom, almost cheerfully for him. They finished the *Kinos* late in the evening and Tom left without staying for the offered drink.

Tom was called to the office on Thursday morning, which interrupted their progress. The old man called him in.

'You don't get on with Robert?'

'It seems to have resolved itself for the moment, sir,' answered Tom. 'We only have the *Queen* to do.'

'Call me, Mr R, Tom, you have been around long enough to know that. Robert can be difficult, awkward, downright rude and drinks too much. Don't forget, I pay his bills, but he is good and he pulled a couple of chestnuts out of the fire for me in the past. So, you will just have to put up with him. Your salvage reports are good, as I would expect, and I suspect he just copies them out, as he does with the Salvage Master, but no matter, he gets us good awards, which is all that matters.'

'Understood, Mr R.'

'I am taking Robert and a few guests out in the *Coseltina*, the company yacht, on Sunday and I would like you

182

to join us. Hilda will be coming too. She has become interested in our business and might join Cosel. She was very impressed by your story and the way you told it.'

The old man smiled. 'Finish off the *Queen* and see you on Sunday at Jurong pier, 1100 sharp.'

'Thank you, Mr R, I will enjoy the trip.'

The *Queen* was finished on Friday afternoon and Tom joined Robert at the bar for a celebratory drink. The wagon trip had not lasted, but when it looked like turning into a session, Tom departed, not wanting to mess up his evening with Shelia. They left on better terms, Robert saying, 'You are better than that illiterate Dutch man,' and laughed.

'See you on Sunday, Robert,' said Tom, as he was leaving the bar.

'Coming up in the world, are we?' said Robert. 'I'll have to nip this in the bud with Mr R,' he continued, only half jokingly. Tom was glad his dealings with the lawyer were over.

The night with Shelia went well, dinner was excellent and they laughed and joked together just like old times.

It was less than a month ago it started, thought Tom, with a shock, discounting the original encounter in the Orchid Inn. They even sounded each other out about living together when Tom was in Singapore, she had her own apartment. The sex was back to being good. They got on well again now Tom had made his stand against Robert and life was on the up. How quickly things change, thought

Tom the following morning, as he lay next to Shelia, contemplating a morning glory when she awoke, his body already responding to his erotic thoughts.

CHAPTER 15

Tom consulted with Shelia regarding the best thing to wear on the yacht, omitting to tell her Hilda would be there. It seemed pointless to cause any problems or suspicions when there were none.

Sunday, the day of rest, dawned fine as the sun rose over a sleeping Singapore. Tom felt guilty he had not been out to the tug since Friday morning, as he looked at the view out of Shelia's sitting-room window, the red orb of the sun quickly turning to molten steel. It was going to be hot, as usual. He consoled himself, however, with the thought that Gonzales was now promoted chief officer and Tom was supernumerary. He could be taken off at any time, without interfering with the proper running of the *Sunda*. Captain Hannibal's leave was cut short and he was back onboard his old tug.

'Making babies,' as he told Tom, when they met in the office when asked if he enjoyed a good leave.

Shelia watched him from the bed as he dressed, her blue eyes sparkling, her blond hair covering the pink pillow. The white shorts were a little tight, he thought, but she approved. The gaily-coloured gold and red shirt, he thought a little gaudy for a sober mariner, but she laughed his fears away. The long, white stockings were of the type that used to be worn on cargo liners, so they at least felt familiar, as did the white shoes.

He left the apartment a little later, slightly dishevelled, and caught a taxi to Jurong Pier, composing himself for the day ahead. He arrived on the pier just as the *Coseltina* was coming alongside, the rest of the party already waiting at the top of the steps. Two uniformed deck boys helped the guests on board while the skipper held her alongside, the numerous craft coming and going, causing quite a little sea. Hilda was very fetching in a short pair of cream shorts and green blouse with yellow flowers, with a female-type Panama hat to protect her delicate skin from the tropical sun. Mr R was in his usual dress, nondescript shirt and trousers, the smart rig of the New Year's Day party, gone. As soon as everyone was on board, the skipper pulled off the pier, the yacht's place being immediately taken by another.

Introductions were made as the *Coseltina* left the harbour. The two bankers merely took off their ties, while the Salvage Association Surveyor, Mike, whom Tom met on the *Kinos*, entered into the spirit of the day and was dressed more like Tom. The lawyer from London, Sebastian Dick, wore a pair of slacks and a plain, grey shirt but looked relaxed and comfortable, unlike the bankers. Robert wore slacks and a gaily-patterned red shirt and seemed in good spirits. Once into the anchorage, the skipper increased speed and Tom felt invigorated by the rush of still warm,

186

but clean, sea air. The deep water was much clearer than Eastern Anchorage, where the *Sunda* was anchored.

Hilda set to work on the bankers and soon had them in swimming costumes, an assortment of which were kept on board, and rubbing suntan oil into their backs. They loosened up quite considerably and after the first couple of beers, became quite cheerful. She even persuaded her father to change into a pair of shorts she found in the main cabin.

It was about midday when the *Coseltina* anchored off Green Island, where there was a sandy beach. Tom was pleased to see a sailing boat anchor under sail, dropping her sails smartly; a well-trained crew, he thought. A few other boats, all white hulls, were in the anchorage, mainly families with children. The smart, white-uniformed deck boys rigged the laser dinghy but at first there were no takers until Tom could no longer restrain himself and said, 'I can sail.'

It felt so good to be at the helm of a dinghy, dependent on his own resources, revelling in the physical activity and he thoroughly enjoyed his sail. He cursed himself for leaving his sun-glasses behind because the bright sun reflected off the white sail. The lawyer whom Robert informed Tom was a Queens Counsel, encouraged by Tom, went out, now dressed in a pair of red swimming trunks. Hilda persuaded Tom to take her out despite not sailing before. 'You can teach me,' she said. While one of the deck boys acting as cook prepared the curries and food, Tom took Hilda sailing. She was wearing a fetching bikini, which showed off her small but well-proportioned body, and was covered with suntan. Tom changed into a smart, white pair of swimming trunks, which he felt were a little too revealing but Shelia had assured suited him. His wet shorts and shirt were drying on the foredeck.

'Fantastic,' Hilda gushed to the assembled company on their return, the skipper and free deck boy taking the painter and helping Hilda. The boat was allowed to drift aft and made fast leaving the sail up, the *Coseltina* heading into the wind at her anchor. Robert gave Tom a hard look but said nothing. He continued to crack jokes, some of which were quite funny, a can of beer permanently in his hand, keeping the company laughing, although the QC looked as though he had heard enough jokes for one day. The bankers indulged in a swim and were in good form. Hilda continued to sing Tom's praises until he gently told her to stop, she was embarrassing him.

Just before the curries were ready, Hilda was helping the temporary cook, another motor yacht turned up with DB at the helm, his wife and family on board. Wayne Dawson with his family, Tony House, wearing the same picnic gear he wore at the *Jurong* trials were also onboard. DB brought her alongside nicely and she was made fast. The children brightened up the proceedings with their laughter and lunch was delayed while they all, including the old man, went for a swim, the skipper keeping watch and a lifebuoy drifting astern ahead of the laser.

It was a very jolly party for lunch. The crew rigged the white canvas awning over the large cockpit, which kept the heat of the bright sun off some very white bodies, a few of which were developing a hint of red. They were all wearing an array of hats. Sebastian Dick kept looking at Tom, which made him feel quite uncomfortable and he began to think the unthinkable, when there was a lull in the conversation. The children were in a group on the foredeck, laughing and joking.

'I've got it!' exclaimed Sebastian. 'I recognised the name Matravers but I couldn't place it.'

Tom felt a chill in his gut and the curry turned sour in his mouth.

'You were on the *Rada*,' the QC continued. 'I represented the company at the enquiry.'

Tom felt the blood drain from his face and the chill turned into ice, the first flicker of fear brushed over him and all the fun of the day fled, leaving him tongue-tied and speechless.

'You were one of the cadets and you were so self-assured when you gave your evidence, that's why I remembered, still a teenager,' said the QC.

'Yes,' said Tom bluntly, feeling the eyes of the company on him, especially Robert's, and the old man, who looked so surprised. Everyone stopped eating as Sebastian went on, relentlessly, it seemed to Tom.

'She was blown up in the Gulf, a deck passenger ship, with great loss of life. Tom was one of the heroes,' continued the QC. 'I wondered what happened to you and am surprised to see you have become a salvor. I would have run as far inland as I could reach and never see the sea again,' he laughed. 'Life is full of surprises.'

It had given Tom time to pull himself together and he saw a silent Robert continuing to look at him with a quizzical gaze, which Tom knew boded trouble.

'Oh, Tom, how exciting! Do tell us about it, I know you are a good storyteller,' said Hilda gaily, rather out of character, because Tom thought of her as quite a serious young lady.

'No,' said Tom bluntly, and then realising he had sounded very rude, continued, 'many lives were lost and now is not the time or place. We were told not to talk about it. The British were pilloried in the Indian and Pakistani press, despite the disaster being caused by a terrorist bomb. How about I take you out for another sail this afternoon, Hilda?'

'Oh, yes, please,' she answered. 'I did so enjoy it, you are such fun,' which broke the stillness and uncomfortable feeling caused by the revelation.

They all resumed enjoying their curries.

The wind increased a little and there were now mini white horses sparkling like jewels on the green water, the sand golden on the beach ashore, highlighted by the green jungle.

Once lunch was over, the women helped the crew pack up the debris. Tony whispered in Tom's ear, 'There's more to you than meets the eye. We must meet up for a drink and a chat.'

DB's boat and families departed, the children all waving and laughing. Hilda enjoyed her afternoon sail, although she said she had eaten too much curry. Tom was careful not to capsize in the increased breeze. Once the laser was de-rigged and brought on board, the anchor was weighed and the *Coseltina* went on a tour of the Cosel fleet.

The *Singapore* was looking smart and sturdy in Western Anchorage, the tug and barge fleet at the mooring was impressive, but the *Sunda* was the old man's pride and joy, her white hull gleaming with 'Cosel Salvage' painted in large black letters along the sides, looking every inch the thoroughbred, ocean-going salvage tug she was. All traces of the scorching from the exploding tanker were gone, a team from the shipyard had been sent out to give her a new coat of paint. The bankers were impressed and it was then, for Tom, that the second bombshell was exploded that afternoon.

'Captain Matravers,' said the old man formally, as they were returning to Jurong Pier and the bankers were changed back into their more formal dress. 'These two gentlemen represent the bank that is financing the purchase of the UK super tug and, sirs, he is going to be her first Cosel Captain.'

Everyone who heard, clapped, and Tom blushed at this completely unexpected good news.

'Thank you, Mr R,' is all he could think to say and he saw Hilda looking at him, smiling.

'Mind you look after our investment, captain,' said the older one, shaking Tom's hand.

Just before they reached harbour, the QC pulled Tom to one side and said, 'I apologise, Tom, I didn't mean to embarrass or upset you, but I saw your face when I mentioned the *Rada*. It was along time ago, almost fifteen years.'

'Thirteen,' said Tom, woodenly. 'The burnt bodies I saw were not mentioned at the enquiry, but thank you.'

'I see, but not sure I completely understand. However, best of luck in your new profession and look forward to hearing more of you. I have been retained for the *Kinos* salvage.'

So that's why you are on board, said Tom to himself.

'I was impressed with your sailing,' said Sebastian. 'I sail a laser at Hayling Island but as you must have seen, I can't make her fly like you did, and it is a lot warmer here,' he laughed.

'Thanks for that,' said Tom, brightly. 'I've been lucky enough to have sailed all my life.'

'It shows.'

It was after five when the party landed at the pier. The guests and Robert, who was well away, singing songs, squeezed into Mr R's luxury car and were swept away by the chauffeur. Tom thanked the *Coseltina* skipper and crew, and found a taxi while Hilda, being the independent modern lady she was, drove away in her small, white BMW, an expensive car in Singapore.

Hilda was very friendly on the yacht and effusive in thanking Tom for her first sail. She was obviously angling to see him again so he invited her for dinner later in the week, knowing Shelia would be working, but he thought he might be playing with fire. He was glad to be back on board the *Sunda* and able to relax, no longer on his best behaviour, and no more Mr Dickinson.

He was enjoying his breakfast on the bridge, slightly sore from too much sun the previous day, when a message from Ops ruined his plans for the day. He was told to report to the Goodwood Park, the lawyer wished to see him. The brightness faded and he knew it was trouble, but he hardened his heart and resolved he would not be brow-beaten come, what may. He had forced the bully to back down and Tom would keep him there.

Robert greeted him cordially when he met Tom in the lobby, an hour late, looking very much the worse for wear.

'Come along to my suite,' he said, 'just a couple of things to clear up on the *Queen* and you can sign the statement. Susan has been working all weekend.'

'He is too cordial, too nice, he has turned on the charm, but his bloodshot eyes belie it and his fingers are working overtime,' said Tom to himself.

It was after 1100 when they finished, which meant the bar was open.

'A farewell drink, Tom, I will be off at the weekend. Captain Rogers' reports are first class and it won't take me long to finish with him,' said Robert, smiling.

Tom could hardly refuse, despite the unpleasant dig at his reports, so joined him for a beer. They sat at a table rather than the bar and Robert talked about salvage, calling the barman over for more beer.

'I didn't know you were on the *Rada*,' said Robert, pleasantly. 'Must have been a bad experience for a teenager.'

Tom was silent.

'I think we should put something about it in your statements.'

'I don't see why,' said Tom, coldly. 'As I said on the *Coseltina*, the British were pilloried by the press and all sorts of accusations were flying around. I think it better to let sleeping dogs lie, it might get twisted at arbitration.'

'Our QC for the *Kinos* didn't have any problems with it, otherwise he wouldn't have mentioned it.'

'I think that is completely different and anyway, I don't want to have it in my statement,' said Tom, quite forcefully, as yet more beer arrived at the table.

'It will enhance your status and as the lawyer for Cosel I advise it should be in,' said Robert, curtly.

'I don't agree. Too many lives were lost and I don't wish to try and make capital out of their deaths. It was thought a blot on the British, despite the enquiry findings.' said Tom.

'Tell me about it and I can make the final decision,' cajoled Robert, the numerous beers beginning to take their toll.

Tom was silent. He had made up his mind he would not talk about his experiences with this man. He did not trust him. The talk with Jan was a completely different matter.

'Were you frightened?' asked Robert, silkily. 'How did that exploding tanker affect you?'

'It's in my statement.'

'It will definitely enhance your status,' said Robert smoothly, smiling.

'No, Robert, I won't do it, leave it alone,' said Tom harshly, keeping his temper in check.

'Just mention you were on the ship when she was sabotaged,' pressed Robert.

'No,' said Tom firmly. 'Robert, enough is enough.'

'Okay, bloke, your funeral,' said Robert nastily, leaving the table and walking out of the bar.

Tom heaved a sigh of relief, finished off his beer and took a taxi back to Clifford Pier. He poked his head into the pier bar, waited for his eyes to adjust to the gloom and artificial lighting, and was thankful to see Frank's red hair in what appeared to be his daytime place, sipping a beer. It was late afternoon before he finally reached the *Sunda* and went to bed.

CHAPTER 16

Tom was preparing himself to go ashore to meet his date. Miguel somehow inveigled out of him that he was taking Hilda, not Shelia. Tom could have bitten off his tongue when he realised his mistake. Miguel made an extra effort with Tom's shore-going clothing, the white shirt was freshly ironed, and it felt as though the little bugger put starch in it. Tom expressly told him not to starch his shirts the stiffness chafed his skin. The light grey trousers were well pressed and his black shoes gleamed. He put on the matching jacket and was pleased with plain light blue tie.

'You must look good for the chairman's daughter,' burbled Miguel, it apparently being important to him, and Tom wondered how much the crew seemed to know. The bosun put out the steel ladder to make it easier to climb into the zed boat, the first time he had done this for Tom, and that was when Tom knew Miguel had been gossiping. I'll wring his neck, thought Tom, then relaxed and laughed to himself. What the hell does it matter?

Rene, his hair seeming even longer, was just pulling away from the tug at a sedate speed when there was shout from the bridge and Ricky waved a piece of paper at him. They returned alongside and Tom landed on the tow deck at the same time as Ricky, a little out of breath from his unaccustomed exercise.

'Sail immediately full speed, South China Sea.'

The message was signed DB.

'Pedro, give him a crew man. Rene, pick up Captain Jan, usual place.'

An AB hopped into the boat and Rene sped away at his normal full throttle. Tom climbed to the bridge and rang down to the engine room but the chief engineer had heard the buzz and beaten him to it, for Tom heard the powerful diesels start up. He went onto the bridge wing with his binoculars and saw the *Mississippi* was not moving. The light was fading fast and it would soon be dark. Gonzales the chief officer, whose Christian name Tom still did not know, Jesus, the second mate and Alfredo, the third mate, were on the bridge in a state of suppressed excitement. It was a month since the *Kinos* ended and no work since.

'Alfredo, watch the *Mississippi*. Gonzales, pick up the anchor, Jesus, lay a course to pass close to Horsburgh Light and check the tides in the straits,' ordered Tom, as he took off his jacket and tie, laying them down on his chair.

The tug was a bustle of activity and with her engines running, it felt like her heart was beating again. The clank of the chain over the windlass told Tom the anchor was coming in. He could see the radar scanner turning, which meant the radar was switched on, and with the 'click click' of the echo sounder, they were ready to go. Within twenty minutes of the shout, the *Sunda* was underway, and Tom turned the tug to head straight out into the main strait, not wishing to alert the opposition by passing her. He had not

197

switched on the navigation lights and was proceeding at a slow speed until Jan was on board.

'Jesus, where the hell is Rene? Call him up on the radio, he should have been here by now.'

'Okay, Cap,' and he picked up the microphone to the company radio, talking in rapid Tagaloc. It sounded like an argument, when Jesus turned and said, 'Five minutes, Cap.'

'Tell him I am heading south, no lights.'

Tom was steering slowly past the closely-anchored ships, keeping a sharp lookout for country craft, with Alfredo on the bridge wing doing the same, while still monitoring the *Mississippi*.

'*Mississippi* navigation lights on!' called Alfredo, the excitement clear in his voice.

'Hard a-port, helmsman, turn on the navigation lights, Jesus!' ordered Tom, walking towards the engine control levers, which he pushed forward, increasing the speed.

'Midships, steady as she goes,' said Tom. 'Jesus, tell Rene our lights are on and we are heading east.'

Now the opposition were under way, there was no point trying to hide, it was more important to be ahead of her.

'Captain coming,' shouted an excited Alfredo and Tom slowed the tug.

'Captain on board,' said Alfredo a few minutes later, in a calmer voice, and Tom pushed the engine levers to give half speed.

The *Sunda* immediately picked up speed and Tom maintained a careful lookout. Jan appeared on the starboard bridge wing, slightly out of breath from his rush up from the tow deck, took a quick look round and said, 'All mine, Tom, full ahead, both.'

Jan entered the wheel house and sat in his chair and Miguel, who just appeared, handed him a cold tin and picked up Tom's jacket and tie. Tom, pushing the engine levers to full ahead, heard the pop of the tin opening and the satisfied sigh as Jan drained it. The tug quickly picked up speed as did the wash. Jan heaved himself out of his chair and stood by the centre window, giving quiet helm orders as he weaved his way past the anchored shipping. Tom watched the zed boat being stowed in its cradle on the port side, the new crane proving its worth.

Some time later, when almost clear of the anchored ships, Jan gave a long blast on the whistle as they overtook the *Mississippi*. The salute was not returned. The green sidelight appeared, then above it the steaming light and shortly afterwards, with a small alteration of course, the red light appeared as well. They were dead ahead of the opposition.

'Not bad,' said Jan, beer in hand, looking into the darkness ahead, the numerous lights of the ships astern fading.

'On board within half an hour of the call, that Rene is a mad bugger, and the tug underway. Poor Frank will be gnashing his teeth, he was quick though from his seat in the bar,' and he gave a great guffaw. 'Life is for enjoying, Tom, enjoy it!'

Their wash, which had rocked the opposition tug when they passed, did not disturb the two new LPG carriers laid up, huge ships with their ugly, immense cylinders just visible in the darkness.

'The tide is favourable,' said Tom.

'Much stronger on the Indon side, starboard five,' said Jan.

'Starboard five,' repeated Pablo, a short, stocky man, dressed in the inevitable jeans and sweat shirt, a good steady man, thought Tom. The bow of the *Sunda* swung to starboard, just missing a fishing boat.

'Midships, steady as you go,' ordered Jan, moving his bulk back into his chair on the starboard side of the wheelhouse, the engine controls just in front of him.

'We don't know the position of the ship yet,' said Tom, but they both heard the clatter of the telex over radio from Ricky's wireless room. Someone had left the chartroom door open, letting in light from the alleyway and Tom now shut it.

The big tug raced through the night at a good sixteen knots plus two for the tide, making eighteen over the ground. Tom watched Jesus put a position on the chart from the cross bearings he took from the bridge wing gyro repeaters. They were on track. Ricky appeared through the door, framed in the alleyway light, and handed Tom a telex message. He looked at it under the chart light.

'Melody, 10,000 GRT drifting.'

'Plot this, Jesus,' said Tom, handing him the message.

The chartroom door opened again and Gonzales appeared. Jesus spoke to him in Tagaloc, pointing at the chart. Tom walked into the wheelhouse as Jan popped open another can.

'Jesus is plotting the position, a 10,000 gross ton ship,' said Tom.

Jan was silent. The lookout on the bridge wing reported yet another light.

'Straits busy tonight. I would like to get over to the Indon side into the eastbound traffic zone and more tide,' said Jan.

Jesus and Gonzales came into the wheelhouse and Jesus said, 'The position is in the dangerous zone off the Philippines.'

Jan got up from his chair, knocking over an empty can, which he picked up and threw out of the door, crying, 'Watch her, Tom!'

'Have a look, Tom,' he said when he came out of the chartroom. 'I think we should head up the Palawan passage, the inshore route. Anyway, I am going over to the Indonesian side,' and he gave a helm order. The tug heeled slightly and then steadied as he gave another order.

Tom looked at the chart. The straight line distance was considerably shorter but they would have to go round to the west and outside the dangerous area and into the roughest seas. Whichever route they took the dangerous area was clearly marked 'un-surveyed reefs.'

'It's rough out there,' said Jan from his chair, his voice raised over the noise of the tug at sea. 'Look at the weather report, strong monsoon and gale force winds further north.'

'Yes,' said Tom, walking back into the wheelhouse. Jan was standing looking out of the centre window. A tanker in ballast was passing close by on the port side heading towards Singapore. The tug crossed the Straits and joined the loaded tankers and container ships bound east. Jan looked into the radar and gave a new course to the helmsman. He then shut the starboard wheelhouse door saying, 'Shut the door, Tom, let the air conditioning do its work.' He grunted as he sat down. 'That feels better, I don't like being on the wrong side of the Straits at night.'

'Will our better speed overcome the shorter but rougher distance, is the question,' said Tom, as they started overtaking a large loaded tanker, her length difficult to see until her mast head steaming light appeared. Miguel turned up, carrying a tray, which he put down on top of the flag locker beside Jan.

'Thank you, Miguel,' said Jan.

'Captain Tom eat in the mess room?' asked the mess man.

'Yes, ten minutes, Miguel.'

Miguel disappeared and Jan said, 'We will have to slow down to normal full ahead, Francisco is overriding the governor at the moment. Barry would have a heart attack if he knew,' and he laughed. 'Better ring down now, Tom.'

'If we go the shortest distance,' continued Jan, as Tom rang down to the engine room, 'and we still don't have a position, except off the Philippines. We will be plugging straight into a very strong monsoon, gale force winds and you know what It can be like from your days with Indo China. We would have to slow down further otherwise we may damage the tug. If we cross over to the Palawan Passage, the sea will be on our port side but we will be able to maintain speed, through the Passage. If we go outside, and the casualty is further south than we think, we might be the wrong side of the dangerous area. The *Mississippi* is much smaller than us and he will have to go the Palawan route. We are a good couple, if not three knots faster than him, especially in heavy weather, so we will arrive there first.'

'I agree,' said Tom.

'Go and enjoy your dinner. I am staying up here until we pass Horsburgh, and are on course for Palawan. You better stand watch with Alfredo, see what he is like.'

'Understood, Jan,' and Tom left to go below. The plates and cutlery were rattling and shaking on the mess room table, despite the damp tablecloth Miguel spread for Tom, as he sat down. A little later, the vibration reduced and the rattling stopped, so Francisco must have slowed down, thought Tom. He did not like the room, finding it sterile and cold, and thought a couple of pictures on the bulkheads would make a big difference.

The swell was felt well before Horsburgh Lighthouse and the *Sunda* started pitching, increasing slowly the further north she ran, until just outside the lighthouse she was shipping water over the bow, the big flare deflecting most of it but the occasional crash hitting the wheelhouse windows. As soon as Jan altered course for the Palawan Passage, the pitching reduced dramatically but she started rolling, a quick, quite violent movement, indicating the good stability essential for a tug.

The passage to the dangerous area was uneventful but fast. The rolling stopped when they turned north eastwards into the prevailing strong monsoon and although there was quite a sea running, it was nothing as bad as indicated by the forecasts for the South China Sea. A couple of container ships reported containers lost overboard, which suggested how rough it was. It was blowing force seven to eight in the passage where they were steaming at full speed, and up to force nine in the main part of the China Sea, a very strong monsoon. The weather was foul, with low scudding clouds and drizzle, at times reducing visibility and making the sea, despite the white horses, grey and uninviting.

The third morning out was miserable, but the drizzle stopped. It was rough, the sea resembling the North Sea in its dirty greyness, the breaking waves seeming colourless under the leaden sky, some spray coming on board over the flared bow. Jan and Tom were in the wheelhouse with the doors closed. Alfredo was keeping a look-out and Jesus was glued to the radar, Gonzales standing close to Alfredo, binoculars hanging round his neck. A look-out was posted on the foremast, standing on the un-railed platform, his safety line clipped on to a ring on the mast, the movement much more lively up there than on deck. Two look-outs were above the bridge on either side of the monkey island. Just north of the latitude of Kota Kinabalu, Jan altered course north westwards, turning the knob on the auto pilot, steaming into the dangerous area full of unmarked reefs.

'Open the door, Alfredo!' ordered Jan, while he opened the starboard wheelhouse door. 'We should be seeing her soon and we are entering the reef area, keep your eyes skinned.'

He pulled back the engine control levers to about three quarters speed, about eleven knots, and immediately the motion was easier and no more spray came over the bow. She rolled more with the sea and swell on the starboard beam.

'I don't like it in this area,' said Jan, uncharacteristically worried. 'We will hit a reef before we see it, especially with no sun unless the seas are breaking on it.'

The look-outs were all carefully briefed. Jan walked out onto the starboard wing and shouted up at them, 'Keep your eyes peeled!'

There was a waved acknowledgement from the fore-mast and an, 'Okay, Cap,' from the monkey island.

'The position they have given is only a DR, a dead reck-oning, and they may not have taken sights for days,' said Jan, back inside the wheelhouse.

Tom read all the messages as well. 'Why not ask him to send a radio signal and Ricky can home in on it?'

'Your idea, Tom, tell him to do it.'

Tom came back into the wheelhouse after instructing Ricky, to hear the raised voice of Jesus, 'Echo ten miles on the port bow.'

'Message from base,' reported Tom. 'Owners say first tug on sight gets the LOF.'

'Echo proceeding same way as us but slower,' said Jesus, plotting pencil in hand, 'so it's not the casualty.'

'Agreed,' said Jan, 'she will be drifting southwards, not north. I wonder if it is the Manila mob? This part of the ocean is claimed by the Filipinos.'

At that moment, the voice of a Filipino came over the VHF channel 16, calling the *Melody*, but there was no re-ply.

'Must be the *Bintour*,' said Jan, with disgust. 'I did not know that ancient thing was still afloat.'

'She is,' said Gonzales, laughing, which surprised Tom as it was the first time he heard the man laugh. Gonzales was normally quite a morose person; must be the tension, thought Tom.

'Captain Hannibal saw her in Manila when he was on leave.'

'Damn, it is turning into a lottery,' said Jan with resignation, 'but we have to win it.'

CHAPTER 17

'Faint echo, twelve miles on our beam,' said Jesus, excitedly.

There was a crash in the chartroom as the door was flung open, almost tearing it off its hinges.

'Bearing 290 relative!' shouted Ricky, his normal placid self galvanised by the chase. '*Bintour* offering LOF.'

'Tell them we have him on our radar and will be there first,' shouted Jan, leaping out of his chair. 'Tom the VHF, Gonzales take the wheel, hard a port steer for the echo. Jesus, tell him when it is ahead,' and he pushed the engine levers forward, flat on the consul. Black smoke poured from the funnel on the port side as the tug surged ahead. She spun round under full helm and power, her bow thrown up by the sea, and lurched heavily to port.

'Coming ahead now!' shouted Jesus, his voice muffled by the radar cover.

'*Melody, Melody*! This is the salvage tug, *Sunda*. Offer you our assistance on the terms of Lloyds Open Form,' said Tom into the VHF microphone, his voice calm.

Silence. Then the voice of an agitated Filipino on the radio offering the same terms for the tug *Bintour*.

The tension on the bridge was electric, the gloom and greyness of the overcast morning dissipated, and the drizzle which just started again, un-noticed.

'Keep your eyes skinned for breakers!' roared Jan from the bridge wing, as the tug rolled in the sea and swell, an occasional wave flooding the tow deck.

'Pray, Tom, the reefs here are uncharted,' said Jan, returning into the wheelhouse, his moustache appearing to bristle in the dampness, his hair in disarray from the wind outside.

There was a cry, almost a scream, from the foremast.

'Breakers ahead, Cap!' an arm pointing frantically and then from above, 'Breakers ahead!' shouted voices, almost in unison.

'Hard a starboard,' said Jan loudly but calmly. 'Can you see them, Tom?' he asked his voice now cool, which had a calming effect on the others on the bridge.

'On the port bow now,' said Tom, 'just a few breaking waves but quite clear.'

'The *Bintour* must have turned,' said Jesus excitedly, his head out of the radar. 'She is approaching rapidly.'

'Ship no tug on the port bow!' shouted the foremast lookout.

'Hard a port and steady,' said the calm voice of Jan.

The *Sunda* steadied on the new course and the white waters of the breaking seas could now be clearly seen on the port side, but she was steaming away from the casualty.

'Damn, I've gone the wrong way! Hard a port, Gonzales, can't let them get this one.'

The tug took a sea over the foredeck as she turned rapidly back towards the casualty, heeling with the tightness of the turn. Another sea hit her side. The breakers were rapidly moving ahead and then crossed the bow and onto the starboard side.

'Twenty fathoms!' shouted Alfredo, whose eyes were glued to the depth sounder.

'Fifteen.'

'Switch to feet,' urged Tom.

'Sixty feet.'

'Fifty feet.'

The depth was shoaling rapidly but the tug was still turning and the breakers were on the starboard beam. The *Sunda* was turning away from the danger, the reef between them and the Filipino tug.

'Forty feet,' Alfredo's voice raised an octave.

'Thirty feet,' and there was not a sound in the wheelhouse, except the remorseless 'click click' of the depth sounder.

'Twenty-five feet,' Alfredo's voice, almost falsetto, but the tug was now steaming away from the breakers, which were out on the starboard quarter.

'Bottom sighted!' screamed the mast look out.

'Midships!' ordered Jan, still calm and unruffled.

Tom admired him even more; the man was facing the loss of his command with apparent equanimity.

'Ship four points on the starboard bow!' shouted the lookout

'Twenty feet!' screeched Alfredo.

Tom looked astern and could see a huge, breaking wave following the tug, built up over the shallow water. There was only five feet beneath the keel. Jan moved the engine levers into the upright and the stern immediately lifted the wave, falling away.

'Twenty-three feet,' gasped Alfredo, and Jan hissed as though he had been holding his breath, the sound like a deflating tyre.

'Twenty-four feet,' said the calmer voice of Alfredo and then, 'thirty feet.'

Jan pushed the levers forward again, the breakers now well abaft the starboard beam.

'Steer for the *Melody*, Gonzales,' said Jan. 'Take her, Tom, I've got to go below for a second.'

The *Melody* was now clearly visible, a large, modern ship with the accommodation aft. There was still no reply to the messages, the VHF was silent. The *Sunda* was now some miles closer to the casualty than the *Bintour*.

Jan returned to the bridge wearing a different pair of trousers. 'That feels better,' he laughed, as he took a cold beer from Miguel, who had appeared with a tray. 'Must be getting old, first time that has happened to me.' He picked up the binoculars and studied the fast-approaching, drifting ship.

'Not answering me anymore!' called Ricky from the chartroom, closing the door with a bang.

'Good heavens, there are breakers almost beside her! She will run aground on a lee shore unless we are quick,' exclaimed Jan.

'Two miles,' said Jesus.

Tom was studying the ship as well. 'Looks like port anchor is down,' he said, his voice well under control, hiding his excitement and apprehension.

'Yes, but not on the bottom, otherwise she would have swung bows into the wind,' said Jan.

Jan continued studying the ship and Tom wondered when he might slow down. The *Sunda* was still at full speed making, fifteen knots, rolling quite heavily at times and shipping water aft. The sea and swell increased the further they steamed west.

'Right,' said Jan purposefully. 'You can see the reef on her port side, the *Melody* is in effect sailing towards it. Do I dare,' he paused, 'and risk all?'

He was silent for a moment, then continued, 'We have no communication with the ship, so must assume no help from the crew. The *Bintour* is not far behind. I have to go inside, between the reef and the casualty if we are to beat her and save the casualty.'

He was quiet a moment, then continued in a firm voice, full of confidence.

'Yes I dare, and risk all. You hitch on to the hanging cable as we pass and I can then cross her bow and out to

212

sea, turning her so she will be sailing away from the reef. We can then adjust the connection as required, once clear of the reef. The Manila tug is not as manoeuvrable as we are and we will be connected before she can do anything. You go aft, Tom, where Pedro and the crew are waiting. Gonzales, you stay on the bridge with me. I am going to switch over to the aft manoeuvre position.'

The ship was close now, as Jan slowed down and Tom moved quickly aft and told Pedro of the plan. A suitable piece of wire joined together to form a loop, the strop, was already on the tow deck. It was connected to the wire forerunner, which was in place right aft. The deck was wet from the occasional wave, which came on board.

'Strop all ready,' said Pedro. 'I will put it round the cable,' and he issued a string of commands in Tagaloc.

Jan was at the aft control as the *Sunda* passed the stern of the ship. Some figures stood on the bridge, on the port side, the black hull rolling heavily, the waves almost reaching her deck. The roar from the breakers on the reef could clearly be heard. Tom firmly brushed aside the first flicker of fear as he wondered if Jan had left it too late to go between the ship and the reef.

He just made it as they passed close to the *Melody*'s hull. Tom thought it most odd that he could see no men on the forecastle and Jan's assumption of no help was correct. Jan slowed more and altered to close the bow. For some reason, Tom looked up at Jan from his position by Pedro.

They were standing right aft, ready to hook onto the cable and connect the strop.

He saw Jan fall. One minute he was standing rock like, his hands on the controls, looking forward on the starboard side, his hair blowing in the wind and the next minute, he was not there but flat on his back on the catwalk gratings.

Tom instantly saw the tug was swinging too far to starboard and would hit, rather than pass the casualty, but no one was at the controls. There was no sign of Gonzales. The roar from the breakers seemed to intensify.

He never moved so fast in his life. The rolling tug might have been as steady as a rock as he flew across the wet and slippery tow deck, up the ladder to the boat deck and then leapt for the rails on the catwalk, heaving himself up and over until he was standing by the controls.

He had no idea how he had managed to get there, but he was calm as he quickly assessed the situation. He instinctively knew what to do and increased power on the starboard engine and slowed the port, leaving the rudder amidships. The tug swiftly turned but she was too close to the black hull with its high accommodation, which rolled and seemed to be right on top of the *Sunda*. For a second, Tom was thankful that the lifeboat had been removed, for it certainly would have been crushed. He increased speed on both engines, the breaking waves on the reef seemed even louder and closer as the tug shot ahead and along the hull. The bow was passed and he went full astern on both engines to stop the tug with the stern alongside the hanging cable, hoping the anchor would not touch bottom or be too close to the surface and hit his starboard propeller. He managed to hold the tug stationary, long enough for Pedro, assisted by an AB, to pass the strop round the cable, which was rising and falling as the casualty rolled, and shackle it back onto the forerunner.

Pedro gave the thumbs up and they moved clear of the wire as Tom went hard a starboard on the small helm lever, and full ahead on the port engine, swinging the tug round the bow and heading out to sea on both engines, slowing down as he regained control.

Tom was suddenly aware of a presence beside him and turned to see Gonzales, kneeling alongside Jan's body. The unblinking staring eyes were most disturbing, along with the slight movement of the body as the tug rolled and pitched. He turned back and concentrated on the tug and tow. He could not afford a mistake or both the casualty and the *Sunda* would be on the reef. Tom thought the reef must be steep to, or the anchor would have touched bottom. Miguel suddenly materialised and was kneeling next to the body, shaking his head, his fingers on Jan's neck and then he pulled the eye lids down, shutting off the staring eyes forever.

'He is dead, heart attack probably,' he said quietly, and burst into tears.

Tom tore his eyes away from the corpse of his friend, and watched as the last of the forerunner slithered over the greased towing gunwale, followed by the shackled connection to the tow-wire, making a clanging sound. The tug pitched as a larger wave than usual passed under the hull and he had to increase power. The forerunner tightened, the towing wire lifted off the tow deck and the ship's cable moved from the vertical, towards the horizontal. The bow of the *Melody* started to turn and there was a cheer from the tow deck. Tom was as tense as he had ever been, totally concentrating on what he was doing.

Pedro knew what Jan intended to do and did not slack out any tow wire until Tom pulled the bow of the casualty round through the eye of the wind and she was on the other tack, sailing away from the reef. Tom increased power and saw Pedro paying out the tow wire. The ship pitched in the heavy swell and as she turned further to starboard, started to roll again.

'Secure Pedro!' he shouted down to the tow deck and Tom, still concentrating, towed the casualty clear of the reef when the tragedy hit him as he looked down at Jan's face, lying on the catwalk, his eyes closed, looking quite peaceful, as though asleep. He started to shiver and shake with delayed shock, and the violent physical activity reaching the controls. It all happened so quickly.

'You okay, Cap? There's blood on your shirt,' said Miguel, who was still with the body, having folded Jan's hands across his chest. Gonzales had disappeared. 'Don't worry about Jan, his spirit is still here.'

Tom looked down and saw blood, pulling out the shirt to inspect his front, which was heavily bruised, the skin on his stomach broken in places. He must have grazed himself climbing over the rails onto the catwalk. Miguel saw the wound and, holding on to the rail, got to his feet. He felt all round the bruised and bloody area with his hands, completely surprising Tom and said, 'No bones broken, I fix you later.'

Two AB's carried the stretcher along the catwalk, Gonzales watching from the bridge. Tom pulled himself together, tucking in his shirt and shouted, 'I am switching to bridge control, keep her on this course and speed.'

Gonzales raised his hand in acknowledgement and shouted back, 'Okay, Cap,' the wind and noise from the powerful engines making it difficult to hear anything.

Gonzales now took control of the tug from the bridge and Tom felt they were free from the immediate danger. He looked down at the corpse of his friend and mentor, the moustache still luxuriant, his mouth closed, never to give one of his loud guffaws. It seemed impossible that someone so full of life and fun could so suddenly be gone. The AB's opened up the stretcher and then lifted the body onto it, almost falling as the tug gave a lurch. They closed it and tightened the straps, securing it in like a straightjacket.

'I was a nurse,' said Miguel, firmly wiping the tears from his face. 'I will prepare his body for burial.'

Tom tried to think to clear his head, detach himself from the grief he felt. Suddenly, he went back in time. He was in the lifeboat as a teenager, with another body face down in the bottom, shaking it until he realised it was dead. When he managed to roll the corpse over, the face was quite composed, like Jan's. He was faced with the quandary then, but the teenager had not hesitated and insisted that the Japanese crew take it on board and they, too, had used a similar stretcher. With a huge effort, Tom brought himself back to the present.

'Miguel, we can put Jan in the freezer? His wife and children will need to see him before they bury him. It is very important for them,' said Tom, his voice raised over the noise of the engines.

'Yes, Captain. I will prepare him and wrap him in sheets. I fix the cook.'

Miguel followed the AB's along the catwalk, dry-eyed now, and Tom brought up the rear. The tow was following well, heading into the wind.

Once on the bridge, the enormity of what had happened hit Tom and he almost started to weep, but he was now in command and with a supreme effort, held himself in check. The moment was broken when a voice on the VHF brought him back to reality and the present.

'*Sunda*, this is the *Bintour*. We have been awarded the LOF, please hand over the tow.'

He grabbed the microphone, the sudden rage he felt almost causing him to lose control. He was about to shout some obscenity when reason prevailed and he put the transmitter down and said nothing.

'Ricky!' he shouted. The chart room door had been left hooked open by the stretcher bearers. 'Get DB on the telex, quick. Have you told them Captain Jan is dead?'

'Been connected to Berne radio and told them,' Ricky called back.

'Well done.'

Gonzales was well in control, the tug almost hove to and clear of the reef. Tom saw Jesus had plotted the position of the reef they nearly hit on a piece of paper, relative to the reef the *Melody* had been drifting towards. The chart was too small-scale and the reefs were not on it, just part of the dangerous area.

'You happy with our position, Jesus?' asked Tom.

'No problem, Cap, I know where the reefs are and we will miss them.'

'Very good,' and he carried on into the radio room and sat down in the spare chair to compose himself. He picked up a pencil and, taking out his notebook, he sketched out the events as he remembered them; so much had happened in such a short time. Miguel appeared with the first aid box and Tom opened his shirt. The iodine hurt and Tom was about to remonstrate.

'DB on the line,' said Ricky.

'Tell him we are connected to the anchor chain,' and looking at his notes, 'half an hour ago. *Bintour* on site and claiming they have the LOF.'

Ricky typed away and the telex chattered and clattered, amazing machine, thought Tom. Miguel told him he did not need any bandages or plaster and left the radio room. A reply was quickly returned.

'LOF awarded to first on site so you have it, especially as you connected. I will deal with *Manila*,' which Tom thought sounded very reassuring.

'Captain Smit died, apparently of heart attack, while making difficult and dangerous connection,' typed in Ricky on the telex over radio to Tom's dictation.

There was silence as the machine stopped. Tom continued dictating.

'Intend bring body to port for passage to Singapore for family, now in freezer.'

'Agreed, congratulations,' came back the answer.

'Where do you want casualty?'

'Awaiting owners' instructions,' came back the reply.

'Okay, Ricky, sign off. Thanks.'

Tom remained seated, happy that they were safe for now. He thought long and hard, then picking up the pencil, he wrote in his note book, his tears blurring the page as he wrote.

'Gerda, Jan died doing what he loved best, manoeuvring his tug to save a ship running aground in bad weather. He was a brave and honourable man. Mourn not his loss but celebrate the good times you had together and your three wonderful children.'

He pushed the paper across to Ricky who was busy writing his log, rose from the chair and left the radio room.

He stood outside the door of the chart room for a while to compose himself, feeling very alone. His mentor, his friend and teacher, was gone.

He walked firmly and purposefully onto the bridge. He was in command and had a tug, crew and casualty to look after.

CHAPTER 18

Something was wrong. Tom could not bring himself to sit in Jan's chair, so he remained in the chief officer's, on the port side. The *Melody* was silent despite repeated calls and offers on the VHF by the Filipino tug until Tom called them and told the Captain, 'Cosel Salvage are salvors in possession. My office is talking to Manila.'

They were clear of the reef and hove to waiting for a destination but Tom was not happy to remain there for long. He wanted to be out of the reef area before nightfall. The casualty was still silent and there was no sign of life, apart from the people they saw on the bridge while passing to make the connection.

'What would Jan have done?' thought Tom, then said to himself, 'No, it's what I should do, Jan is gone.'

Miguel appeared with a can of cold beer but Tom said, 'Thanks, Miguel, I am not Jan. I prefer tea and if I want a beer, I will ask.'

'Captain Jan is in the freezer,' said Miguel quite cheerfully, which surprised Tom.

'You cheerful, Miguel? I thought you liked Captain Jan,'

'Of course I liked him, he was a real man, but he gone. We should bury him at sea,' said Miguel, seriously.

'His family need him,' Tom pointed out.

'It's just dead meat now,' said Miguel, still serious, which shocked Tom and it showed in his face.

'It's the spirit that matters and I am sure he has not gone yet, he still here to make sure we okay,' continued Miguel, still deadly serious.

The tug pitched quite heavily as a strong breaking swell passed and Tom stood up to watch the tow. She pitched, but the motion was quite gentle at this low speed. It was still overcast but the drizzle had stopped, the sea now leaden. Tom felt the germ of an idea stir; he simply could not stay here. Then it came to him and it was quite clear what he should do.

He walked back into the wheelhouse and into the chartroom where Jesus was writing up the log, his face serious, concentrating.

'Lay off a course to Labuan, Jesus,' said Tom, 'make sure we miss that reef.'

'I only have a DR but I know where the reef is relative to the other one. No worry, Cap, we won't hit it,' said Jesus, smiling, his white teeth prominent.

'Alfredo, tell Gonzales to send a lookout up the foremast, I'm altering course. The wind and sea will be on our port side. Make sure the tow wire is free running. You understand?'

'Okay, Cap,' said Alfredo brightly, repeating what Tom said. He was younger than Jesus, his face fresh and unlined. He was quick witted and learning fast.

Tom slowly increased power to about half, the tow wire tightening satisfactorily, lifting the chain out of the water, the anchor still not visible. As the *Mercury* picked up speed, the chain went down back into the water. It was clear that a good deal of cable was out and the reef where the *Melody* almost fetched up was very steep to, or the anchor would have touched bottom.

'Starboard easy, Rene,' said Tom, noting Rene's long hair was neatly tied into a pigtail, keeping it off his face. He moved from the starboard wheelhouse door near the engine controls, and walked to the wing where he could clearly see the tow and tow wire. There was a man on the tow deck, greasing the towing gunwale.

'Keep your head down!' shouted Tom. 'Midships, Rene.'

But the tow wire started to move towards the unsuspecting man. Why is he there, thought Tom, when I told Gonzales we were altering course?

'Hard a port, Rene!' shouted Tom urgently, and Rene frantically spun the big wheel, realising something was wrong. He pressed the button, sounding the ship's electric horn and the man looked up at the sound to see Tom waving madly, indicating he should duck. He fell to the deck as the wire passed over but Tom did not see whether it hit him or not. The tug started turning to port under the hard a port rudder and the wire passed back over where the man was lying on the deck.

'Midships, Rene,' said Tom in a more normal voice. He saw the man pick himself up off the deck and, keeping his head down, run off the tow deck. Tom gave a huge sigh of relief and started the turn again with no-one on the tow deck.

'Bring her round easy to the new course, Rene,' said Tom. 'Silly fool on the tow deck nearly lost his head.'

He returned to the wing to watch the tow wire and tow. Alfredo returned and an AB was climbing the foremast.

'The reef should be on the port side!' shouted Tom, and the lookout raised his arm in acknowledgement as he clipped himself on.

'Did you tell Gonzales we were altering course, Alfredo?' asked Tom sharply, watching the casualty beginning to turn, the tow wire was out on the starboard beam.

'Yes, Captain,' replied Alfredo.

'The reef does not show up on the radar, too much clutter from the sea,' said Jesus, looking up from the screen.

'Keep a sharp look out, Alfredo,' ordered Tom.

'On course,' reported Rene, and Tom saw the tow settle down and take station on the port quarter, her aft accommodation acting as a sail, pushing the bow up into the wind.

Tom felt quite happy with her there, rather than yawing. He walked back into the wheelhouse and sat down firmly in Jan's chair, emphasising to himself he was the Captain, the port chair being for the chief officer. Ricky walked into the wheelhouse, his face rather pasty compared to the rest of the crew who spent time out in the fresh air and sun.

'Weather forecast, Cap, still the same. Strong monsoon.'

'Thanks, Ricky,' said Tom, taking the flimsy. 'Tell Singapore something wrong on casualty, no communication nor sign of life, am proceeding Labuan Bay. Strong monsoon, presently wind NE force 8 rough sea.'

'OK, Cap, I will bring it out when I've typed it.'

Tom nodded and Ricky turned and left the wheelhouse. Tom rose from his chair and walked out onto the port wing to look at the casualty. She was in the same position and he was satisfied all was well with the tow, if not on board her.

'Breakers on the port bow!' shouted the lookout, as Alfredo did the same, rushing out and pointing. Tom lifted his binoculars to his eyes and, adjusting the focus, saw them, spray spouting up into the air.

'Sixty fathoms!' shouted Jesus. Gonzales appeared on the bridge wing from the boat deck.

'Sorry about the AB, it was Pablo, on the tow deck. It was a misunderstood instruction,' he said.

'Well, he nearly lost his head,' said Tom sharply, 'let it be a warning. Captain Jan never lost a man in all his years in command and I don't intend to start now.'

'Fifty fathoms,' shouted Jesus, his voice rising.

Tom shook his head as though to clear his mind from the near death of Pablo. He thought about the the shoaling water, the hanging anchor worrying him because he did not know how much cable was out. There was no communication with the casualty so he could not tell them to heave it in.

'Starboard twenty, Rene,' ordered Tom, thinking to turn the casualty away from the shoaling water, as the *Melody* was closer to the reef than the *Sunda*.

'Forty fathoms!' shouted Jesus, with real concern in his voice.

Tom saw the vertical hanging chain begin to lead aft and the tow wire tightened. The anchor has touched bottom, thought Tom. The tug was still turning to starboard, the tow wire moving amidships as the bow of the *Melody* started to turn to port under the pull from the anchor on the bottom. The main tow wire tightened even more, and the chain from the bow of the casualty was almost horizontal.

'Midships, steady as she goes,' said Tom, turning his face to the wheelhouse door so Rene could hear.

'Steady,' said Rene and spun the wheel.

The *Melody* was still following but much further out on the port quarter and the *Sunda* had slowed down, even though Tom had not touched the engine controls held back by the dragging anchor.

'Forty-five fathoms,' called a relieved Jesus, and Tom moved back into the wheelhouse and over to the engine controls, pushing the two levers forward to increase power. He walked back to the port side and watched the tow from the doorway through his binoculars and saw the port anchor cable tend off to the port bow, indicating the bow was being pulled to port.

'Fifty fathoms,' and Tom knew they were in the clear.

He was sweating profusely, his heart pounding. Miguel appeared with a mug of tea but Tom said, 'Cold coffee, Miguel,' who smiled, and produced a can from his pocket.

Tom continued watching, after taking the opened can and drinking, handing it back to the waiting mess man. He saw the chain swing back to the vertical; the anchor was off the bottom. He sat in his Captain's chair and called to Gonzales, who was still on the port bridge wing.

'We are clear back into deep water,' said Tom. 'I'm going to slow right down and let the tow come up to us, hoping the strop will slip down the chain to the anchor, we then have proper control. I can keep the anchor off the bottom and we can shorten the tow wire to allow for the amount of chain out, which I estimate at about four shackles.'

'Good idea, Cap, maybe I slacken the tow wire at the same time?' he queried.

Tom thought a little.

'Yes,' he said.

Gonzales walked out through the chartroom and Tom moved to the controls. With the controls on the starboard side in front of his chair, and the tow on the port quarter, it was difficult to coordinate the slowdown, so he told Jesus to man the levers while he watched the tow.

'Sixty fathoms,' said Alfredo, who was now watching the depth sounder.

Jesus moved the levers to Tom's commands and the tow, pitching and rolling, slowly approached the tug, the bow still tending to port as the wind blew on the aft accommodation. The chain from the bow to the strop slowly moved into the vertical position and Gonzales, standing at the stern, signalled to Pedro, who was slacking the tow wire, which was pinned between the raised dolly pins, the two movable pins on top of the towing gunwale. The tow deck was occasionally awash as a wave came on board. The bow was very close to the tug and Gonzales gave the 'thumbs up' signal and said into his radio, 'I think it has slipped down, Cap.'

Tom told Jesus to increase speed and Gonzales moved forward into the shelter of the towing drum house and off the tow deck. The dolly pins were lowered and the wire was free running again. The speed was slowly increased once the tow wire was secured until Tom decided about three quarter power was enough. He set the course to Labuan. The anchor appeared briefly at the surface so Tom knew the strop was near or around it. The *Melody* stayed out on the port quarter as before, and followed well.

'The tow is following well. Jesus, it's your watch, put her on automatic steering and thank you, Alfredo, you can go below,' said Tom.

The tow settled well and Tom relaxed in his chair with a fresh cup of tea. It was still a dull and dreary day, the tug's pitching and rolling much reduced by the tow wire. He was suddenly almost overwhelmed by the loss of Jan and felt so sad for Gerda and the children, who so obviously doted on him. Tom made a conscious effort to thrust such thoughts from his mind and concentrate on his charges.

He thought it very odd that there was still no sign of life on the casualty and no communication. By nightfall they were well clear of the dangerous area and into the Palawan Passage traffic. The *Melody* switched on her navigation lights but Tom was unable to instruct them to turn off the white steaming lights, so he sent a TTT, warning other ships of his tow.

Base sent a message which Ricky brought out as night was falling.

'Owners lost communication with *Melody*. You are not, repeat not, to make an attempt to board casualty. We have chartered *Mississippi* to pick up police contingent to board vessel on arrival Labuan,' and the message went on to give the anchorage co-ordinates.

The *Bintour* stayed with them until dusk and then turned northwards. Back to Manila, thought Tom. The VHF remained silent. He cat-napped through the night, the tow continuing to follow well in the reducing sea and swell, the strop holding firm. The three Filipinos were competent enough watch-keepers and Tom left them to it.

Miguel brought him toast and tea at dawn, with the sun rising over Malaysian Borneo, the sky almost clear of cloud, which gave a good lift to his spirits.

'Captain's cabin ready for you, Captain,' said Miguel. 'I pack Captain Jan's things and clean.'

Tom had not said a word about moving cabins, and surmised there was much more to Miguel than met the eye. It was time to move on; Jan was not coming back; he was the captain now.

'Thank you, Miguel. You told me you were a nurse. How come you're mess man on a salvage tug?'

Miguel's face closed in and he shut his eyes and Tom thought he was not going to reply.

'I was a good nurse,' he said firmly, opening his eyes and looking at Tom. 'I train and am qualified, I pass all the exams. Someone died and the doctors blamed me, but it is not my fault. I no strong man like Captain Jan and run away to sea. I lucky to get job and good captain so I look after you now.'

He turned and left, leaving Tom wondering at the vagaries and vicissitudes of life.

Tom showered and changed into the clean whites Miguel laid out in the bedroom of the spotlessly clean cabin. All trace of Jan was gone, his own few pictures were hanging on the bulkhead.

The convoy entered Labuan Bay late in the afternoon and Tom ordered the tow to be shortened so the anchor cable did not drag on the bottom. The *Mississippi* was waiting at the anchorage, her ensign at half mast, as was the *Sunda's*. He told Frank over the VHF about Jan and he could go alongside the casualty at any time. No one seemed to know what was wrong on the *Melody* and the police on his tug were armed.

As Tom slowed so the anchor went deeper into the water, and Pedro slacked out the tow wire until certain it was on the bottom, the *Melody*, overran it at first, but fell back in the light breeze. Tom anchored the tug, while still connected, noting the *Mississippi* was alongside the casualty and presumed the police were on board.

Sometime later, a rubber boat was launched from the *Mississippi* and Tom could see the red hair of Frank, sitting upright on the middle thwart, the boat being driven at a very sedate speed. Rene, who was on the bridge, laughed. Pedro saw the boat and rigged the metal boarding ladder.

Miguel served the cold beer in the captain's air-conditioned day room, Tom and Frank comfortable in the arm chairs, nuts and crisps on the table.

'The head policeman, a very smart man, told me they would be taking the entire crew ashore with the dead body after the initial interviews.'

'Dead body?' said Tom, surprised, thinking of Jan in the freezer.

'Yes, the captain,' said Frank, making the most of the moment. 'Unfortunately, they did not put him in the freezer and he has been some days in his cabin, so you can imagine the smell.'

Tom took a sip from his glass.

'I don't know the whole story yet, but no doubt on the way into port I will find out. However, you will have a dead ship so perhaps you had better get your mob on board once the police leave and secure the engine room?' said Frank

'Thanks for that. It will be dark, maybe I will go alongside,' said Tom, thinking about lighting.

It was after dark when Alfredo came down from the bridge with a message from the *Mississippi* that the police were ready to leave. Frank stood up, thanked Tom and left. From the bridge wing, Tom watched the boat return to the *Mississippi*.

CHAPTER 19

Once the *Mississippi* left, Tom called Gonzales and Jesus to the bridge. Alfredo was already there, having been on duty all day and he rang down and invited Francisco to attend. The *Melody* was lying quietly to her anchor, in complete darkness, with the *Sunda* anchored ahead. The sea was almost calm apart from a slight current.

'I am going alongside the casualty for the night and provide lighting. Francisco, you check out the engine room make sure no leaks etc. We will prepare her for towage tomorrow, dead ship. The cook will have to check the contents of the freezer and we will have to ditch, otherwise it will go bad and cause more problems. We are still on LOF so the more we do, the bigger our bonuses,' he laughed, and the others smiled politely.

'Gonzales,' he continued, 'tell Pedro to heave up the tow wire and instruct the welder to cut the strop, easiest way to disconnect. Rig the mini Yokohamas on the port side and I will go alongside 69 port side to her starboard. Tomorrow, Francisco, you can check the windlass and see if we can supply power to raise the anchor, otherwise it will be a long and hard exercise.'

It did not take long to disconnect, the tug perfectly steady in the calm sea with no swell in the bay. Amazing, Tom thought, how calm it was, considering how rough it was outside. Gonzales heaved up the anchor and Tom, perfectly confident, manoeuvred the tug alongside, more gently than Jan but no less effectively. She was quickly moored, kept well off the black hull by the fenders. The electrician soon rigged some temporary lighting and an anchor light shining forward. Enrico, so Tom heard, was married to a beautiful wife and had twelve children. He was a scruffy individual with a smooth, almost unlined face, and was almost bald, but he was an excellent electrician and a real asset on salvage.

Tom noticed the men crossing to and fro, from the tug to the casualty, using the fender as a bridge and a rope ladder, and told Gonzales to rig a proper gangway. Francisco reported the engine room secured for the night. Tom gave a short message for Ricky to telex to Singapore.

At last relaxing, Tom dragged out his chair onto the starboard bridge wing and sat down cold beer in hand and looked up at the star-speckled sky, the moon not yet risen. He felt completely comfortable in command. The short time onboard the *Singapore*, along with his sea trial on the *Jurong*, even though it was only a day, gave him the taste and the inkling he could handle tugs. The *Sunda* held no surprises for him. He sailed with Jan long enough to have the feel of the tug and the instinctive knowledge he displayed when he took control after Jan dropped dead, emphasised this. Handling the *Buron* was completely different, but somehow he just knew what to do; it was not something taught, but an instinct he could not explain.

The night was cool after the heat of the day and all activity stopped. Tom thought back over his time with Cosel, especially that with Jan, and gave thanks for knowing such a man; he missed his guffaw and his exuberance for life. He knew something irreplaceable was gone. There was no going back now, he was entering a new phase, almost a new beginning, but he was on his own. His ambition was fuelled, he would build on what Jan taught him, facing and overcoming his fears, but he had not reached a plateau like Jan. He was still single, although he wondered about Sheila, and the future seemed very bright, not least the promised command of one of the world's super tugs, which held no terrors for him; he could not wait for it to begin.

The next morning, soon after sunrise when there was good daylight, Tom crossed the gangway to the casualty. It was an eerie experience, the first time onboard a dead ship. Nothing was running, no generators, no pumps, the engine room was quiet, silence pervaded the whole ship. The cabins, all with the same brown curtains open, letting in the sunshine through the round portholes, still contained their former occupants' personal effects. Photographs of girlfriends or wives and family were on the bulkheads, in some, clothing was lying on the deck, magazines on the bunks, their colours bright, all suggesting an abandonment.

He walked through the alleyways, which needed a clean, and up onto the bridge, where he could look down on the green, painted deck of the *Sunda*. Pedro and his men were rigging the towing gear, connecting the white nylon spring between the forerunner and the main tow wire. Gonzales appeared.

'Make sure all the cabins are secured and the doors shut, I don't want any charges of looting. The personal effects are to be left alone.'

'Okay, Cap, the cook and mess man are looking into the freezer.'

Tom went down and found Durano and Miguel.

'Not much in the fridge,' said the cook, 'they were very short on food. Can we take anything?'

'No,' said Tom, emphatically, 'and I want a full inventory of the freezer. We will be ditching it tonight and I want to make sure the owners cannot accuse us of stealing.'

Durano looked at Tom, as if to say, how are they going to know if it is thrown to the fishes or in the *Sunda* freezer, but sensibly said nothing.

'No need to bother about the dry stores, just leave well alone,' said Tom.

'Okay, Cap,' said Durano, tonelessly.

Tom found Francisco and his men working in the engine room, lit by temporary lighting.

'No problem securing the propeller,' said the chief engineer, 'and I have been down into the steering flat. We can fix the rudder amidships, but you better secure it with wires.'

The two divers were working on the tow deck and Tom gave them their instructions, telling Rene to launch the zed

237

boat. Pedro would secure the wires on deck once attached to the rudder.

'When you have done that, I want patches on all the sea intakes.'

'Okay, Cap,' said Eduardo, who was thickset and very tough, glad to be diving and using his special skills. Libre, who was small and wiry, smiled his agreement.

'And I want a sketch of both the rudder and patches when you have finished. We are still on LOF,' added Tom.

Tom retired to the bridge and inspected the log book which, during most salvage manoeuvres, was written up by Alfredo and Jesus. He added a few times to his notes and was satisfied with the compilation of a good log.

Ricky called through the open chartroom door. 'Message from Singapore, 'tow to Singapore'.'

The wheelhouse doors were closed and the air conditioning was working well. Alfredo and Jesus were on the casualty, so Tom had the bridge to himself. He decided to use the time and started writing his salvage report. The preparations would not be completed until the next afternoon, the windlass was electric and the electrician made it work using power from the tug. Tom decided to connect up and leave at daylight the next day. The contents of the freezer would be ditched in the evening.

The cloud returned on sailing day when Enrico started the windlass and heaved in the anchor cable. Tom let the tug and tow drift while Gonzales and Pedro secured the anchor and removed the gangway, leaving three men with

Gonzales to start the tow. They were to make sure the chain bridles to which the towing gear was secured did not move. It was a simple movement to let go the lines, turn the tug and head out to sea, Pedro slacking out the tow wire. Tom increased to about three quarters power, which gave a good speed; no point wasting expensive fuel, he thought. Gonzales reported on the walkie-talkie that he had made a thorough inspection, including the engine room, and all was in order.

'Launch the zed boat, Rene, and pick them up,' said Tom. 'Alfredo, you have the watch,' and he left the bridge with Rene.

Pedro drove the crane and Rene started the engine just as the boat touched the water, the propeller biting as it went into the water. Rene increased power and signalled for the painter to be let go, speeding away from the moving tug. Very neat, thought Tom. He returned to the bridge and when the zed boat returned, watched Rene skilfully disembark his passengers and then ride with the boat when lifted out by the crane. Tom did not slow down.

The tow to Singapore was uneventful. Once clear of Labuan Bay, it was rough but the wind and sea were behind and the tow yawed from side to side, but Tom was not worried. Once they turned westwards to cross the bottom of the South China Sea, the tug rolled but the *Melody* stayed out on the starboard quarter of the tug, the accommodation acting as a sail. Two visits were made to the tow, Tom slowing down each time in the rougher weather before launching.

All was in order, reported Gonzales, Alfredo joining him on one visit, for experience. Tom went across himself on the third visit and felt very odd, seeing his command without him; the eeriness and silence on board the dead tow more pronounced at sea, it was almost like being on a ghost ship.

Tom adjusted speed to make Singapore Eastern Anchorage at daybreak but at the last minute he received a message, diverting him to Sembawang, and he picked up the pilot at the beginning of the Straits. The pilot left him to it, passing the new airport to port and the green jungle on the other side, until they reached the shipyard where the yard tugs assisted. He put the *Melody* alongside the grey concrete wharf with its huge, tall cranes, it not being so easy to slip the chain bridles. Tom wanted to make the manoeuvre and complete the salvage. The tide was ebbing, going downstream, so it was not difficult, he simply stemmed the current and let the harbour tugs gently push the *Melody* alongside, putting the *Sunda* alongside in the vacant berth ahead.

Pedro and his men walked along the quay to climb aboard the safely moored casualty and slip the chain bridles. They brought back all the *Sunda* equipment and heaved in the tow wire with the chains making considerable noise as they were pulled over the gunwale. The blue-uniformed customs and immigration officers took time and completed a mountain of paperwork before they allowed the undertakers to take Jan's frozen body ashore, wrapped in white sheets. Tom ordered the ensign at half mast to be fully hoisted.

Tom steamed the tug round to Singapore feeling very flat. No one appeared from the office; when he thought about it, why should they? He was somehow expecting a thank-you, a pat on the back, after all, it is not every day a tug master is brought back dead after a successful salvage.

He anchored the *Sunda* close by and to sea ward of the *Mississippi* and went ashore. Rene was back to his usual, high-speed behaviour, despite the darkness. Tom went no further than the pier bar, where he found Frank in his usual place.

'You are a jammy bastard, Tom, you really are! You have the luck of the devil,' said Frank, his red hair neatly parted, sipping his beer from a glass, rather than the usual bottle.

'You'll have to get a bigger tug,' laughed Tom, already feeling better for seeing his friend, even if he was still the competition. 'Tell me, what happened on the *Melody*?'

'The policeman was quite forthcoming over a beer on the bridge, returning to port,' said Frank. 'He thought the European master was keen on boys or something and it was a mixed crew. I don't understand owners, it's well known there's nearly always trouble with mixed crews, be it race or religion. Anyway,' and he took a long draught of his beer, 'looks like the old man who was quite young, only in

241

his early forties, nicked someone's boyfriend and got himself murdered for his troubles. Everything broke down after that, and the two religions had a fight. The Christians won, locking up the others, leaving the ship, which had broken down, to her own devices. They'd been drifting for some days. At some stage the radio room and VHF on the bridge were smashed up. Someone escaped or something, it's very unclear.'

'That would explain why the communication stopped because my radio man received a radio signal, which we were able to home in on, and then silence. Just goes to show, you should never mess around with your crew. Which reminds me, my crew seem to have accepted me,' said Tom.

'That's because you are, as I said, a jammy bastard,' and Frank laughed. 'Seriously, you have shown you are competent, can handle the tug, and so far have been lucky. What more do a crew want?'

Frank signalled to the barman for more beer.'I should think there will be some fun and games in Labuan with a dead body and a crew with a murderer amongst their midst, the jail will be full. The diplomats will have to do some work for a change.'

Tom laughed. 'Still, not for us to wonder the why anything happens, just for us to solve the problem, preferably on Lloyds Form.'

'Jan's funeral in two days' time,' said Frank. 'Looks as though the whole of maritime Singapore will be there.'

'I'm not looking forward to it,' said Tom, gravely. 'I'm seeing Gerda and the children tomorrow and I'm not looking forward to that, either.'

He took a sip from his fresh beer. 'I expect they'll return to Holland. I don't think Singapore holds anything for Gerda without Jan.'

'Well, look on the bright side,' said Frank refilling his glass, 'if you have got to go, what a way to do it.'

Tom was silent, remembering the moment and the resulting bruising on his front from the rails he climbed over. He told Frank in great detail exactly the circumstances leading up to seeing Jan fall, the rough weather and greyness, Jan's all-or-nothing decision, almost daring himself to go between the casualty and the reef to save the ship from running aground on a lee shore. The courage and confidence to do it, the figure standing rock-like with his hands on the controls, and the fall. Frank listened intently, his face a mask of concentration, as though he was putting Tom's words into pictures.

'Fantastic,' is all he said when Tom finished and then, 'he was a man.'

He refreshed his glass from another bottle placed on the bar by the barman, who was smart enough to say nothing. Frank pondered on what Tom had told him, then shook himself, as though shaking off the images in his mind. Changing the subject, he said, 'Well, you have a fine tug, Tom.' Looking him in the eye with a mischievous grin,

continued, 'And my spies tell me you are the master desig-
nate to the super tug, how lucky is that?' and he laughed.

'How the hell do you know that?' said Tom, not both-
ering to deny it, thinking of the few people who knew.
There were not many secrets either company could keep
from each other, despite management's best endeavours.
Frank stroked the side of his nose and smiled.

'Our big bosses are coming from Amsterdam to assess
the Singapore operation in the light of your expansion,' he
said.

'We heard,' said Tom, 'and what you don't know is, Mr
R is going to meet them, joint venture perhaps.'

'You must be joking!' said Frank, shocked. 'The Dutch
would never do that.'

Tom laughed. 'You never know what's around the next
corner, Frank, look what has happened to me.'

Frank was silent, then said, 'Chinese?'

'Why not?' agreed Tom, feeling much better. Telling
Frank about Jan's death had been very cathartic.

Hilda and Shelia were out of town. He hoped to start
moving in with Shelia but that seemed in abeyance for the
moment, so he was glad of his friend's company.

It was late when they returned to Clifford Pier and chartered a launch. Tom did not want to call out Rene unneces-
sarily and they went out together, Tom leaving first. The
watchman was alert and came onto the tow deck as Tom
climbed on board, giving him a helping hand.

244

CHAPTER 20

Tom felt in a better mood the next morning and he was glad he spoke with Frank about Jan's death. After an early breakfast on the bridge just after sunrise, he set to work on his *Melody* report, and made good progress. Miguel kept him well supplied with tea, taking the handwritten sheets to Ricky for typing. He told Jesus to draw a sketch of the relative position of the two uncharted reefs and the route taken by the *Sunda*. He knew the Arbitrators would be impressed if his report contained good sketches and diagrams, which the lawyer would no doubt incorporate into his statement. He shuddered at the thought, relieved Mr Dickinson was not in Singapore.

Tom arranged with DB for the *Sunda* to come round to the yard and temporarily shut down so the whole crew could attend the funeral. Steve would put one of his engineers on board to keep the generator running so the freezer was not stopped and thus spoil the frozen food.

As soon as it was daylight, he obtained permission from port control to move round to Jurong, arriving at the yard mid-morning. He used the Cosel harbour tugs to tow the *Sunda* into the creek, not wishing to risk his propellers in the shallow, debris-strewn waters. The sun was bright and many of the office staff came out to admire the white-hulled tug, now famous in the company, standing out amongst the black-hulled barges and a coaster under repair.

At 1300, the entire crew left the tug. Tom felt proud of them, all smartly dressed, unlike some of the clothes worn on board; no jeans and sweat shirts for Jan. The officers wore suits and looked very different. Even Rene managed to look respectable, his hair tied in a bunch, rather than the usual pig-tail. Alfredo looked particularly dapper and handsome, with his classic aquiline nose and firm chin, in a white shirt with a black tie and dark grey suit, with black, polished shoes. The three, white company vans with *Cosel Salvage* painted on the sides in black lettering took them all to the cemetery. It was to be an open-air affair, making it easier for all religions to attend, with Cosel laying on the refreshment afterwards. Tom acknowledged Frank's hand greeting, having spotted his red hair amongst the many people in the marine world who knew Jan. The sun was hot and some of the ladies were carrying parasols. The green grass among the white headstones had a cooling and soothing effect.

A few minutes before the service was due to start, while the priest was testing the microphone, Tom's pager sounded. He had forgotten to turn it off for the ceremony.

'Too bad,' he thought, he had not brought his radio, then remembered the vans. Moving as unobtrusively as he could, he left the assembled crew and quickly made his way to the parked vans.

'Base Mike, five,' he called.

246

'Ship broken down Malacca Straits, request assistance of a tug,' the duty man said.

Ishmael was at the funeral along with the other Cosel people, all well-dressed, the men wearing suits and the women frocks.

'I have spoken to the owners and they will agree LOF on arrival.'

Tom was in a quandary as to whether he should sail on his own recognisance. The decision really was DB's, or the old man. They were both there, but the ops man was right to contact him so as not to alert the competition. Everyone in the marine world was at the cemetery so all the opposition were there and would notice any senior Cosel person moving away.

'Okay, I will round up my crew. Tell the owner we will sail within the hour. Tell port control.'

He returned to his crew and instructed Gonzales to marshal them all into the vans and then looked around for the drivers who were attending the service. He saw Ishmael had noticed what was happening, although the crowd were listening to the priest who had just started.

Tom felt awful and sent up a little prayer.

'Sorry, Jan.'

He swore he could hear the guffaw encouraging him to go.

He found one of the drivers and decided not to waste time looking for the others, but to drive one of the vans himself; they would all have to squeeze into two. He did

247

not think to check whether his license covered driving a mini-van in Singapore.

It was lucky the priest was interesting, holding the attention of the large crowd, because Tom managed to sneak away unnoticed with his crew. Miguel, very smart in a suit, was weeping quietly, being comforted by one of the divers.

He picked up the position from ops and the *Sunda* was away within the hour, towed by two Cosel harbour tugs into the main channel, one of them, the *Jurong* still looked new. Tom quickly increased to full power and thundered out through Western Anchorage, the usual huge wash making it pretty obvious to any competition tug that something was up. The duty ops man cleared the tug with port control and the open-dated port clearance was on board. She must have made a fine sight, thought Tom, her white hull shining in the late afternoon sunshine, the red funnel in stark contrast. He wondered if the large black tug anchored off Sultan Shoal would follow.

The crew were all changed back into their normal working clothes, very different from the smart men at the cemetery. It was an uneventful rush through the early evening, up the Malacca Straits. Tom became more impressed by the third mate Alfredo, each time there was an emergency and was now content to let him continue his watch while he cat-napped in his chair. It was just after 2200 and the moon had risen, when they came up with the ship, her deck lights rather obscuring the anchor light. She was a small container ship of about 5,000 tons, *Container Three*, a most uninspiring name, thought Tom.

'*Container Three*, this is salvage tug *Sunda*. I will come alongside on your port side,' said Tom on the VHF.

'No,' said a firm, continental-sounding voice, German, thought Tom. 'Assistance not required.'

'LOF was agreed,' said Tom, perturbed.

'Repeat, assistance not required,' and a little later the deck lights and anchor lights went out and the navigation lights came on, the two steaming lights and red side-light indicating she was heading north. Not even a thank you, thought Tom, as he told Alfredo to turn the tug and head back to Singapore at economical speed. He walked into the radio room and told Ricky to inform Singapore.

It was a fine night, although there was lightening far to the north on the horizon. The stars were bright above and the moon almost full, casting an eerie glow on the Straits, which was full of traffic, the southbound passing well to the west. Tom was cat-napping, his tea now cold, confident Alfredo would wake him if necessary, when he heard what he thought was a muffled 'May Day' on the VHF channel 16. He was instantly awake and alert. He picked up the notebook and pencil he kept by the radio ready to take down the message, in particular the position. Suddenly, there was a crash as the chartroom door was flung open and Ricky shouted, 'Captain!'

Tom rushed into the chartroom and snatched the message from him, scanning it for the position, and said urgently, 'Offer LOF, quick, before anyone else gets in.'

He plotted the position and shouted to Ricky, who was busily sending in the radio room, through the still-open door, 'We will be there in twenty minutes!'

He moved quickly into the wheelhouse and said, 'Alfredo, take the wheel steer south,' as he pushed the engine controls levers to full power.

'Pablo, alert everyone, passenger ship on fire.'

He pressed the electric fire alarm button three times, his signal that there was a salvage. In very short order, Gonzales and Jesus were on the bridge, followed by Pedro and the Chief Engineer, Francisco.

'Whether we have agreement or not, I am going straight alongside to fight the fire,' said Tom.

'I've got him on the radar, I think,' said Jesus excitedly, his head still in the radar. 'Twenty degrees on the starboard bow,' his hand holding the plotting pencil.

'Steer two hundred degrees, Alfredo,' ordered Tom. 'We should see her, unless the fire is on the other side.'

The figures standing in the wheelhouse were indistinct in the darkness. A clap of thunder in the distance and a flash of lightening added to Tom's sense of foreboding and he made a mental effort to shake it off and concentrate on the matter in hand: the tug rushing towards a burning ship, only a few miles away.

'Have the Yokohamas ready. I don't know which side yet. When we reach the casualty, start the fire pump and be ready with the foam. Have all our hoses ready with the portable foam attachments. We'll have to get inside the accommodation as soon as possible. Gonzales will remain on the tug, I will be boarding the casualty.'

The thought of impending action banished all sense of fear, even though it was a passenger ship, and Tom gave a quick thanks for the meeting with Jan on the *Buron*. Amazing, he thought, how a confrontational talk, a confession really, helped him control the fears and panic.

'Call her on the VHF channel 16, name *Seahorse*!' called Ricky from the chartroom door.

'Three miles,' said Jesus. Twelve minutes, thought Tom.

'I can see her,' said Gonzales. 'Looks like emergency lighting only and I think the fire must be on the opposite side to us.'

Tom picked up the VHF microphone.

'*Seahorse* this is salvage tug, *Sunda*,' he said. 'Offer you my services on the terms of Lloyds Open Form.'

His voice was cool and steady, inspiring confidence, he hoped.

'Agreed,' replied a very English voice.

Tom felt elated and he could feel the excitement in the others on the bridge.

'Log it, Alfredo,' commanded Tom, seeing Pablo was back and taken over the wheel, 'and tell Ricky to inform Singapore.'

'Yes, Cap,' he replied, trying to keep his voice calm.

'Fire on my port side, started in the first class galley and spread aft. Been let down by my crew,' continued the voice of the captain.

'There is not much wind, I will come alongside on your port side and attack the fire with my monitors,' said Tom.

'Yes, but don't bank on anyone taking your lines, the lifeboats are turned out on the starboard side. I have four hundred and fifty passengers on board.'

'Have the grapnels ready, Gonzales, starboard side to,' said Tom.

'I can see your stern and about to alter round it,' said Tom, dropping the microphone and pulling the engine control levers back, slowing the *Sunda*.

'Alfredo, tell Ricky to man the VHF, then go down and assist the Chief Officer.'

Tom could see the white hull with its counter stern, a few emergency lights showing, and altered course round it, close to. He slowly went ahead along the hull of the burning ship, the fire a red glow ahead with occasional flames flickering out of the hull through the smoke. He turned on the searchlight situated on the monkey island and directed it from the wheel house control handle on the deck head to shine on the fire area.

'Fenders secured, Cap,' said the voice of Gonzales, through the company radio.

Tom indicated to Pedro, who was manning the foremast monitors with an AB, where to direct them and put the tug gently alongside the drifting ship just abaft the fire, Pedro already directing the jets on to the hull.

'Use the grapnels, Gonzales,' said Tom into the radio round his neck, and he watched from the starboard wing, feeling the heat of the fire. He heard the clang of the grapnels hitting the metal railings under the still-stowed lifeboats.

'Jesus, go and assist Gonzales,' ordered Tom, and then into the radio, 'Gonzales, Jesus and Alfredo to lead the teams onto the boat deck and into the forward lounge. There will be a stairway down to the galley deck and we attack the fire in what looks like the dining saloon. Once anyone is on board, lower the lifeboat ladders.' The whole area was well lit by the powerful search light.

Rene, his hair now loose, had climbed one of the grapnel lines and was letting down the wooden ladders. Tom climbed a ladder onto the boat deck, followed by his crew carrying portable equipment and heaving lines. The lines were soon used to heave up the fire hoses and tins of foam, while Tom found the door into the lounge, hesitating before opening it, in case he created more ventilation for the fire. Rene was behind him with a hose.

'Open up Cap or we can't get at the fire,' he said, which brought Tom to the practicality of the situation, thoughts of his previous passenger-ship fire dissipating.

The lounge was not on fire but very warm and the deck was hot underfoot, lit up by the light from the searchlight. He soon found the stairway, billowing smoke making it difficult to see, although he could see the red glow of the fire through it, reminiscent of what he saw as a teenager. He vigorously thrust it from his mind.

Rene dropped his hose, coughing, and disappeared. Tom could hear the water from the monitors hitting the hull. Three men clad in breathing apparatus passed him and climbed down the stairway into the smoke, one returning shortly afterwards, gesticulating to Tom for the water to be turned on.

Tom spoke into the radio and shortly afterwards the hoses filled with water under pressure, bucking and moving like snakes until the men controlled them. Tom knew that too much water was going to cause stability problems.

'Ricky, tell chief engineer switch on the foam both monitors and fire main,' he said into his radio.

Jesus and Alfredo came into the lounge, followed by Rene dragging another hose. Tom remembered noticing the galley portholes and some of the cabin portholes were open, and said into his radio, 'Gonzales, tell Pedro to aim his monitors into the open portholes.'

Gonzales was directing the firefighters on the tug.

Tom wondered if he should flood the lounge. The deck was becoming hotter and it might not be too long before it caught fire. He thought about the stability and decided to wait, hoping his men would put out the fire in the dining saloon below. He thought he was hearing things, apart from the noise around him, the monitor jets hitting the hull, the muted sound of the main engines and generator from the tug, the whine from the fire pump, but there was something else, something unearthly: music, voices, singing hymns. It must be the passengers, thought Tom. There was no sign of the ship's crew.

'Jesus, you stay here, Alfredo you come with me,' said Tom, raising his voice, and led the way out onto the boat deck.

He climbed down a lifeboat rope-ladder, back onto the tug, followed by Alfredo, who was coughing, on another ladder. On the aft deck, Tom found what he was looking for, the stores loading door in the side of the *Seahorse*. If he could open it he could send in another team and fight the fire from aft as well as forward. He saw there was already less smoke and the flames in the dining saloon had died down, but the galley and cabins aft of it were burning fiercely. Pedro, relieved by an AB at the fire monitor, was leading his men directing hoses into the open port holes and the monitor jets were covering those in the galley.

Alfredo stopped coughing.

'Tell Gonzales I am going to try and get that door open. I want you to lead a team and attack the fire from aft,' said Tom, pointing.

Tom swiftly made his way onto the bridge, manned only by Ricky, and called up the *Seahorse* on the VHF. The Captain answered.

'Can you get anyone to open the loading door?' asked Tom, urgently.

'No. My crew are in a funk.'

Tom was surprised. 'Your engine room OK?' he asked.

'Yes, except the main engine breakdown.'

'Make sure your bilge pumps are working. Quite a lot of water is going into the accommodation.'

'Of course.'

'What about stability?' asked Tom.

'Not good, we are due to bunker in Singapore.'

'Ballast a couple of fuel tanks, Captain,' ordered Tom.

'Can't do that, contaminate my fuel.'

'Better that than capsize with all your singing passengers on board. Please, do as I say,' ordered Tom, firmly.

There was silence, then a subdued, 'Of course, I was not thinking.'

'Fire in the dining saloon seems to be out,' reported an excited Jesus on the walkie-talkie. 'They are moving to the galley.'

'Well done,' said Tom, noticing Miguel heaving up a bucket containing water bottles and glasses, and then disappearing into the lounge. And he thinks he is a weak man, thought Tom, with wonder.

He returned to the tow deck, collecting Alfredo on the way.

'The ship's crew won't open the door,' said Tom.

'Maybe I could get in through an open port hole, I'm thin enough,' Alfredo laughed.

'Look, there's Rene, try with him.'

The hull of the burning ship just forward of the *Sunda* was covered in white foam, which was slowly sliding down with an unpleasant, animal smell, but it was both cooling the hull and much of it had entered through the portholes. The white foam was still pouring out of the monitors at pressure and Tom thought of the foam tank and the speed it must be emptying.

He watched as Rene and Alfredo climbed up onto the aft Yokohama fender. Rene gave Alfredo a leg-up, and then pulled himself into the open porthole. Rene pushed him through, it was a tight fit.

'Ricky, ring down and tell Francisco to stop the monitors,' ordered Tom into his radio.

He noticed the *Seahorse* was now listing to port but she was upright when they arrived. It made Tom increasingly nervous about stability. It was a feature of passenger ship fires; too much water is pumped in and the ship capsizes due to the free surface affect. It is what capsized the *Rada*.

Rene was looking up into the porthole through which Alfredo had disappeared. He tensed himself, leapt, holding onto the rim, and hauled himself through.

'My word,' thought Tom. 'He is fit.'

Shortly afterwards, the loading door opened and the grinning faces of Alfredo and Rene appeared.

CHAPTER 21

Tom approached the two divers on the tug's deck, who were tending the fire hoses leading into the lounge of the casualty, and instructed them to put on their breathing apparatus and take hoses in through the open loading door. He climbed over the Yokohama fender and entered the burning ship with a sense of foreboding, even though there was no fire in the immediate vicinity. The *Rada* was suddenly fresh in his mind, the burning tween deck full of smoke, the screaming. He made a huge mental effort to break free from the images, free himself from the flashback.

'Come Alfredo,' he said, his voice hoarse, 'we must find our way to the fire.'

They made their way forward along an unlit alleyway with a green deck, their torches the only light, until it was blocked by a white, watertight door, tightly closed. Tom was now firmly in the present, Alfredo's presence a calming influence.

'Ricky,' Tom spoke into his radio, 'tell the *Seahorse* to open the watertight door by the loading area, port side.'

He walked back along the alleyway and across the ship to the starboard side, where there was another watertight door, similarly closed.

As Tom returned, Ricky called over the radio. 'You can open it now, Cap.'

Tom and Alfredo turned the handle and pushed the door open. The smell of burning lingered and they could see little wisps of smoke.

'We're on the deck below the galley, Alfredo, there must be a companionway or stairs up somewhere.'

They walked forward and found it. Tom climbed into what he thought was B deck, where the galley was situated, but found it was C deck, hence the lack of smoke, he thought. They needed to climb up another deck. With a little searching in the alleyway, they found their way and Tom could see through the acrid smoke to the red glow before them. The fire crackled as wood burnt and he knew they were being foolish, attempting this without breathing apparatus. Alfredo started coughing again, so Tom signalled to him, and they returned to the loading door as the two divers climbed on board the casualty in their apparatus, pulling two hoses. Pedro directed the men remaining on the tug to assist the divers.

'Alfredo, you show the divers. Be careful and come back if there is too much smoke for you without breathing apparatus.'

'OK, Cap, no problem.'

Eduardo, the stocky diver, gave Tom the thumbs up as he heaved a hose along, two AB's with towels around their faces following behind. Tom left them to it, crossed the Yokohama fender and returned to his bridge. The fire in the

260

galley seemed much reduced as the firefighters on board fought it, but the accommodation aft was burning strongly, tongues of flame appearing out of the open portholes and licking the paint on the hull, setting that alight, also. Tom was worried about the amount of foam being used. If the foam ran out before the fire was extinguished, they would be in trouble. Water alone would disturb the foam carpet and might cause the area already put out to reignite. On top of that, the list on the *Seahorse* had increased noticeably. Tom called up the captain on the VHF.

'Are you ballasting, Captain?' Tom asked.

'Yes,' came the firm reply.

'Good, your list has increased.'

'I know,' was the curt reply.

'Fire is out in the dining saloon and my firefighters are in the galley but aft of that is all alight. I have men coming from the loading door to attack it from aft as well as forward,' continued Tom into the VHF microphone.

'Thank you. My crew have let me down.'

'How are the passengers?' asked Tom.

'Singing hymns, they're mainly in good heart and can't see the fire. The lifeboats on the starboard side are lowered to embarkation level, ready in case we have to abandon.'

'I heard. For a moment I thought I had gone to heaven,' said Tom cheerfully, which elicited a slight laugh from the worried captain.

'We have the *Sealion* arriving in a couple of hours and if necessary we will transfer them.'

'With luck we will have the fire out well before then,' Tom assured him. 'We have another tug on the way.'

Tom saw that the hoses leading through the loading door were thick, indicating water and foam were going through, so the divers were fighting the fire from aft.

'Captain, you must have foam.'

'Yes, in a tank.'

'Can we use it through your fire main?' asked Tom.

'I suppose so. I'll ask the chief engineer. His men are okay.'

'If it is possible, please turn it on and I will use it, connecting my hoses to your fire main. Jesus, Alfredo,' Tom ordered, switching to company radio, 'check where the nearest fire main connections are. The ship is going to run foam through it. Connect up once you see it running.'

'Okay, Cap,' said Jesus.

'Divers attacking fire in accommodation,' reported Alfredo between coughs.

'You okay, Alfredo?' asked Tom, concerned.

'I am okay, Cap.'

Tom returned to the *Seahorse* and up into the accommodation but could not reach the divers who were almost hidden by the foul smoke, the red glow of the fire ahead of them, the noise quite loud. They were progressing forward and with the forward party moving aft, Tom was hopeful they would have the fire out before the foam ran out.

'Fire in galley out,' reported Jesus on his radio. 'We are moving into the cabins.'

Tom made his way back to the *Sunda*, passing Alfredo, who was coughing badly but insisted he was okay, and Miguel, who was supplying water to the firefighters. The electrician had already rigged some emergency lighting, making it much easier to move around. Back on his bridge, Tom could see the fire was much reduced and he was confident they would have it out shortly. He could see the navigation light of ships passing but they were keeping well clear. It was a fine night and the moon gave everything a ghostly glow, highlighting the smooth sea, so smooth it was reflecting like ice.

'Foam from ship,' reported Jesus on the company radio.

'Connect up some of our hoses, and you, Alfredo.'

'Okay, Cap,' he coughed, his voice sounding harsh on the radio.

In the light of the searchlight, Tom could see how the white paintwork on the hull had been scorched and blistered by the fire, and in places the metal was bare, already rusting from the firefighting. The foam on the hull was mainly gone, except where it had dried. A few figures, obviously passengers, appeared on the boat deck, watching the action. Tom assumed they were younger ones, but was concerned about them, preferring them not to be there. He was concerned the bolder ones might eventually hinder his men or trip over a hose and injure themselves.

'Seahorse, captain, keep your people off the port boat deck,' said Tom, quite firmly, over the VHF. 'I don't want an accident.'

'Will do,' the captain replied.

It was not long before an excited Jesus came over the radio.

'Cap, fire is out,' he said.

'Well done,' congratulated Tom, his voice conveying some of his own excitement at their achievement. 'Maintain a fire watch and keep the foam running until you are absolutely sure.'

'Okay, Cap.'

'Alfredo!' called Tom.

'We have met with Jesus team and all cabin fires out,' he coughed, barely able to make himself understood.

'Alfredo, I am ordering you out of there, now!' said Tom, sharply. 'Is Rene there?'

'Yes,' coughed Alfredo. Tom kicked himself for not ordering him out sooner, he was the only one seriously affected by the smoke.

'Give him the radio and tell him to bring you back here, now.'

'Okay, Cap,' came Rene's voice.

Something was seriously wrong with Alfredo and Tom was worried. He saw Pedro on the tow deck and ran aft along the catwalk to the aft controls. The white hull of the *Seahorse* towered above him, illuminated by the tug's deck lights.

'Pedro!' he shouted. 'Help Alfredo back.'

Pedro waved his hand in acknowledgement and moved towards the loading door. Tom returned to the bridge and Ricky handed him a telex.

'*Coselvenom* departed Singapore with foam and Salvage Master, *Singapore* proceeding.' It was signed, DB.

'That is all I want, the Salvage Master after the fire is out.'

Tom remembered Jan's words at the *Kinos*.

He will be too late to do anything, won't arrive until tomorrow morning, he thought. He realised they had only been at the burning ship just over an hour, and were lucky to have caught the fire before it really took hold. She was an old ship with lots of inflammable materials.

Tom saw Pedro and an AB help Rene bring Alfredo on board the tug across the black Yokohama fender and lay him out on the tow deck. Miguel appeared, gesticulating to get him into the accommodation.

'Well, thank heavens for our nurse,' thought Tom. Miguel had been busy, taking water to the firefighters, seemingly fearless of the fire.

'Fire definitely out,' reported Jesus on the radio.

Gonzales left the bridge earlier to take charge on deck, so it was just Ricky and Tom on the bridge. He was pleased to see the Radio Officer kept a good log of the company and VHF radio traffic, together with a brief note of the content. Tom rang down to the engine room and told them to turn off the fire pump.

'Seahorse,' Tom called on the VHF, 'fire is out,' and gave the time.

'Well done, and thank you very much,' said a much relieved captain. 'Are you coming on board?'

'Indeed, be with you shortly,' said Tom. 'Get some of your people into the burnt out area and remove the debris, and bring fire extinguishers in case there is a flare up.'

'Very good,' agreed the relieved voice.

'Gonzales, get some fire extinguishers into the burnt out area and maintain a fire watch. I am going to see the Captain. Make sure the towing gear is ready, I am hoping to tow her,' said Tom into his radio.

'Okay, Cap.'

Tom took the completed Lloyds Form. Ricky was efficient putting it in a stout envelope, clipped to a board with a biro attached. Tom climbed on board the casualty, made his way through an unlit accommodation where only the emergency lighting was on, and found the captain sitting in his chair, looking exhausted under the wheelhouse light. He was a thin, elderly man with startlingly white hair, a narrow, drawn face and brown eyes. He was delighted to see Tom and when he stood to greet him, Tom realised he was a tall man, dressed in No 10's tunic, long white trousers and white shoes. He shook Tom's hand with both of his.

'I can't thank you enough, you have really saved my bacon,' he said, his military bearing out of place with his hand-shaking, and Tom felt quite embarrassed.

266

'Your engine not fixed yet, Captain?' Tom said.

'No, the chief says another couple of hours. My name is Captain Owen, but please, call me Charles.'

'Captain Tom Matravers,' said Tom. 'I'd better tow you to Singapore, no point hanging around here. Gonzales,' he said into his radio, 'get the slip-hook on board and make it fast up forward, we're going to tow him to Singapore.'

'Okay, Cap. Fire watch okay, ship's crew clearing up. You will need to turn the tug, Cap.'

'I tell you what, Charles, we better regularise everything. If you sign here, it's done,' said Tom, taking the LOF out of the envelope and clipping it onto the board, indicating where the Captain should sign with the biro.

Captain Owen signed with no comment. Tom was elated, even though the LOF was valid with the verbal agreement over the radio and logged by Ricky.

'The quicker I get him under tow, the better,' thought Tom.

'Ricky, telex Singapore, LOF signed,' Tom said into his radio.

CHAPTER 22

'My chief officer will prepare a slip-hook which makes slipping the tug easy,' said Tom, walking out onto the port wing of the bridge of the *Seahorse*. 'Yes, Charles, they are getting it ready now. I will have to turn the tug.'

He walked back into the wheelhouse. 'How are your passengers?' he asked.

'No air-con,' said Charles, which is why so many port-holes were open, thought Tom. 'So of course, they have been moaning about it, but that was before the fire. During the fire they were very good, did what they were told, now all drinks are on the house. Food is no problem, the second class galley is still working, once we get some power on. The electricians are working on isolating the burnt area and then we will have power elsewhere.'

'My electrician is a wizard, I'll send him to your chief engineer,' said Tom, and spoke into his radio.

'The *Sealion* will be here shortly. Look, I think it is that blaze of lights, but I am loath to transfer the passengers unless it is really necessary, most of them are not in their first youth and some are really very old. Someone is bound to get hurt. They are much better on board here, until we can disembark them in Singapore.'

'I agree,' concurred Tom, 'Singapore is only about twelve hours away. I reckon we can tow you at more than eight knots, the *Sunda* is a powerful tug and you'll be able to steer at that speed. Time would be less if you get your own engines.'

'Yes. The list has stabilised and expect to finish ballasting shortly. We picked two small tanks.'

'Good. We are maintaining a fire watch and I will leave those men on board, your people are already clearing up. My people have put some small portable pumps on board to pump out any pockets of water that have not drained down, especially in the dining saloon,' said Tom.

'Captain,' called Ricky, and Tom knew something was wrong from the tone of his voice. 'Miguel has called and said Alfredo has died.'

Tom felt as though someone had cut him open, and all the pleasure, sense of achievement and excitement of the salvage poured out of him, leaving him empty and bereft. He knew he should have ordered him out of the fire area much sooner.

'My third officer has died,' said Tom in some distress. 'You must have a Doctor, can you send him over to have a look at him?'

'Of course, I am very sorry, I thought we were going to get out of this with no casualties,' said Captain Owen, picking up the telephone receiver and dialling immediately.

'I will meet him at the loading door,' said Tom, and he left the bridge, taking the signed LOF with him.

The doctor, also dressed in number 10's, was waiting for him. Tom helped him to cross the black fender to the tug, and could not help but smell the drink on his breath, although he seemed in full control.

When they reached the mess room, they found Alfredo, stretched out on the formica-topped table. His arms were crossed over his chest and his eyes closed, his smooth, handsome, unlined features, light toffee-brown skin almost dark cream, quite composed, as though he was asleep. He was dressed in a long-sleeved, blue shirt and jeans, which were still wet from the firefighting, flecks of foam showing up against the blue of his clothing. Miguel, dry eyed, stood by him. Tom thought back to the corpse in the lifeboat and poor Jan. He shook himself to get rid of the images.

'I did my best, Cap,' said Miguel, distressed, 'He would not stop coughing and his heart just stopped, I tried pumping his chest but he was gone.'

'Miguel was a nurse before coming to sea,' said Tom, in answer to the doctor's raised eyebrows. He was a plump man in his mid forties, with a full head of brown hair and a moustache to match, his face showing the signs of good living, his uniform quite out of place on the tug.

The doctor bent down and examined the body, concurring that he was indeed dead, but it would require an autopsy to establish why. Tom asked if he should put him in the freezer but on being told they should reach Singapore in twelve hours, the doctor said the air conditioning would be sufficient to maintain the condition of Alfredo's corpse.

Tom assured Miguel he could have done no more and instructed him to move the body to Alfredo's cabin. It was with a heavy heart that Tom escorted the doctor back to his own ship.

Back on his bridge, Tom sat in his chair and took stock, pushing Alfredo out of his mind. He saw there were lights on in *Seahorse* lounge.

'Looks as though Enrico has worked his magic,' said Tom as Francisco appeared on the bridge, wiping his hands on his white boiler-suit.

'Yes,' said Francisco quietly. 'Just heard about Alfredo. His parents will be destroyed, he was the apple of their eye. He was engaged to be married, too. Our families knew each other well in Manila. A fine young man.'

'Yes,' said Tom, 'he was turning into a good salvor. I am very sorry.' He paused in respectful silence, then continued, 'We are going to tow the *Seahorse* to Singapore.'

'No problem, leave Enrico on board the casualty,' suggested Francisco.

'Yes, unless they send him back. Expect the chief has already found out what a wizard he is, especially as the *Seahorse* is an old ship.'

'Need to turn the tug, Cap,' said Gonzales on the radio. 'All ready for you. Pedro has disconnected all the hoses, divers are ready with two of the fire watch team to take the tow, *Seahorse* chief officer here and windlass working.'

'Very good. Once connected, you stay on the *Seahorse* bridge and co-ordinate our people on board. Enrico is on board as well,' said Tom, standing and holding onto his radio. 'I will turn her now.'

'Okay, Cap.'

There was a light wind on the starboard side of the casualty, so the *Sunda* would have been pinned on the port side of the casualty but for the Yokohma fenders. Rene was waiting to let go the lines. It was a simple manoeuvre for Tom to swing the stern out, the port engine ahead and the starboard astern, then full astern both, Jan style, and the tug moved astern passing the stern of the casualty now all lit up. He turned her and once he was in position, waited for Pedro to move the fenders onto the port side of the tug. He then went gently alongside the lines being taken by the men who had been sent forward. The stern and aft deck of the *Sunda* was now under the bow of the *Seahorse*.

It did not take long to lift the heavy slip-hook on board the forecastle of the *Seahorse*, the crane just long enough to reach the foredeck illuminated by the ship's own lights. Tom turned off the searchlight and Rene was lifted back on board the *Sunda* by the crane as Tom wanted his boat driver on board the tug. Pedro then used the crane to lift the forerunner, which was pulled on board the *Seahorse* through the port bow fairlead and the connection was made onto the slip-hook that had been secured. All was ready within half an hour of the fire being extinguished, which Tom thought was pretty good going.

Gonzales walked along the foredeck of the casualty and spoke to Tom who was on the bridge wing of the tug. He confirmed his instructions.

'Keep Captain Owen company and keep me informed at all times. The list has reduced. All our equipment is on board. The fire watch team can pump out any remaining water. Inspect every now and then, both teams have radios.'

'Okay, Cap, don't worry,' said Gonzales.

'Ricky, give Gonzales three spare batteries for the radios, don't want any of them to run out,' said Tom.

A line fell onto the bridge deck as Ricky returned with the green batteries and the waste paper basket. He tied on the line and Gonzales heaved it up.

'Okay, Gonzales, let go the lines and go on to the bridge. Make sure they steer once we get going.'

Tom used the engines to manoeuvre the bow off the casualty, then using power, went ahead so the stern was clear of the drifting ship and turned her quickly to starboard, with the tow wire free-running onto the starboard side of the towing gunwale. The tug was now facing the same way as the tow and Tom moved ahead of her, Pedro paying out the tow wire until he heard Tom's instruction to stop on the internal intercom. He slowly increased power, turning the *Seahorse* to the south, the *Sealion* taking station astern a blaze of lights from the starboard side of the casualty.

'Jumped the gun a bit,' the *Seahorse* Captain came over the company radio.

Gonzales must be on the bridge, thought Tom.

'Thought we better get on with it, Charles. If you get your engines, it is easy enough for my men to slip the tow. Please switch on just your sidelights and stern light.'

'Sorry about that, upset routine,' he laughed. 'The chief has not reported back.'

'We are doing a good speed,' said Tom cheerfully, 'have you in Singapore by noon.'

It was now after midnight and much had happened in less than two hours but everything was overshadowed by Alfredo's death. Gonzales reported the fire watch party and divers were fed by the ship and there was no sign of fire. The ship's crew were working and the fire area was being cleared. All was well with the tow, the forerunner being greased where it passed out through the fairlead on the tow. Enrico seemed to have worked his wizardry and the fire-damaged area was blanked off, allowing lighting to be switched on in all the remaining areas. There seemed to be an electric fault in the air conditioning but he was working on it. The passengers were in good spirits, no doubt helped by free drinks, and the band was playing cheerful music. Those whose cabins were damaged by the fire were camped out in the first class lounge and food was served from the second class galley. The ship was almost upright and was following well, steered by a man on the wheel. The *Sealion* was steaming at slow speed, following on the starboard quarter. Tom had good cause to feel pleased with himself and his crew. Poor Alfredo, he thought, but told himself not to dwell on it.

274

Early in the morning, the *Singapore* arrived and Tom told Captain Hannibal to take station ahead on the starboard bow to warn any ships who came too close. The *Coselvenom* arrived about an hour later and the Salvage Master asked Tom to slow down as he wished to go alongside.

'Paul, I don't think that's a good idea,' said Tom into the company radio. 'I don't wish to disturb the tow, it's following well. The sooner we can get the passengers off in Singapore, the better.'

'I am the Salvage Master and I am in charge,' said Captain Rogers, somewhat angrily.

Tom's heart sank; everything was going so well and now this. He had that sick feeling in his stomach but realised he must assert himself. As far as he was concerned, it was his salvage; he had put out the fire, signed the LOF and started the tow. Jan's words following the *Kinos* fire came to him: 'Always arrives after the fire is out,' along with Jan's warning that Rogers thought Tom a threat, he would knife him, 'a silver knife.'

Oh, dear, Tom thought, confrontation but not in public.

'Paul, the Captain has one of our radios. I will send Rene to pick you up and bring you to the *Sunda*.'

'I will come alongside you if you slow down,' ordered the Salvage Master.

'Paul, I am not slowing down.' Tom was firm. 'I am the tow master as Jan was on the *Kinos* tow. You are not to come alongside me. I repeat, I will send my zed boat across to pick you up.'

275

There was silence and Gonzales, who must have heard their exchange, said over the radio, 'All okay here, Cap. Captain Owen asleep.'

Tom was so short of men on the *Sunda*, with more than half the deck crew on board the casualty, that he had dispensed with the lookout, staying on the bridge with Jesus, which meant they would be on watch until they reached Singapore. Miguel materialised on the bridge with fresh mugs of strong tea, giving one to Jesus and one to Tom, his small figure indistinct in the darkness of the wheelhouse.

'Don't you sleep, Miguel?' asked Tom, pleasantly.

'No, Cap, I keep a vigil for Alfredo until his spirit ready to go,' he said and Tom wondered at the depth of the man who said he was weak but kept the firefighters supplied with water, apparently oblivious to the danger.

'Anyway, you need tea,' he said, more cheerfully, and gave a little chuckle. 'Not like Captain Jan.'

'Tell Pedro and Rene to launch the zed boat and pick up the Salvage Master from the *Coselvenom* and bring him back here.'

'Okay, Cap,' and he disappeared.

A few minutes later Tom saw the crane lift the zed boat with Rene aboard and Miguel tending the painter. Rene roared away as soon as he was afloat, his hair flowing behind his head, just visible in the moonlight, an almost ghostly figure. A very angry Salvage Master appeared on the bridge some time later.

'Your boat driver is crazy and he needs a haircut! It's a wonder he has been allowed into Singapore by the immigration.'

Tom took a deep breath, not wanting a blazing row while towing. He was tired but knew he was going to have to establish his own authority. This was not like the confrontation with the lawyer.

'Rene is an exceptionally brilliant boat driver,' said Tom, quietly. 'Paul, listen to me a minute. I know you are a very good Salvage Master but this is my salvage. We put out the fire with no help from anyone else, the ship's crew did nothing. I have started the tow. I have two men forward watching the tow, Gonzales, my chief officer, is on the bridge with the Captain, the electrician is with their chief engineer and has got the lighting back on. I have a three-man fire watch in the burnt-out area. I don't see whatever you can do that I have not done.'

'I saw the loading door on the port side was open, it should be closed at sea,' pointed out Captain Rogers.

'I had it opened. In fact, we opened it to fight the fire. It was an escape route for the firefighters and now is providing ventilation. The dead third mate opened it.'

'Dead?' said the Salvage Master, shocked.

'Yes, dead. He died as a result of the smoke and probably heart attack.'

'I am sorry.'

'So are we.'

'I would like to be taken to the casualty,' Captain Rogers said, sounding more conciliatory.

'Look, Paul, I rather you did not go on the casualty yet. It is the middle of the night and everything is fine. Gonzales has a good rapport with the elderly Master. If you want to help so I can put your services in my report, why not send your efficient and capable Juan with some men to back up my crew who are pretty tired. Don't forget, we fought a major fire.'

'I am here to take charge,' he said, visibly suppressing his anger, his southern hemisphere accent more pronounced. Australian, thought Tom.

Tom took a deep breath.

'No, Paul,' he said, firmly. 'I do not want you on the casualty. You can assist as I have suggested or just escort.'

He sighed with relief; he had made his stand, but he could see from the look on the Salvage Master's long face, faintly lit by the chart table light, that he had made an implacable enemy. He would need to heed Jan's warning.

'Captain,' called Jesus, formally.

Tom walked quickly into the wheelhouse.

'On the starboard bow.'

Tom immediately saw what Jesus reported, the searchlight from the *Singapore* shining on a small coaster with no lights proceeding slowly in the same direction as the convoy.

'*Sunda*, this is *Singapore*,' said Captain Hannibal over the radio. 'Starboard bow.'

'Seen, thank you, *Singapore*,' replied Tom. 'We are passing clear at the moment.'

'Okay, Cap,' and Tom returned to the chart room.

He could see Captain Rogers appeared to have a change of heart, or perhaps he was planning his attack on Tom.

'I will send Juan across with half a dozen men,'

'Thank you, Paul. Juan can co-ordinate with Gonzales.'

Tom walked back into the wheelhouse and saw they were clear of the coaster being overtaken, still illuminated by the *Singapore* searchlight. He stood in the doorway and saw Rene take Captain Rogers back to the *Coselvenom*, which Juan brought close to the starboard side, maintaining the same speed. Not long afterwards, he saw the heavily loaded zed boat speed across to the casualty. Rene's skill was apparent: Tom had not slowed down and they were making well over eight knots. *Coselvenom* slowed and disappeared behind the stern of the *Seahorse*, ahead of the *Sealion*, and took station on the port quarter where Tom could not see her. Tom saw the zed boat safely loaded and shortly afterwards, Rene appeared on the bridge.

'Bosun and five men, Cap,' he reported.

'No, Juan?' asked Tom, surprised.

'No.'

'Well done, Rene, and thanks,' Tom congratulated Rene as he walked off the bridge and along the boat deck to the stowed zed boat.

Tom wondered what Captain Rogers was up to. He realised he needed to be careful, or his own success would be his downfall. He was sure Paul Rogers now considered Tom a threat to his position and would try and get rid of him. He could hear Jan's warning, ringing in his head. He shook himself mentally, and found himself shaking, physically.

So be it, he thought, if that is the way it is, then I will fight. It will be a fight to the end, either him or me. What a pity, he thought, but he was resolved to win.

CHAPTER 23

The tow continued uneventfully to Singapore, the *Cosel-venom* out of sight and soon out of mind. Tom had other, more important things to worry about.

The *Sealion* was very visible, escorting on the starboard quarter of the *Seahorse*, and the *Singapore* ahead on the starboard bow of the *Sunda*. It was a fine morning with just enough white cloud to make the sky interesting, highlighting the the lush green of the Malaysian mainland, while the water of the Malacca Straits was its usual muddy brown, although smooth as silk. Singapore port control gave permission for the convoy to proceed straight to the berth in Keppel harbour. The Pilot boarded the *Seahorse*, entering the anchorage, and his assistant boarded the *Sunda*. Tom had shortened in the tow so the casualty was close to the stern of the tug, with the nylon stretcher above the water making it easy to manoeuvre. At times, the burnt patch on the port side was clearly visible on the white hull, smoke damage and blisters from the heat making it appear much larger than Tom envisaged.

In all the activity surrounding the arrival – the messages on the VHF and company radio, the arrival of the harbour tugs and pilot boat, *Coselone* with the old man and DB visible on deck, numerous launches with journalists, photographers and TV people on board – Tom almost missed seeing the *Coselvenom* zed boat come round the stern and the Salvage Master board from the pilot ladder.

Trouble, thought Tom, the battle is beginning, then thrust it from his mind, concentrating to ensure the final berthing was successful, for they were still bound under the LOF contract; no cure, no pay. The boat decks on the *Seahorse* were full of passengers waving at the press, some with coloured streamers, turning the arrival at the berth under the bright sun into a tumultuous welcome. The damaged side alongside highlighted to the well wishers ashore the danger from which the ship had been saved. The ship's orchestra and band playing on deck added to the occasion.

Tom and the Singapore senior pilot on board the *Seahorse* discussed the berthing. The Pilot knew his stuff, having berthed dead ships before and luckily, there was little wind.

'The timing is good,' he said, 'the tide will be against us going in through the narrows and at the berth, but coming up to slack water so that makes it easy. Just tow to the berth and the tugs can push her alongside.'

'There is room ahead for me?' asked Tom.

'No, that is the only difficulty.'

'I am on a slip-hook so my men can slip me at any time. I have two of my own people standing by with a radio.'

'Cosel efficiency again,' laughed the Pilot. 'I will connect a harbour tug before slipping your tug, but if we get it right she will have a headline or two ashore.'

The tow proceeded at slow speed through the anchorage to the narrow entrance of Keppel Harbour, where Tom increased power to get through. Harbour tugs seemed to be everywhere and two were connected astern of the *Seahorse*, making it easier to control her. The *Sealion* gave three blasts on her deep ship's whistle, turned and proceeded to her own berth, her escort duties completed. Coming up to the berth, the headlines were towed ashore by the two line boats and once fast ashore, the pilot gave the order to slip the *Sunda*.

Tom suppressed his rage and anger when Gonzales reported to him over the radio that the Salvage Master arrived on the bridge and ordered him forward. Not wishing to have a public row on the radio at this critical stage of the arrival, Tom said nothing.

'Slip, Gonzales,' said Tom into his radio. He looked aft and saw the forerunner fall into the murky harbour waters from the bow of the *Seahorse*. He held the tug off until Pedro recovered the towing gear. The *Coselone* came alongside and the old man and DB shouted their congratulations and then Tom saw the lawyer waving from inside the cabin, a little smile on his face. Enemy number one is planning something, thought Tom, and his heart sank.

Why should success always cause trouble from others? The whole salvage has been a triumph for Cosel, salving not just the ship but the passengers, too, Tom said to himself.

Once the towing gear was heaved on board, with a slight delay when the shackle to the stretcher caught at the towing gunwale, Tom looked to go alongside the *Seahorse* and pick up his gear and men. His way was blocked by the *Coselvenom,* which was alongside the loading door on the starboard side where Tom wished to go.

'*Coselvenom, Sunda,* move astern so I can come alongside and pick up my gear,' Tom politely called into the radio.

'Captain Rogers told me to remain here,' replied Juan, his chief officer, sounding apologetic.

'Just move astern, Juan. It is the best for me,' said Tom, quietly.

The radio was silent and then Tom saw the *Venom* moving astern.

Sensible man, to do it quietly, thought Tom. It's started, preliminary skirmishing, and he sighed.

There were no passengers on the boat deck when Tom put the tug alongside in the 69 position, they were all on the other side taking part in the welcome. The tide was slack, making the manoeuvre easy. Tom boarded and made his way over to the burnt area where his crew were collecting up the pumps, fire hoses and equipment, and carrying it across to the *Sunda*, supervised by Gonzales.

'If you need to move the tug forward to collect the slip hook, do so,' said Tom. 'I am going to see the Captain.'

'Okay, Cap, nice man,' he smiled. 'He was not very pleased when the Salvage Master arrived.'

284

The burnt area was cleared from most of the debris but the place stank of the foam, which was made from animal waste, burnt wood panelling, fabric, paint and other un-nameable material. Tom put his handkerchief to his nose. The deformed metal, twisted and buckled as though some giant hand had been in a frenzy, was already starting to rust, indicating the intensity of the fire and Tom realised just how lucky they were to have extinguished it so quickly.

Tom found his way up to the bridge through the accom-modation but the Captain was in his day-room, one deck below. He was talking with officials, organising immigra-tion and customs for the disembarkation of his passengers, and was dressed in fresh white shorts and shirt with epaul-ettes, long white socks and white shoes, looking very smart and every inch the Captain, unlike the worried man of the previous night. The Salvage Master was sitting in an easy chair, the greenish-coloured covers matched the car-pet and curtains, rather a sickly decor and not one Tom would have chosen for himself. Captain Rogers was dressed in blue working shorts and shirt, short black socks and shoes, looking completely out of place, his inevitable notebook in hand, writing.

Captain Owen spotted Tom, who had changed into fresh whites himself, and stood up from his chair.

'My saviour,' he said, and laughed.

The Salvage Master looked daggers at Tom, pen in hand.

'Let me finish here and then we can have a celebratory drink. In fact, you can come with me and say goodbye to the passengers, they are dying to meet their hero.'

Tom sat in a vacant chair and immediately a Goanese steward, very smart in his No 10's, appeared and asked what he would like to drink. The ensuing beer tasted delicious and Tom started to relax, the tension and excitement of the last fourteen or fifteen hours beginning to drain away.

'The port health officials say the funeral people can take Alfredo away,' said Ricky over Tom's radio. '*Coselone* has taken the ship's papers to get a new port clearance.'

Tom immediately felt guilty. He had forgotten about poor Alfredo.

'Does anyone need me?' asked Tom.

'No, Cap.'

'I think champagne is more in order,' said Captain Owen jovially, as the last official left the cabin, 'steward.'

The silver ice bucket and champagne were ready in the fridge, which was hidden by a wooden door under the Captain's desk. The Captain ceremoniously opened the *Dom Perignon* himself, handing the opened bottle to the steward to pour. The Salvage Master ostentatiously refused to take a glass.

'To the hero of the moment,' laughed Charles and raised his glass, 'and to my immediate retirement.'

They drank but the Salvage Master continued writing.

'Look after the Captain here, steward,' said Captain Owen, gesturing to the seated man in blue working gear. 'We are going to meet the passengers,' and walked out of the room, indicating Tom should follow.

'Funny fellow, your man,' said Charles as they made their way down to the first class lounge. 'Had to tell him to mind his P's and Q's, coming onto my bridge and ordering around your chief officer, Gonzales, I think that was his name. Good man, Gonzales, I could have done with him on my ship, might not have needed you if I had had someone like that as my chief officer. The chief said your electrician is some kind of genius, he's even got the air-con going. Where on earth do you find these people? I am retiring, as I said. I'll never be given another command so better pre-empt the inevitable. Anyway, I have decided I'm past it. The fire was a wake-up call, time to go. Just a warning, the passengers are in general a friendly lot, all dying to meet you, but free drinks have been available since the fire so some are, how should we say? A bit boisterous!'

The first class lounge was full, all sign of the temporary camper site gone. A buffet ran across the starboard side and forward of it a temporary bar had been set up. The afternoon sun streamed in through the windows but the air-conditioning kept the food cool. Enrico's doing, thought Tom. Some were outside on the boat deck where there was apparently nothing wrong, but underneath was the charred, burnt-out area and the hull, bare and rusty, the paint on the edges curled and blackened. Coloured streamers still littered the deck and the dock side. The public address system was working and the Captain, standing very straight for a man of his age, led Tom to the platform and the microphone, on the opposite side of the lounge.

'Ladies and gentlemen, quiet, please,' and the lounge became silent. 'I would like to present Captain Matravers, the Salvage Master, who is my, and your, saviour.'

Prolonged applause followed, along with shouts of, 'He's a jolly good fellow!' which left Tom squirming with embarrassment, wishing he was anywhere but that lounge and remembering Alfredo's body was at that moment being carried ashore beneath them.

'My thanks are to him and his fine crew. But for their timely arrival and bravery the outcome would have been very different.'

Charles spoke clearly and in measured tones, which gave added emphasis to the words.

'I apologise for the drama but thank you for your forbearance and good nature, and give thanks none of you were hurt.'

More clapping and cheering broke out. A tall, distinguished, white-haired man stood and walked purposely to the microphone. When the noise died down, he spoke in a mid-Atlantic accent.

'On behalf of the passengers I would like to thank Captain Owen for the way he handled the emergency, and Captain Matravers for his timely intervention.'

There was more clapping and cheering. Captain Owen took Tom by the arm and led him into the crowd, saying, 'You will have to shake hands with them.'

For the next half hour, Tom was clapped on the back, his hand shaken, sometimes more vigorously than was pleasant, until it felt as though it had been put through a mangle.

'Everything on board and ready, Cap, including Enrico.'

Tom just heard Gonzales' voice above the noise of the crowd, holding the radio close to his ear.

Captain Owen and Tom then escaped what was turning into a very lively party at the company's expense. The more mature certainly knew how to enjoy themselves, thought Tom.

Back in his day-room, Captain Owen sat down.

'I see your man has gone,' he said, as the steward poured another glass of champagne. 'I've had a long and interesting life and as I said earlier, it is time to go. This type of passenger ship has had its day, they are on the way out, fire being a particular hazard as we know to our or my cost. The world is changing. Thank the good Lord no-one was hurt, but very sorry for your man lost. I shall have to turn the drink off soon or the passengers will never leave,' he laughed. 'Well, don't need you now, so better sign you off.'

'I need to borrow a typewriter, please, Charles,' said Tom.

Captain Owen picked up his telephone.

'Send the writer,' he ordered into it.

A very smart Asian appeared shortly afterwards, immaculate in whites, which set off his smooth, light coffee-coloured skin and black hair.

'Dictate and Rico will deliver,' ordered Charles. 'I will miss all this,' he added, and laughed.

Half an hour later, Tom returned to the *Sunda* with the signed termination letter in his pocket. He was full of champagne and beginning to feel tired, the action and drama-filled, sleepless night catching up with him. There was no sign of the *Coselvenom* and Tom knew there was trouble ahead. He put it aside as the ship's crew, organised by Pedro, let go the lines and Tom steamed the *Sunda* round to her normal anchorage, noting the *Mississippi* was still in the same place. It was late afternoon and once anchored, Tom fell into his bunk and was instantly dead to the world. It seemed only minutes, not the couple hours in his dreamless sleep, when Tom was woken by Miguel, with a message in one hand and a cup of tea in the other.

'Report to the Mandarin Hotel at 1930, lobby bar.'

CHAPTER 24

Tom was not in his bunk on the tug when he awoke and he felt completely disorientated. His head throbbed and pulsed as though Hercules, striking the gong at the beginning of a film, was inside it, a deep, body-shaking sound. He lay still, frightened to move, and tried to think back. He was not sure if he felt sick and his mouth was dry and tasted foul. Hercules began to turn into a more normal man with a smaller gong, and his beaten brain slowly began to work.

He drank a beer on the *Sunda* while dressing, to clear his head from the champagne earlier in the day. Miguel fussed around, brushing his suit and shining his shoes. Rene drove him ashore at a sedate pace, befitting his dress code. He called in at the pier bar, the lights bright after the darkness outside, and drank a quick couple with Frank, who was mad with jealousy but happy for his friend's success.

The lobby bar at the Mandarin was something else again, thank heavens he had the sense to wear his well-pressed suit! A whole crowd of strangers stood and applauded when he entered. The old man beamed and even DB had a smile on his face. Everything was still a blur, champagne at the hotel reception, white and red wine with the dinner, brandy with the coffee, the speeches. Captain

Owen of *Seahorse* gave a short, measured speech, confirming his retirement and praising Tom. It was all so embarrassing but he was stuck, he could not just leave. The lawyer was there, too.

Tom brought himself back to his present surroundings. It was an even smaller gong now, with a midget, and he looked around: pink pillows. He turned his head to see a mass of blonde hair. Good heavens! It was Shelia, still fast asleep, with a little smile on her face. He felt below; he was naked.

Tom's thoughts were in a whirl. Hilda was at the hotel reception, he thought she was in Hong Kong, but she must have flown down. Help! The old man made an announcement, something about Hilda joining Cosel after Christmas. It must have been after the dinner date he missed she had teased him that she was so unimportant he had not bothered to tell her he was not coming. She had phoned ops to find out. What else had happened, he wondered? God! He had given an interview to some journalist but he could not remember what was said. Snippets of conversation returned to him. What had the lawyer said? 'It's too late now, so go with the flow, bloke.'

What was too late, he asked himself?

He could see the sun low over the city through the half-closed curtains. He sat up and almost passed out. Never again, he thought, I am going to be teetotal from now on.

Very gingerly, he moved onto the edge of the bed. He did not want to wake Shelia, who was still smiling. He simply could not remember even meeting her, let alone getting into her bed. Hilda had looked particularly ravishing in a tight cheongsam, blue to match her eyes. God, what had he said to her? '…would see more of her if she was living in Singapore…' Must mean she was leaving Hong Kong. Oh, Shelia!

He slowly stood up, feeling dizzy. The room eventually stopped revolving and he walked unsteadily to the bathroom and relieved himself, wrapping a towel around his middle. He poured himself a glass of water from a bottle on the table in the bedroom, opened the French windows enough to walk out, and sat down in the chair on the balcony. The sun was further up over the city, a small red disc in the haze, and he could feel the early morning heat on his naked skin. He looked over to the anchorage and could see the *Sunda,* her white hull with the black lettering standing out. He sipped the lukewarm water and began to feel better. No doubt he would find out soon enough if he had blotted his copybook.

Some time later, Shelia came out onto the balcony, with a big smile on her face, wearing only her flimsy, see-through nightdress and carrying a cup of tea, the *Straits Times* in her other hand.

'My hero,' she said, putting the tea down first, then more slowly, the newspaper with its front page uppermost.

'Cadet Hero Now Saves Ship.'

The main picture was of the fire-damaged *Seahorse* being towed by the *Sunda,* alongside a picture of the burning

Rada to the left, then one of Tom in his suit on the right, with what he thought looked like a soppy grin on his face. He had no recollection of having his photograph taken. He felt awful and embarrassed looking at it and the word 'Cadet' incensed him. Only one person could have been responsible for that, he thought.

'What are you looking so sad about, Cadet Hero?' and Sheila laughed.

'It's so embarrassing, I can't remember much,' he almost moaned.

'Oh, don't be so wet, Tom,' laughed Shelia. 'Not surprised you can't remember much, the state you were in. It's called blackout, dear, in case you didn't know.'

'Never again will I touch a drop of alcohol,' said Tom, holding his head in his hands. Then through his fingers, he added, 'It's that damned lawyer.'

'It's happened, Tom,' said Shelia, seriously, 'so you might as well enjoy your fifteen minutes of fame, it won't last long. You can't put the clock back. You never told me you had been blown up.'

'The ship was, not me,' said Tom. 'I don't talk about it.' He remembered Jan's words on the *Buron* and was silent.

'Too late now, the whole world knows,' Shelia laughed. 'Drink your tea.'

'Hilda…' he stopped when he saw Shelia's face and wished he had said nothing.

'Hilda what?' she almost hissed.

'Hilda has come back from Hong Kong and I think, if I remember rightly what the old man said, has joined Cosel in Singapore.'

'Oh,' said Sheila, sharply. 'She's not called me.'

Trouble, thought Tom, it is all going to be trouble.

He picked up the paper and began to read as Shelia sat in the other chair. It was all there, school, horses, sailing, the *Rada*, a full account ending with the praise from the Wreck Commissioner, a brief account of the *Melody* and Jan's dramatic death, fulsome praise from Captain Owen of the *Seahorse*, and the announcement, 'Captain Matravers will be the Cosel Captain of the super tug, which he will bring to Singapore shortly.'

'Shortly!' said, Tom surprised. 'I thought the takeover of the new tug was not for months yet.'

'I saw that,' said Shelia. 'Perhaps it's writer's license. I was hoping for a bit more time with you now you have moved in.'

'Last night…?' asked Tom, hesitantly.

'Nothing happened, you weren't in a fit state to do anything. I had to undress you, not so easy with a drunk, a dead weight,' said Shelia, and then more brightly, 'Breakfast to face the day?'

'It was the lawyer getting his own back,' said Tom. 'Oh, well, as you say, it's too late now so might as well enjoy it. Come to think of it, might as well enjoy you, too, sitting in that revealing outfit,' he said, standing and giving her a kiss. Breakfast was delayed.

295

He reached the office rather later than he intended, to find numerous copies of the *Straits Times*. There seemed to be one on every desk. The lawyer was not yet in for which Tom was grateful. Mr R's secretary saw him and beckoned, pointing at his door and the old man stood as she ushered Tom in.

'Well done, Tom,' he said, shaking Tom's hand enthusiastically. 'The publicity is really good for Cosel and Singapore, we are really on the salvage map now.'

Tom saw Hilda looking at him. She was sitting on the sofa, so Tom decided to take the seat in front of the old man's desk. As he did so, he noticed two yellow pins stuck in Japan on the chart behind him.

'As I told you last night, Hilda is going to work for Cosel here in Singapore. We've appointed a Hong Kong man to run the new representative office that she opened. I want her to have a full understanding of the whole business so she'll be with me for a couple of weeks then attached to the various departments, marketing, personnel, accounts, law, insurance and so on,' said Mr R, looking at her.

Hilda smiled at Tom with a look that struck him as a little more than just a smile, almost an invitation and right in front of her father, too.

'Did she know about Shelia?' Tom asked himself.

'Now, you,' said Mr R quite sharply, bringing Tom out of his reverie. 'I want to capitalise on this stunning success and am hopeful we can bring forward the takeover of the super tug. We've decided to call her 'Dover', good European name for the Arbitrators, *Dover Straits*,' he laughed.

'Now, we have a problem if we manage to arrange this,' he said more seriously, looking at Tom. 'Good captains are not easy to find, especially with salvage experience. You're a bit of a one-off. We've bought two more medium-sized tugs in Japan to be named *Rhio Straits* and *Taiwan Straits*. Daniel Bang is recruiting in Manila now.'

No wonder there has not been a replacement for poor Alfredo thought Tom.

'We hope to pinch a couple from Malayan Towage,' he laughed, 'we pay better, but we're worried about the *Sunda*. With Jan gone and you to UK for the *Dover*, the *Sunda* has no captain.'

'What about Captain Hannibal?' asked Tom.

'Daniel sounded him out, he does not want her, too big.'

'My chief officer, Gonzales, is not ready for the *Sunda* but he would make a good captain for the new ones in Japan or the *Singapore*.'

'Noted,' said Mr R, scribbling on the pad in front of him. 'Daniel tells me you are friendly with the captain of the *Mississippi*.'

Nothing is secret in Singapore, thought Tom and replied, 'He was hoping the Dutch were going to bring a bigger tug to Singapore to combat the *Sunda*. The big bosses are due any time.'

'And no doubt you know I am going to meet them,' laughed the old man.

Hilda looked fascinated at this interchange and kept smiling at Tom whenever he looked at her.

'Offer him the *Sunda*,' said Mr R, suddenly.

'He will want more money than he is getting now,' said Tom, after thinking silently for a moment.

'No problem. If he is interested, tell him I want to talk with him. Can't be here or at my house, tell him we can meet in the American Club, not too many mariners there. Let me know as soon as possible, Tom.'

'Very good, Mr R.'

'Mr Dickinson is here to take your evidence for the *Melody* and the *Seahorse*. I want quick settlement or arbitration, that shouldn't be a problem with your reports.'

The old man smiled, picking up his telephone and pressing an intercom button.

'Come,' he said.

'Thank you,' said Tom, taking it as a compliment.

The door opened and DB entered. He was a tall man, Tom noted, as he sat down next to Hilda.

'Now,' said Mr R, looking stern. 'Complaints. Our Salvage Master has complained to me, in confidence, that you did not obey his instructions during the *Seahorse* tow.'

He was sitting very upright in his chair, the fingers of one hand drumming on the table and those of the other twisting his sparse hair.

The silver knife is not so silver, thought Tom, then took a deep breath.

'Captain Rogers arrived after the fire was out,' he and said, quietly, with as little emotion as possible, 'and the tow had already started. In fact, he arrived after the *Singapore*. We had a fire watch with our own people while the ship's crew were cleaning up. I had the two divers forward, watching the towing connection, my chief officer, Gonzales, had established a good rapport with Captain Owen and was on the bridge, my electrician was working his wizardry with the chief engineer and had the lighting and air conditioning working, we were doing a good speed and the *Singapore* was escorting. Captain Rogers wanted to take the *Coselvenom* alongside, which meant I would have had to slow down and disrupt the tow, and for what? I didn't want him on board, usurping Gonzales and upsetting the Captain. I felt it was very much my salvage. If the fire had not been put out or we had not started the tow, then no problem. I hope, if I had been in Captain Rogers' position, I would have been big enough to leave well alone.'

Tom felt relieved he had been honest but wondered what Mr R and DB would think.

'I see,' said Mr R, looking at DB. 'We know Captain Rogers of old and I knew Captain Jan well. May be it was our mistake to send him but don't forget the fire was not out when he left Singapore. What do you think, Dan?'

DB was silent and his face expressionless.

'I am sorry, Mr R, that Captain Rogers and I did not see eye to eye on this occasion. He has been very helpful to me, the car carrier and the *Buron*. However, you mentioned

Captain Jan, and I must tell you he warned me if Captain Rogers considered me a threat he would try and get rid of me,' said Tom, firmly.

'I just said we know our Salvage Master of old. You both have very different skills and he is very good at what he does and we receive good awards due to his paperwork. On the other hand, he will never command the *Sunda* or the *Dover*. You are both prima donnas so makes it very difficult for us, Cosel needs both of you. You will be away for a while soon, if I am successful next week.'

He looked at DB, who nodded.

'Don't fight Mr Dickinson,' Mr R laughed and waved Tom away with a flick of his wrist.

Tom was relieved to leave the office, but glad he made his position clear, and it seemed to have been taken in good faith. He was not so sure about Hilda; he was convinced she was flirting with him, but he could not really believe she would do so in the chairman's office! He walked down the passageway towards ops when he was waved into Tony's office.

'Congratulations, Tom! Not the rising star but the risen star,' he laughed. 'It's a bit early even for me, otherwise I would offer you a drink. That was a good bash Mr R put on at such short notice and fantastic publicity for Cosel.'

'Thanks, Tony,' said Tom, smiling. 'And now for the super tug *Dover*. He's bought two more tugs in Japan.'

'Yes,' said Tony, 'he's really on the move. Not my scene at the moment, I'm still very much tugs and barges,

300

but I can see he's going to need employment for them, they can't all be on salvage stand by. *Melody's* and *Seahorses* don't come around every day. Anyway, bully for him! By the way, it's about time you joined the Tangle Inn Club, I can put you up.'

'That's very kind of you,' said Tom, leaving the office. 'I might just take you up on that.'

In Ops, Ishmael shook Tom's hand enthusiastically.

'Congratulations, Tom' he said, 'the Dutch will be gnashing their teeth!' He laughed. 'Mr Dickinson said to send you down to him when the old man finished with you.'

'No secrets, even from the lawyer,' laughed Tom, walking out into the bright sunshine, the heat hitting him like a furnace door had been opened.

CHAPTER 25

The van dropped Tom off at the Goodwood Park, the sliding door making him feel slightly *infra dig* outside such a smart hotel; he could have sworn the doorman looked down his nose at him. Tom stood on the steps of the entrance, admiring the gardens in the bright sunlight. The grounds were looking good, with well-tended, rather coarse green grass and the flower beds in vibrant red and yellow.

He went inside and found Robert Dickinson sitting at the bar, nursing a beer.

'Well, here comes the conquering hero,' he said, sarcastically, one hand clutching the glass, the slender fingers of the other hand drumming on the polished wooden bar. 'Have a beer.'

'No thanks, Robert. So, it was you who let the cat out of the bag?' asked Tom, quietly.

'What cat?'

It was going to be one of those days, thought Tom.

'Orange juice, please, barman,' he said, settling himself onto the bar stool next to the lawyer and resting his elbows on the shining bar.

Tom was firm. 'You told the press,' he said.

'Told the press what?' asked the lawyer, awkwardly taking a sip of what was obviously not the first beer of the morning.

Not yet noon, thought Tom, and those fingers are working ten to the dozen.

'About the *Rada*.'

'Actually, no. The old man rang up a public relations friend of his. I merely made sure the information was correct, for which you can thank me. Don't forget our little trip on the *Coseltina* and Seb Dick, the barrister, who is a Queens Counsel, where he told all.'

Tom felt deflated and humiliated. He was so sure the lawyer was responsible for the leak to the press, he had forgotten about the earlier episode.

'I apologise,' said Tom.

'It is very good publicity for Cosel and the old man is very pleased,' said the lawyer. 'It's put the Salvage Master's nose out of joint and he's threatening to resign.' He gave a nasty little laugh which did not reach his bloodshot eyes, and signalled to the barman for another beer.

'Resign because of a Cosel success?' Tom was incredulous.

'It's not his success, it's yours and you disobeyed his orders,' said the lawyer, sharply.

Tom was silent, his brain whirring; the possibility of the Salvage Master leaving opened up a new avenue for him.

'Don't believe all you hear from Captain Rogers,' said Tom, tartly. 'I've been with the old man this morning.'

'I know you have and the old man knows Captain Rogers and all his stories, but he doesn't want to loose him. He's useful. I expect it will wash over but you are a new part of the equation, something very different from the past,' said the lawyer, looking at him.

It was obvious to Tom that no work would be achieved today.

'Robert, if I go back to my tug I can finish off the *Melody* and bring it ashore for you tonight. I can finish the *Seahorse* in two days, working flat-out. You can dictate the *Melody* statement to Susan while I'm doing the *Seahorse*. I can be here afterwards to answer any questions.'

'Ordering me about now, are we?' There was an unpleasant note to the lawyer's words.

'No, Robert,' said Tom, keeping his temper in check, 'just trying to be practical and finish the work. Good for you, good for me.'

'Makes sense, I suppose,' agreed the lawyer. 'The old man is in a hurry, buying all these tugs. Okay, come up here each night at 1800 sharp. I can ask questions each day.'

'Okay, agreed,' said Tom, relieved.

'Any photos of the *Seahorse* fire?' asked the lawyer.

'It was dark, Robert.'

'So?'

'Well, Ops have the film we took but don't expect too much,' said Tom.

'Heard you lost the third mate,' commented the lawyer, his thin lips curling almost into a sneer, the fingers on his left hand still drumming away.

'No, Robert, I did not lose him. The young man died of some sort of latent lung disease, triggered by the smoke. It was very quick and very sad.'

'Still adds a bit to the dangers. We'll make a bit of a thing about it. Risks to the salvors and all that,' and the lawyer smiled to himself.

Tom felt sick but then thought if it means poor Alfredo contributing more than just his work, so be it.

'He was engaged to be married,' said Tom.

'Adds a bit of pathos, a bit of human drama. Still, expect she'll find someone else,' added the lawyer, waspishly. 'That reminds me, life salvage.'

The lawyer was silent, obviously thinking of what he was going to say next.

'Life salvage?' queried Tom.

'Don't repeat me,' said the lawyer, sharply. 'The passengers were all on board when you arrived in Singapore?'

'Yes,' replied Tom, firmly.

'Could they have been transferred to another ship?'

'Yes.'

'Why didn't you?'

'Because Captain Owen, whom you heard at the reception, said it was better to keep them on board. Getting the old ones into a lifeboat in the dark would have been difficult and someone would have bound to be hurt, so he thought it was better to keep them on board, especially as the speed of our intervention seemed to contain the fire. My electrician helped them get the lighting back on and fixed the air-con.'

'Good, got notes about it?'

'Yes.'

The lawyer sat up straight and Tom saw the fingers had stopped drumming.

'Make sure you make a thing about it,' he said, confidently. 'Safety and comfort of passengers, etc. Life salvage is a funny thing. You can claim it but the Arbitrators don't like it. There is a duty to save life at sea. There is no value in a life, although a life insurance policy can make a difference. The principle is to stop, in an extreme case, picking up those with a perceived value and leaving those with no value. In death it is quite simple, such as an air crash, the values are quite clear because the carrier is being punished for killing them. Saving life is a different matter. So what we do is not mention life salvage but show the Arbitrator that we have salved them. We have made extra effort to look after them so he can give us an enhanced award without mentioning life salvage. There is plenty of salved value in the ship, so the value of the lives doesn't come into it.'

Tom was impressed. It was the first time he had heard the lawyer speak in such a way and understood for the first time why the old man stuck with him. It then occurred to him that there was something similar about the *Melody*.

'What about the *Melody*?' asked Tom. 'If she had run aground the crew might have been lost. They would never have been able to launch their lifeboats in the surf on the reef.'

'Now you are thinking, bloke,' said Robert, surprised and smiling. 'Enhancing the award, that's what it is all about. Salvage doesn't come around every day and you have to make the best of it when it does. Say something in your report and I can expand on it in your statement. The Arbitrators are there to encourage salvors but if it's not in the evidence they can't use it.'

'Understood, Robert,' said Tom.

The lawyer sat back relaxing into his bar mood. The fingers resumed their tapping on the bar top. Tom decided it was time to move and start on the *Melody*. There was now a good chance the work would be completed speedily.

He looked in at the pier bar but Frank was not there and he noticed the *Mississippi* was gone from her usual anchorage position. He took a country craft boat out to the *Sunda*, the smell of the sea and fresh air a welcome change from the air-conditioned life of the lawyer.

'Where's the *Mississippi*?' he asked Jesus, who was in the chartroom, working on the charts, when he arrived. It was a hot afternoon and the wheelhouse doors were open, the afternoon breeze blowing through.

'Keppel shipyard for engine repairs. We told base when we saw her move this morning.'

Tom worked hard all afternoon in his office and kept both Ricky and Miguel busy, the one typing and the other making tea, among his other duties. The *Melody* report was finished by 1900 and he made a point about the dangers to the crew. He was able to include Alfredo's sketches of the towing connection, as well as those Jesus drew of the route to the casualty. The divers sketches of the sea intake patches and rudder securing wires were included competing a very comprehensive report. Jesus even traced out a copy of the South China Sea chart and picked out the routes from and to Singapore via Labuan Bay in different colours, with a sketch of the *Sunda* and her tow. Yes, Tom thought, I am pleased, this is all good work. Rene dropped him off at Clifford pier, which was busy as usual, and Tom was glad he held a briefcase to keep the documents dry. He photocopied the sketches and drawings in the shop by the Cellar Bar and dropped the originals off at the Goodwood Park without seeing Robert. He would arrange for a van to pick up the copies in the morning and deliver to Ops.

It was late when he finally reached the flat. Shelia was not in a good mood and Tom thought it better to keep quiet. This was the life he had chosen to lead, and he thought she had accepted it. He did not enjoy his plain omelette, as he sat watching TV in silence; later, in bed, they each kept to their own side.

Saturday dawned, a half-day in Singapore, but Tom decided he would work all day. He left a note for Shelia when he left soon after daybreak, suggesting supper at the Hilton

Rooftop. She was still sleeping and looked particularly alluring, with her blonde hair on the pink pillow, a smile on her pretty face. It was pleasantly cool outside as Tom waited for his taxi; it was going to be another fine day.

The *Seahorse* report went well and he finished the section on the firefighting, having told Jesus which sketches he wanted. He emphasised the passengers on the boat deck wearing life jackets, with the lifeboats lowered to embarkation level so they could leave quickly if the fire spread out of control. The salvors had made that unnecessary. He made a point of the difficulties facing elderly people getting into and out of lifeboats in the dark. He stretched his legs on the bridge every hour or so, enjoying the fresh air and the sights in the anchorage, although it was a hot day. The new third mate had not turned up and Tom made a mental note to chivvy Daniel Bang. Tom arrived dead on six o'clock at the Goodwood, to find the lawyer in the bar, drinking soda water.

'Your *Melody* report is okay and I like the references to the crew dangers, quite good,' said Robert. High praise indeed, thought Tom. He must be in a good mood.

'I like the sketches, the Arbitrators love them. I will need the log and I want the radio log for both salvage jobs.'

'No problem.'

'Have a beer,' offered Robert.

'No thanks, if you don't mind, Robert, I have a date,' said Tom.

'Not Hilda, is it?' asked Robert with a leer.

'No,' said Tom and left.

When Shelia arrived, she was in a much better mood and they enjoyed a cheerful supper on the rooftop by the pool, looking out over the city. They discussed making the tentative temporary arrangement of Tom moving in more permanent and that he should buy a car once they knew when the super tug was ready to be taken over. If sooner, then there was no point; if later, then he would buy one straightaway. Tom brought up the vagaries and impermanence of a salvor's life, never knowing, when the phone or pager rang, if it was an invitation for a drink or a ship on fire. It was the life he had chosen and he found it exciting and fulfilling, utterly different from any other seafaring, and the opportunities for the future with Cosel were good. He liked living in Singapore, a world apart from the England he knew. Shelia said she would try to accept it, no worse than the military, she supposed, or lawyer. There appeared to be a high turn over of wives in the legal firm he worked for in London.

'They have to keep working to pay the maintenance,' Tom laughed. Shelia was not so amused. They enjoyed the evening, talking about England and their lives before Singapore, so completely different.

Tom finally signalled to the waiter for his bill, when his pager went off. He walked over to the bar, Shelia watching despondently and dialled the Cosel number, his heart racing, he could not believe there would be another salvage so soon but, as he knew, it was often feast or famine.

'Mike five,' he told the duty ops man.

'Mr R has invited you to join him on the *Coseltina* at 1100 sharp, Jurong pier, tomorrow.'

'Okay, tell him I will be there,' said Tom, his heart sinking. He knew Shelia now would be alone on the first full day they promised to spend together in a long time. She did not take it well and he made it worse by reminding her of their earlier conversation where she accepted the vagaries of his life as a salvor.

'That Hilda will be there,' said Shelia, bitterly.

'I don't know, Shelia, I can hardly turn the old man down. I am the only captain he has ever invited out, as far as I know, and consider it an honour and good for my prospects in Cosel. You know as well as I do that out here social and business life are intertwined, much more so than England,' and he thought of the UK in the latest cold snap, a million miles away, in more ways than one.

'Well, I don't like it. I think you could have turned him down,' she said her face betraying her unhappiness in the dim light. Tom remained silent.

Sunday dawned fine and Tom was woken by the rising sun, shining through a gap in the curtain. The party on the yacht that day was jolly and Tom was feted by the guests, including Hilda, who persuaded him to take her sailing, which also pleased the old man. Robert behaved himself, remaining almost sober all day.

'Understand you're getting on well with the evidence,' said Mr R, smiling. He was in a good mood. 'And between

311

you and me, I will know next week when you can take over the *Dover*,' which reminded Tom to start work on Daniel Bang for the crew he wanted.

He would have liked to have taken the *Sunda* crew, lock, stock and barrel, but he knew he could hardly swing that.

The day ended well, everyone was in good form and Tom went straight home to the flat where he found Shelia in a better mood. She spent the afternoon at the pool but had caught the sun. She accepted Tom's offer to massage her back with after-sun lotion, which later led to more intimate activities, which Tom felt was encouraging for their more permanent relationship.

It was still dark when he left the flat and returned to the tug for breakfast on the bridge, and Tom was in good spirits. Rene was back on form and the high-speed drive through the anchored ships cleared any cobwebs from Tom's mind. He worked hard on the *Seahorse*, emphasising the passengers remaining on board for the tow and their safety, and he finished it later in the afternoon. Together with all the sketches and plans, he was pleased with the result. New log books were started and after photocopying the completed ones he took all the originals to the hotel that evening. He listed everything and told Ricky to send the list in a message to DB. Just in case, thought Tom; he would never completely trust Robert again. Robert was still in a good mood and asked Tom to supper. Poor Shelia, Tom thought, but we have discussed it and she says she has accepted. He could hardly turn down the lawyer, now they were getting on so much better.

Supper was quite a jolly affair in the smart hotel restaurant, white tablecloths and napkins, smart waiters and pleasant décor. Some other lawyer was in town whom Robert knew and Tom was really there as an audience for their jokes. It was quite amusing at first, but a good deal of wine was consumed, no doubt at Cosel's expense, thought Tom, cynically. He could hardly refuse to join their drinking, but it began to pall. He was very much the worse for wear when he finally arrived home. Shelia was not amused.

'What happened to the teetotal?' she said, as she helped him to bed.

It was a subdued Tom who left the flat at the same time as Shelia the next morning, a little peck on the cheek was all he received in farewell. He arrived at 0900 as instructed, to find Robert still in bed. He spent the morning reading the *International Herald* and the *Straits Times* and the lawyer eventually surfaced just before noon, so no work was done until after lunch. He seemed satisfied with the *Seahorse* report but Tom was not sure he had even read it.

Tom was home early and had a quiet evening in with Shelia, which pleased her.

The next two days passed swiftly, the evidence was finished, the statements signed, the photos had come out better than expected and Tom enjoyed adding captions. He was very pleased with his efforts and parted on good terms

313

with the lawyer, who was not sure when he was returning to London as he had other evidence to deal with.

'You are not the only one in Cosel, you know,' he said, waspishly.

Tom's relations with Shelia improved no end, because he continued to arrive home in good time each evening.

CHAPTER 26

After the excitement and blaze of publicity surrounding the *Seahorse* had died down, it felt good to return to his old Salvage stand-by routine once the evidence with the lawyer was finished. Normally, he would be on the tug until the afternoon, when he would call in at the pier bar for a quick one, pick up any local marine gossip and then go home to Shelia. A very pleasant existence, he thought, with mainly fine, hot weather. Frank was away up-country for a short leave while Keppel repaired his engine, and the Dutch took the opportunity to dry dock the tug as well.

Sheila was pleased with the settled routine and Tom was beginning to appreciate the delights of living together, wondering if he was falling in love. He held no illusions at the beginning of the affair; they both fancied each other and they had a good physical relationship, but Tom felt it was turning in to something much deeper, and Shelia felt the same. They discussed it and decided to see how it went. They would take their leave together, although Tom was not due any for some time. There was no further word of the *Dover* so Tom assumed the old man had not been successful. He was bullying Daniel Bang for a new third mate. Daniel kept assuring him the new man would be onboard any day.

The *Mississippi* arrived at the anchorage one afternoon and Tom met Frank in the bar. After the usual pleasantries, Tom said, 'I hear you spoke at Jan's funeral.'

'Yes,' said Frank, opening his second beer. 'Thirsty work driving a tug,' he laughed.

'All of a couple of miles from Keppel,' Tom pointed out.

'It's the traffic,' said Frank.

'Tell me about the funeral,' asked Tom.

'You remember you told me all about it in this bar, you were a bit cut up,' said Frank seriously.

'Yes,' Tom said.

'Well, I sometimes have quite a good memory. When it came for the time for someone to speak about Jan some of us saw both you and your crew leaving. I knew something was up but I'd not been paged. You said you were going to say something, so on the spur of the moment I stepped into your shoes and pretty much word for word relayed what you told me. I must say, it went down very well. A hero's death, it was reported almost verbatim in next day's *Straits Time*.'

'I didn't see it but thanks, Frank.'

'No, well, another hero, a live one this time, was bringing in the *Seahorse*. You have the luck of the devil, Tom,' he said, his admiration obvious.

'We lost the third mate, Alfredo. Well, I say lost, he died. He was a good man, turning into a real asset.'

'I heard,' said Frank. 'Bit young for his heart to pack up.'

'No, it was his lungs, couldn't stop coughing. Must have been a weakness all round. Surprised he passed the medical. A real shame, handsome fellow and engaged to be married.'

'How are you and Shelia getting on?' smiled Frank.

'What do you mean? I've never mentioned her to you,' said Tom, looking directly at him. Frank's question surprised him.

'Singapore is like a village, Tom. Don't think you can shack up with a girl and keep it secret!'

Tom was silent, then said, 'Just between you and me, it might be a bit more permanent than I thought, but she doesn't like the unsettling business of never knowing when I'm rushing off somewhere.'

'What female does?' laughed Frank, signalling to the barman for another round.

'How are your big bosses getting on?' asked Tom, refilling his glass.

'Been and gone, as I'm sure you know. No news yet, not sure they want to make the commitment,' said Frank seriously.

'Why not join us, Frank?' Tom suggested.

'Why should I do that? I'm quite happy where I am, the Dutch are okay to work for,' replied Frank, taking a drink from his glass.

'Cosel will give you the *Sunda*,' said Tom, quietly. Frank looked round at Tom, surprised. 'And top your present pay.'

'You must be joking!' laughed Frank.

'I don't joke about things like this,' said Tom, rather primly, and then more robustly, 'Listen, Frank,' and he touched his arm in his earnestness. 'Cosel is on the move, the old man's bought two more tugs in Japan. They'll have Filipino masters and I'm going at some stage, probably fairly soon, to pick up the super tug to be named *Dover*. The *Sunda* is yours for the taking, they want a European on her. The Dutch will never give you command of a bigger tug, you know that, Frank, you're the wrong nationality. It's a great opportunity, expanding company, in on the ground floor, good to work for.'

'I will have to think about it,' said Frank.

'Well, don't think too long, and when you've decided yes, the old man wants to see you. He suggests the American Club.'

Frank sat up straight from his usual bar slouch. 'The old man is involved?' he asked.

'Yes, I told you I wasn't joking. I haven't made it up. He asked me to sound you out. Look, here is his office direct line, you can give him a ring,' urged Tom, handing him a number typed on the chairman's memo paper.

Frank, still sitting straight, opened the fresh beer sitting on the bar and ordered a whisky chaser. They discussed the matter for some time, Tom urging Frank to be bold, and they spent longer in the bar than usual. Shelia was not too pleased when Tom turned up later than expected.

'Company business,' Tom smiled.

'In a bar?' asked Shelia, disapprovingly.

'In fact, yes,' said Tom. 'I've been on a recruiting drive. Let's go out to supper at the *Top of the Hilton*.'

Shelia thawed and it turned into quite a jolly evening. It was a fine night and from their table by the pool at the top of the building, they could see the brightest stars through the loom of the city lights. They joined another couple that Sheila knew from work, who helped them to drink the wine and who were fascinated to hear of Tom's work and his salvage stories.

All was good until Tom's pager went off. Shelia stiffened and went quiet, her face closing in, losing its easy smile. Tom walked quickly to the bar telephone, but someone was chatting away on it. His pager sounded a second time, so Tom tapped the man on the shoulder and told him he had an emergency call to make, waving his pager. The man rather ungraciously told the person at the other end he had to go, and slammed the receiver down.

'Mike five,' said Tom briskly when he was connected to Ops, throwing off the effects of the alcohol he had consumed.

'Big container ship aground just outside Western Anchorage. Salvage Master proceeding with *Coselvenom*. *Sunda* to be on standby, instant readiness,' said the duty man.

319

'Tell them to send the zed boat meet me at Clifford Pier in half an hour,' ordered Tom.

The afternoon and evening indulgence seemed to slip away as his brain raced with the possibilities of salvage.

'Got to go,' said Tom, giving Shelia a quick kiss.

'I still can't get used to this,' he heard Sheila complain, and he felt a stab of remorse when he heard her burst into tears as he walked quickly towards the lifts. He resolutely thrust it away; this was his life, his worthwhile work and he wondered how permanent the relationship could be, despite what he told Frank in the bar. What about children, he thought in the taxi. Gerda had seemed to be quite happy with Jan, but Gerda was very different to Shelia.

He banished such thoughts from his mind on arrival at Clifford Pier, where he found Frank trying to bribe Rene to take him out to the *Mississippi*.

'Rene, you can take the bribe but drop me off first,' he said, stepping into the bobbing zed boat. As usual, the wash from the launches and country boats was causing a lopple around the concrete steps.

'Come on, Frank, Rene will drop you off,' urged Tom, and Frank jumped in as Rene took off in his usual style, throwing Frank against Tom who laughed, 'Best boat driver in Singapore.'

'Mad bugger!' said Frank, clutching onto the hand ropes attached to the hull as Rene raced through the anchored ships, bouncing over the occasional wave at full speed. When they reached the *Sunda*, Tom climbed out and over its towing gunnel, which had been freshly greased, staining his shore-going trousers.

'Hold on, Frank,' he shouted as Rene tore away.

'More work for Miguel,' thought Tom, but he was pleased that preparations for towing had been made.

The anchor was aweigh, Gonzales was in the wheel-house and Jesus forward when Tom arrived on the bridge. The message from the office told him to proceed at full speed. The tug was at half speed but increasing when Rene returned. Pedro was ready with the crane and Tom watched as the boat was lifted out of the water with Rene inside it. At that moment, a launch shot alongside the tow deck. A figure was standing outside the towing gunwale, held by two AB's, who helped her jump on board. The launch swerved away and disappeared into the night. Tom was so surprised, he was unable to speak or move. The tug was moving fast now, so all his concentration was required to avoid a collision with either an ill-lit anchored ship or one of the numerous launches and country craft carrying passengers and goods to and from the shore. When he had time to take stock, he saw they were well ahead of the *Mississippi*, which was all that mattered. He needed the strong tea Miguel brought him.

'Who was that I saw jumping off as we left?' asked Tom.

'Don't know, Cap,' said Miguel.

The Straits were quite busy but the eastbound ships, bound for the China Sea, were on the Indonesian side, so

321

well clear. He watched for those he was overtaking and any coming out of the anchorage before Raffles Light. Jesus was back on the bridge, manning the radar. It was now cloudy, a stark change from the starlit evening at the Hilton. Tom could feel spots of rain and shut the open wheelhouse window. The *Sunda* was approaching Raffles Light at over sixteen knots, dragging a huge wash behind her when the heavy shower hit them, reducing visibility to almost nil. Jesus reported the rain clutter obscured everything on the radar screen. Tom felt there was no option but to slow right down because for all intents and purposes they were running blind although he had seen no ships between the tug and Light. However he would not see anything before the tug hit it and the lookouts could see no more than he could. No third mate was onboard yet, Tom thought rather irrationally, but missing Alfredo. He thought he would send send a telex about it which the old man would see. The rain made a hissing sound as it hit the windows, the clear view screen whirring, but Tom could see nothing. He had noted the time and distance to Raffles Light when the rain hit and altered course on the dead reckoning, although Jesus could not pick up the lighthouse on the radar screen and no-one had seen the Light.

A tense few minutes followed before the rain stopped as suddenly as it had started and it became clear, all the lights visible. Tom was relieved to see Raffles was behind them and Sultan Shoal Light just forward of the beam. There was still no traffic ahead of them so Tom increased back to full speed. Sultan Shoal was behind them and Tom was about to alter course and skirt the Western Anchorage boundaries, when the company radio came to life.

'Anchor off the casualty and await instructions,' ordered the Salvage Master.

'Understood, *Mississippi* behind us,' said Tom, into the microphone.

'Anchor close to the bridge on the starboard side where the master can see you. There should be enough water. No contract yet,' the toneless voice continued.

'Understood.'

So, thought Tom, I will make a bit of a show and make sure the captain sees how big and powerful we are.

He continued to skirt the boundaries, altering to the north at the western end, and then saw the casualty, the light beacon flashing away just ahead of her.

Odd place to go aground, thought Tom. It was mud if he remembered correctly from his study of the chart, shouldn't be too difficult a salvage.

The grounded ship was on the port bow of the *Sunda* and the lights of Singapore to starboard in the distance. When the ship, lit up by all her deck lights, was abeam, he turned and headed for the bridge at full speed, only stopping when close to and letting go the anchor.

'They saw you,' said Captain Rogers over the radio, as the wash from the *Sunda* hit the container ship, causing the

323

Coselvenom to surge against her lines alongside. The *Mississippi* arrived a little later and anchored on the other side where Tom could not see her.

Pedro was launching the zed boat with Rene aboard when the Salvage Master came over the radio.

'You are not required here, Captain Matravers.'

So that's the way it was going to be; he was going to get his own back for the perceived slight on the *Seahorse*. Foolish man, thought Tom.

'The *Mississippi* Captain will be over shortly. I would be a good counter-weight,' suggested Tom.

'I will call you if I need you.' Captain Rogers was forceful.

Tom settled down to wait and told Gonzales to tell the crew to make sure any friends were off the tug before they moved, in future. He was not going to make a scene about it but guests were only allowed on board with the Captain's permission, and then daytime only. Miguel brought him another strong tea.

I can go and have a look with Rene leaving Gonzales in charge, he thought.

He set off, with Rene driving the zed boat, the two divers and a sounding line. It didn't take long to make a sketch of the depths around the ship and see where she was aground. He took the mean draught as a guide and calculated she was stuck many feet into the mud. He wondered if it would antagonise the Salvage Master when he decided to call on his radio.

'Paul, I have taken soundings around the ship, if it is of any help.'

There was silence, then a few minutes later, 'There is a pilot ladder opposite my salvage vessel.'

Tom was greeted by Juan, the chief officer, when he boarded the *Coselvenom*.

'He is in a mood, it is very difficult for me,' was Juan's somewhat bitter comment.

'Perhaps you'd better join me on the *Dover*,' said Tom, mischievously.

'Yes!' cried Juan, touching his arm. 'I can't stand him much longer. Nice one minute, horrible the next.' His face was a mask of misery, pale in the artificial deck lighting and Tom thought he was going to weep. He patted him on the back

'Cheer up, Juan, it can't be that bad,' he said.

'It is,' Juan said, wiping his eyes. 'Whatever I do is wrong and I have been with Cosel nearly five years now. Make sure you ask for me to be your chief officer on the *Dover*, I will make a very good one,' and he tugged at Tom's arm in his urgency.

Tom was taken aback at this outburst. He knew how competent the man was.

'I'll ask and get you to come with me to UK Juan,' he said, and shook his hand.

'Thank you,' said Juan more calmly as Tom started to climb the ladder up the side of the huge container ship, wondering why Rogers would alienate such a good man.

He put this aside as he climbed the outside ladders to the bridge, where he found a cluster of men inside the lit wheelhouse. Captain Rogers was wearing his blue working clothes and Frank, with his red hair standing out, wearing a white boiler suit with the Dutch Company logo. The Salvage Association senior surveyor Mike whom Tom had met on the *Kinos* salvage, was also there. The Captain was dressed in khaki. Tom was glad he was wearing his whites with Cosel embroidered on the chest. There were some others present, whom Tom could not place.

He was introduced by the Salvage Master and the Captain said, in a very American drawl, 'Tell us about your tug, Captain.'

Tom handed the sketch of the soundings to Captain Rogers, who studied it as Tom launched into an exposition the *Sunda*'s power and effectiveness, as well as pointing out how manoeuvrable she was, just the thing to pull his ship free.

'You will need the power, Captain,' said the the Salvage Master when Tom had finished. 'Look, your forepart is more than twenty feet into the mud,' he pointed to the sketch in his hand.

'Is that so?' said the owners' rep, a large man wearing jeans and a coloured shirt, who took the sketch. 'You lot stay here while we go below and discuss the matter.'

'High tide is just over an hour away,' Captain Rogers pointed out.

'Is that so?' he drawled again, and left the bridge with the party, leaving just the salvors and the officer of the watch on the bridge. Tom could not help being partly mesmerised by the beacon flashing just ahead of the ship.

'What's wrong with him?' asked Frank quietly as Captain Rogers moved away.

'In a mood,' said Tom.

'If I join Cosel, am I supposed to put up with him? I like to enjoy my salvage.'

'Don't worry. As long as he doesn't think you are a threat you'll get on fine with him, he can be very pleasant. He taught me a lot in that car carrier and the *Kinos* salvage,' said Tom.

Frank was silent then said, 'I'm supposed to meet the old man tonight.'

'Good news,' said Tom, jubilantly. 'Don't worry, he'll know what is happening if you don't turn up.'

About ten minutes later, the Salvage Association surveyor came into the wheelhouse, his pleasant lived-in face serious.

'The owners have agreed to offer you a joint Lloyds Form which both of you sign,' he said. 'They want you both connected now and an attempt to be made at this high tide. You will have to be quick. This is a container ship and time is money, hence the haste. The bottom is mud, as your sketch indicates, Captain Rogers, so we don't think the hull will be damaged.'

'What do you think, Tom?' asked Captain Rogers.

'Agree,' Tom answered instantly, surprised to be asked.

'I will have to ask my owners,' said Frank.

Tom was disappointed in his friend's answer and said quickly, 'Frank, agree and we make the re-floating attempt now. Half a Lloyds Form is better than no Lloyds Form.'

'Cosel Salvage agree,' said the Salvage Master, and produced a blank Lloyds Form which he started to fill in.

Frank took a deep breath.

'We agree,' he said, glancing at Tom as if to say, 'If this goes wrong for me it's all your fault.'

CHAPTER 27

The Lloyds Form was filled in and signed by both Captain Rogers and Captain Ings. Once signed it was taken below by the Salvage Association Surveyor for signature by the Master. Mike said the master would hold on to it while the salvors left to connect their tugs.

'You better be quick about it if you are going to make this tide, speed is of the essence, gentlemen,' he added.

The Salvage Master held a short meeting where it was agreed that he would be in overall charge of the salvage, with his crew standing by aft to make the connections. There was no time to bring across the heavy slip hooks, and it was agreed the forerunners should be made up round the bitts, not the eye over them. The *Mississippi* would connect on the port side and the *Sunda* on the starboard side of the casualty. It was coming up to slack water so there was little current running.

'I don't see why we can't both connect at the same time,' Tom suggested.

'I am single screw and no bow thruster,' Frank pointed out.

'No problem,' said Tom, 'I will keep out of your way. I think we should have oxyacetylene to hand, so in an emergency the *Coselvenom* crew can cut the forerunner as we don't have time for the slip hooks,' he added.

The Salvage Master was silent. Tom called on his radio and told Gonzales to pick up the anchor and start heading to the starboard quarter of the casualty. When he met Juan on the deck of the *Coselvenom* Tom told him what was happening.

'I wonder, Juan,' he added, 'if you could have your welder and the oxyacetylene gear ready to cut the tows in an emergency and make sure the eye of the forerunners is not put over the bitts but is made up round them, so easier to let go.'

'Okay, Captain, I will do that,' Juan replied.

On his way back in the zed boat to the moving *Sunda*, Tom saw that the sky was completely clouded over, looking very dark and threatening, with black clouds to the north. There was quite a breeze blowing across the stern of the casualty, presaging the rain to come from the heavy cloud, and the zed boat felt the wavelets. Once back on board his tug, Tom took over from Gonzales and manoeuvred her off the starboard quarter of the *Mr President*. Juan, efficient as ever, threw a heaving line neatly onto the tow deck and the *Sunda* was quickly connected. It started to rain, quite lightly at first.

'Mike four, this is Mike five, *Sunda*, connected,' Tom reported on the company radio.

'Good. Get a company radio across to the *Mississippi*,' ordered the Salvage Master.

Tom could see the *Mississippi*, a blur in the rain, her almost indistinct navigation lights indicating she was heading towards the *Sunda*. *She was* still close to the *Mr President*, whose outline was faint and the deck lights hazy in the increasing rain. This was not going to be the easy salvage Tom thought it would be; the rain was reducing the visibility, making it very difficult so see anything. If they lost sight of the casualty it would become very dangerous, especially if she re-floated.

Tom instructed Pedro to secure the main tow wire and was steaming gently, maintaining his position easily with the wind on the port side blowing quite hard. Suddenly, nearby, there was a clap of thunder, all the more frightening because it was so unexpected. Tom's heart sank and he felt his insides turning to jelly. He held on to the bridge front while looking at the faint outline of the *Mississippi* out of the starboard wheelhouse door. A thunderstorm and squall were the last thing they needed during the re-floating attempt and at night, too. In fact, Tom thought, if he was in charge he would abort the attempt and wait for daylight and the next tide.

'Jesus, collect a radio and spare battery from Ricky in the radio room and take it across in the zed boat to the *Mississippi*. Tell Rene to leave the boat in the water when you get back.'

'Okay, Cap.'

The *Mississippi* and the casualty were in VHF contact but Tom did not hear any communication from either of

331

them. The Salvage Master carried the Company radio and if there was one with Frank it would be easier to coordinate and control the operation. Tom saw the zed boat disappear into the rain, which was beginning to hiss against the wheelhouse windows. In the light over the tow deck Tom could see the droplets bouncing off the surface of the sea, like a cauldron boiling bubbling and spitting liquid contents. The *Mississippi* was almost invisible in the downpour and pitch darkness, but Gonzales said he could still just see her on the radar and she did not appear to have moved. It was almost high water and Tom was worried for his friend.

'*Mississippi*, this is Mike four, what is your position, please?' asked Captain Rogers on the VHF.

'Just connected and paying out,' Tom was relieved to hear Frank's reply.

'*Sunda,* tow at full power on your quarter, *Mississippi*, tow at full power on your quarter when you are ready,' ordered the Salvage Master on the VHF.

Tom, who was still watching for the *Mississippi*, pushed the engine control levers in front of him slowly forward, increasing to full power, relying on Pedro to warn him if anything was wrong because he could not see the wire in the rain. It was free to run across the towing gunwale, so he could manoeuvre the tug easily.

'*Mississippi* moving closer,' said Gonzales from the radar.

'Get the two Yokohama fenders out on the starboard side quickly, Gonzales, just in case.'

'Okay, Cap,' said Gonzales, and left the bridge.

Tom was happy that the steady and dependable Pablo was on the wheel, but he was missing a third mate, and thought of Alfredo. Jesus appeared, dripping water on the deck and said, 'Radio delivered, Cap,' and moved over to the radar, a pool of water collecting around his feet.

'*Sunda*, this is *Mississippi*, I will secure when I am parallel with you if I can see you through this rain,' said Frank on the company radio, his Scots accent more distinct than normal indicating the stress he was under.

He saw the *Mississippi* appear in the rain close to, and remained on the same heading as the *Sunda*.

'Mike four, this is *Mississippi*, secured and towing at full power,' reported Frank, his voice now sounding less stressed.

'Thank you, *Mississippi*, we are going astern on the main engine and will be increasing to full astern. It's almost high tide,' said Captain Rogers.

A great clap of thunder sounded overhead, much louder than the earlier one, and lightening lit up the two tugs, the extreme darkness making it seem even more bright. The lightening seemed to sizzle as it wriggled through the rain and hit the sea, apparently boiling with the power of the rain. The noise of the engines was completely blotted out and Tom momentarily wondered if they had stopped. The

333

visibility was reduced to almost nil but Tom sensed something had changed. It was the wind, now blowing hard on the other side of the tug, the starboard side, and Tom was concerned it might blow the *Mississippi* onto the *Sunda*.

Gonzales came on to the bridge, completely drenched through, pouring more water onto the already wet deck, and reported, 'Fenders rigged, Cap.'

'Frank, wind change!' called Tom on his hand-held radio.

'I know and my dolly pins are jammed, my tow wire is held amidships and I am having difficulty holding her up into the wind,' Frank's Scots accent more pronounced again.

'Don't worry, you can come alongside me, my Yokohama's are rigged.'

'Thanks.'

Tom suddenly remembered Rene and the rubber boat.

'Jesus, where is zed boat?'

'Starboard side, it was the lee side before the wind change,' he answered, lifting his head out of the radar.

Tom realised it was too late to do anything and just hoped it would not be crushed, that the fenders would hold off the other tug far enough. The *Mississippi* loomed out of the rain and Tom felt, the *Sunda* heeling slightly as she came alongside quite heavily. He ordered more starboard helm as Pablo reported she was falling off to port, and he noted the gyro clicking quite rapidly as the heading changed. The wind would keep the other tug alongside, there was no need for mooring lines.

'Mike four, this is Mike five. *Mississippi* is alongside the *Sunda*. I suggest you treat us as one unit,' reported Tom on the company radio.

'Mike five, yes. *Mr President* is on full power astern, no sign of movement yet and it's high tide. Commence salvage yawing!' ordered Captain Rogers in reply.

'Commence salvage yawing,' repeated Tom. 'Hard a starboard, Pablo.'

Tom sensed the wheel being spun but could not see it in the darkness.

'You copy that, Frank? I am going to starboard first to try and get upwind.'

'Understood.'

'I think we are moving slowly to starboard but the rain clutter is almost completely obscuring the casualty,' said Jesus from the radar.

Tom knew the heading had changed because Pablo reported it, but that did not mean the two tugs were moving sideways up against the wind, they could still be being blown downwind.

'Hope you are right, Jesus,' said Tom, with a mirthless laugh.

The rain was heavier then ever, although there was no more thunder, only the occasional bolt of lightening. Tom was so tense, he felt his nerves at breaking point. It was not being able to see anything, and the knowledge that the huge

335

ship behind them was going full astern on her massive engine. They might not know when she actually re-floated and the *Sunda's* manoeuvrability was severely hindered by the *Mississippi*. The wind was blowing even stronger. Tom felt he was not in full control of events and that the tugs were in considerable danger. They might even be over run by the *Mr President*, but there was nothing else he could do. Miguel appeared with a welcome mug of tea for those on the bridge.

'Rene says the zed boat is between the two tugs and he can't move her,' said Miguel

'I know, tell him too bad, we'll sort it out later, Miguel. Leave the boat alone.'

'Moving,' an agitated and excited voice came over the company radio, its Australian accent very strong and Tom did not immediately recognise it as the Salvage Master. Quite suddenly, the sound of the diesels changed, speeding up, despite Tom not touching the engine controls. This suggested the load on the engine had reduced, which could only mean they were moving ahead. The visibility was still almost nil and there was no word from Jesus, but the land was completely obscured by the rain so he would not see anything, either.

Tom opened the downwind door of the wheelhouse and walked out into the rain. He was drenched in seconds, as if he was under a waterfall. The water was running in mini rivulets along the deck pouring in streams down the side of the wheelhouse. He could still not see the casualty, so he did not know where she was in relation to the tugs.

'I am totally reliant on the Salvage Master,' he thought.

It was becoming obvious that the speed was picking up and the heading was changing, but there was no word from the casualty. Tom stood in the wheelhouse door, partly sheltered from the rain, when he thought he saw a glimmer, a blur of light. It then increased as the rain started to reduce and quite soon, almost stopped. *The President* was well out on the starboard side of the tugs, the stern swinging away from them, the wind was still keeping the two tugs together.

'Hard a port, Pablo,' shouted Tom as he reached for the radio microphone, having left his portable one on the locker by his chair before walking out into the rain.

'*Mississippi,* this is *Sunda*! We are going to be in trouble if you are not slipped, Frank.'

'I can see.'

'Mike four, this is Mike five, I think we should slip the *Mississippi*, his dolly pins are jammed and his tow wire pinioned.'

There was silence. The two tugs started to move apart, the *Sunda* turning to port and under control, thought Tom, but the *Mississippi* was being pulled around by her pinioned tow wire.

'Juan,' said Tom crisply, 'this is Mike five, slip the *Mississippi*.'

'Can't slip, the ship's crew put the eye over the bitts before I could stop them,' said Juan, urgently.

'Cut, Juan, cut quickly, or she is going to be in trouble!'

'Frank, hard a port!'

'I am but she is going the wrong way,' said Frank, the concern showing in his voice.

'I've told Juan to cut you,' said Tom, calmly.

The President was moving fast astern and the very thing Tom was worried about, being over-run, was happening. The casualty should stop her engine and go ahead. The tow wire on the *Sunda* was right out on the port beam, but the stern of the casualty was beginning to go ahead of the tug. The *Mississippi*, however, was in a far worse state and in a very dangerous situation.

'Mike four, this is Mike five. The *Mississippi* has lost control and I am losing it as well. Please, go ahead on the casualty engine. You are afloat and there is plenty of water.'

'Roger that, stopping engine now. We got a bit disorientated in the rain,' said Captain Rogers, apparently quite cheerfully, not realising the imminent danger to the tugs.

Suddenly, the *Mississippi* shot ahead and Tom gave a huge sigh of relief; his friend and the tug were safe. He felt he had aged ten years since the rain started, which was not more than a quarter of an hour previously. What a difference, now he could see what was happening. *The President* was moving back astern of the *Sunda* and with the tow wire free running he was back in control.

338

'*Mississippi*, cut,' said Juan on the radio.

'*Sunda*, this is Mike four, we are going to slip you and anchor. When ready, come and anchor close by,' said Captain Rogers on the company radio.

'Understood,' said Tom.

'*Mississippi,* this is Mike four, anchor close by *The President*,' ordered the Salvage Master on the VHF.

'Understood,' replied Frank.

Rene came on the bridge from the boat deck, still in his wet clothes. 'You have cracked my boat,' he said, accusingly.

'Sorry about that, Rene, I am sure you can patch her up,' said Tom, trying his best to soothe him.

'Yes.'

'Go and get the radio back off the *Mississippi*, take a diver,' ordered Tom.

Rene left the bridge by the boat deck ladder without a word, his long hair wet and hanging ragged below his shoulders. So that's the way it is, thought Tom; he feels it's his own boat so takes care of her better. Got to have him on the *Dover*.

'Slipped,' reported Juan on the radio, and Tom moved the engine control levers to upright, the engines in neutral. Pedro and Gonzales, both left the bridge when they heard Juan, went aft and heaved in the towing gear. *The President* was anchored, her deck light still blazing, almost obliterating the anchor lights. She looked huge, thought Tom, and he shuddered with the vision of her over-running the tugs.

The zed boat disappeared into the darkness at Rene's usual speed; not much wrong with the boat, thought Tom. As soon as the towing gear was on the tow deck, which had taken longer than usual because the mud had to be hosed off, Tom steamed slowly to the starboard side which was the inshore side. The casualty was heading away from Singapore, the tide had turned, and Gonzales let go the anchor. The diver returned the radio and battery to Ricky while Pedro lifted out the boat with Rene in it.

'We are being terminated,' said the Salvage Master on the company radio. 'You can return to your salvage station in Eastern Anchorage and stand by. Submit your report to ops as soon as possible, the lawyer is returning to Singapore tomorrow.'

Tom relayed this to Frank on the VHF and suggested he contact Captain Rogers directly for instructions. He felt tired. The session with Frank in the pier bar and the supper at the *Top of the Hilton* with Shelia, together with the intense activity of the last few hours, not least the drama of the re-floating in the thunder storm, had taken its toll and Tom felt utterly exhausted. The thought of running back to Eastern Anchorage was almost beyond him. He decided to steam further away from *The President* and anchor, hoping the Salvage Master would be too busy to notice. He was beginning to feel chilly, still in his wet clothes, and went below to have a hot shower and change.

CHAPTER 28

'Tell me, Captain Matravers, what were your exact words to your mate, Frank?' he asked. He was obviously serious.

'I told him half a Lloyds Form was better than no Lloyds Form,' replied Tom, surprised at the unusual intensity of the man.

'You are sure you said half?'

'Yes,' replied Tom, firmly.

'Good, I will want that in writing. We will make out an affidavit to that effect,' he said, pleased.

'What's the problem?' asked Tom.

'I don't want an argument with the Dutch,' replied the lawyer. He was animated now. Tom had never seen him so alive and interested, as though he was on a mission, and he noticed the fingers were still.

'Listen, Tom, the arbitrators love co-operation between salvors when they mostly spend their time fighting each other and we don't want two sets of lawyers involved, and two sets of costs, with what is essentially a simple salvage. If I have control I can make it into a saga of the sea. Just watch, instead of nit-picking with the other salvor about which salvor did the most work, we treat it as one salvage, with one salvor, and enhance our award. I need to persuade the old man to agree a fifty-fifty split with the Dutch and I take charge of the case for both companies.'

'Fifty-fifty,' said Tom, slightly outraged. 'We had the bigger tug and the salvage master and the *Coselvenom*, we should get the bigger slice.'

'My whole point, bloke, small mindedness. Think big, not nit-pick with the lawyers trying to score points from each other, which detracts from the overall award. I can get a bigger award, which would give more to Cosel, on a fifty-fifty split, than a smaller award and bigger slice for Cosel. Enhancing the award, that's what matters. So the Dutch are not going to reject a fifty-fifty agreement with half a tug, which had to be cut free,' and he laughed, a full-bodied laugh, which was the first time Tom heard one from him. 'Or that is how I would present it if we were not co-operating. Instead, I will turn into an asset, highlighting the dangers and getting a bigger award. This is what I am good at doing, turning what is essentially a straight pull-off with not much danger, into a major salvage and we have eliminated the alternative assistance,' and he laughed again, his face lit up, almost a different person from the one Tom dealt with last time he was in Singapore.

'I see,' said Tom, thoughtfully.

'So that's why I have got to persuade the old man to agree what on the surface is a bad agreement,' and the lawyer walked importantly out of the office. And in that mood and frame of mind, thought Tom, you could persuade him to do anything. He was impressed with what he had seen

342

and it emphasised why Mr R stuck with him. He was back after only twenty minutes.

'He's agreed and will fix the Dutch, so don't need your affidavit. It's full speed ahead and I am in control, so I will start with you. Got your notes, log, etc? What about photos?'

'It was dark and raining,' said Tom.

'Well, get an underwater camera,' said the lawyer sharply. Tom felt remiss because, the divers owned one and he had not thought to use it. He made a mental note to ask them.

Tom was sitting in the office assigned to Robert in Jurong. It was too soon for him to have written his report. The rest of the day was spent with Robert, exercising skills which would make him the asset to Cosel the old man thought he was. He admired the way the lawyer put his statement together from the raw material. Tom's notes which were partly illegible from the soaking when he walked out onto the bridge wing in the rain, the ship's log and the radio log and questioning him. He brushed aside Tom's objection that the Salvage Master ordered him to make the sounding sketch, which, of course, he had not and gave the order to cut the *Mississippi* forerunner.

'Oh, don't be so wet, Tom! Didn't you listen to me about nit-picking? We have to show the Salvage Master was in charge, the best thing since sliced bread, it's the award that matters, not your petty squabbles. I can show why speed was so necessary, not just the commercial aspect of maintaining their schedule but that the longer she stayed in the mud the more difficult it would be to re-float. Might have had to discharge containers and of course, it was the top of high water springs, the tide would not have been that high again for another two weeks. I am sure I can find an expert on mud who will write a report telling us what we want.'

Tom subsided, admonished, and watched Robert turn round the chaotic re-floating into a success, full of dangers but skilfully contained and overcome by the Salvage Master.

'It's the award that matters, not you, bloke,' emphasised the lawyer. 'You had your success with the *Seahorse*, the information was all there for a really good award. Additionally, we have the newspapers and TV footage. It's making something quite mundane like this into a good award, which is the challenge.'

It was an interesting and wearing day, not just for Tom, but also for Susan, who took the dictation, which could not have been easy. Tom saw a completely different Robert Dickinson.

It was quite late and they were nearly finished when the telephone rang.

'We are busy,' Robert said quite curtly, but then he was quiet and his face changed into a smile. 'Oh, it's you, Hilda. I didn't recognise your voice at first... No, he's here,' and he passed over the receiver.

'Hilda here, Tom. I am resurrecting the dinner date when you stood me up. Tonight, 1930, Mandarin Grill. Mr R wants to talk to you.'

'Okay, Hilda, I will be there. Thanks,' said Tom, and put down the receiver. Poor Shelia, he thought, they were due to be having supper at the Tangle Inn with friends of Shelia who were out from England.

'Hilda, eh?' said Robert, a leer playing on his face.

'No, it's the old man, he wants to talk to me,' said Tom, firmly. He wanted to quash any gossip Robert might spread. He knew Hilda was working with her father, learning the business, but as Frank had told him, Singapore was like a village.

He took a van back to the flat for a shower and to change into his suit. The Grill was a very smart restaurant, jacket and tie only. He received a very frosty reception from Shelia. Nothing he said would change her mind. He should have said no, so rather than have an argument, he kept quiet, but it put a damper on his mood.

Dinner was not what Tom was expecting. It was just the three of them, in an alcove. The decor was subdued elegance and muted colours, nothing to distract from the food, wine and company; no band, no music, a thick carpet so the waiters' movements were soundless, no loud conversation, soundless air conditioning, with the temperature just right, belying the fact Singapore was situated almost on the equator. This was a serious place for serious business. The food was very good, the wine was excellent and Tom was careful to limit his intake, especially in view of the conversation, which was something Tom could never have anticipated. He was being propositioned and his initial reluctance, almost outrage, was being turned into a dare.

'My father has been talking of selling out,' stated Hilda over the Norwegian wild smoked salmon, 'and I have told him he is mad. Cosel is just starting in the big league.'

She was dressed in a smart grey business suit, which looked very good on her, and the pearl necklace set off her delicate skin.

'The share price of the holding company is sky high and I have received a tentative offer for my shares,' said Mr R, who was dressed in a very smart suit and blue tie, suggesting Hilda played some part in it, so very different from his normal, dowdy appearance. 'I am not getting any younger.'

'I have told him I will help him, which is why I am in the Singapore office, as you know.'

'A woman in this business is a curiosity but will not be taken seriously,' said the old man. 'Believe me, I know.'

There was a silence and Tom began to wonder why he was here, what this had to do with him. The smoke salmon plates were whisked away by the silent waiters and with some ceremony the lobsters, resting under silver covers, were served, the covers lifted simultaneously. A different wine was served.

'I want you, Tom, to help me and ultimately, we will take over from him,' Hilda said, quietly and forcefully, looking him in the eye. 'He will stop being what he really is, the chief executive, and be the real chairman. I can't take over as chief executive because even if I had enough experience, I am a woman.' She paused and said, 'But you can,' and she paused again, looking at her father who nodded. 'On one condition, you must marry me.'

Tom was completely floored and speechless, shocked to his very core and a picture of his father, the Archdeacon, flashed across his mind, the outrage showing on his lined face. It was something so outside his whole upbringing, so outside the society in which he lived in England. This was, in effect, an offer of an arranged marriage. And what about Shelia, whom he had come to believe he loved?

They both looked at him, expecting an answer, not the rather vacant gaze as Tom withdrew into himself and his two sides debated. His adventurous side, the one that had brought him to Singapore and earlier Hong Kong, said what an opportunity this was: Singapore the Far East, expanding and growing, not stuffy, old, declining England. The other side of him opposing it as a base betrayal of everything he had been brought up to believe was good about marriage and behaviour.

'You would be selling yourself,' a voice whispered. 'Rubbish! It's the opportunity of a lifetime,' said another.

Not that he did not fancy Hilda, but he had Shelia.

'A business marriage, a marriage in the interests of business, not love,' said Tom in a shocked voice.

347

'Nothing new in that, especially out here and Hong Kong,' said Mr R. 'You two seem to get on together.'

'This is how it would work,' said Hilda, briskly taking advantage of Tom's silence. 'You take over the *Dover* next week, my father has just signed the contract with the new date, and bring her out to Singapore. I will be at the takeover ceremony and our engagement will be announced then. Gives me time to organise the wedding, which will be a big Singapore affair, the ceremony in the cathedral. All good publicity for Cosel. Once we are safely married and after the honeymoon, you will be appointed chief executive.'

Tom was silent, still collecting his thoughts, his brain racing. The good food and wine seemed to enhance his thought process.

'Why do we have to be married?' he asked.

'To bind us together for life. It's not just a business arrangement but a lifetime commitment and it will be my father's legacy, a thriving Cosel Salvage. If my father sells, he is just another rich man and I am just another rich man's daughter. If he is chairman, he retains his status as not just a rich man but the founder and chairman of a successful salvage company of world repute, which opens doors which otherwise would be closed to him. He is courted and wanted, a good reason to be alive and useful. For me, I am the working wife of a successful chief executive and when my father goes, we will be Cosel. What more could I want?'

'Children,' Tom blurted out.

'Of course, we will be married, I am a reasonably normal woman,' said Hilda, brightly.

The conflict must still have been showing on Tom's face.

'I dare you,' Hilda said, in a low voice, full of hidden meaning. 'Yes, it's a dare.'

THE END

Printed in Great Britain
by Amazon